Among Strange Victims

Among Strange Victims

A NOVEL BY
Daniel Saldaña París

TRANSLATED BY
Christina MacSweeney

COFFEE HOUSE PRESS
MINNEAPOLIS
2016

Originally published in Spanish as
En medio de extrañas víctimas
by Sexto Piso, Mexico, 2013

Coffee House Press books are available to the trade through our primary distributor, Consortium Book Sales & Distribution, cbsd.com or (800) 283-3572. For personal orders, catalogs, or other information, write to info@coffeehousepress.org.

Coffee House Press is a nonprofit literary publishing house. Support from private foundations, corporate giving programs, government programs, and generous individuals helps make the publication of our books possible. We gratefully acknowledge their support in detail in the back of this book.

Library of Congress Cataloging-in-Publication Data

Names: Saldaña París, Daniel, 1984– | MacSweeney, Christina, translator.
Title: Among strange victims / Daniel Saldaña París ; translated by
    Christina MacSweeney.
Other titles: En medio de extrañas víctimas. English
Description: Minneapolis : Coffee House Press, 2016.
Identifiers: LCCN 2015033493 | ISBN 9781566894302 (paperback)
Subjects: | BISAC: FICTION / Literary. | FICTION / Humorous.
Classification: LCC PQ7298.429.A43 E513 2016 | DDC 863/.7–dc23
LC record available at http://lccn.loc.gov/2015033493

ACKNOWLEDGMENTS

Daniel and Christina would like to thank the OMI International Arts Center for including them in its Translation Lab residency, which allowed them to work together on the final proofs of *Among Strange Victims* and to get to know each other better as author and translator.

PRINTED IN THE UNITED STATES OF AMERICA

23 22 21 20 19 18 17 16   1 2 3 4 5 6 7 8

On park benches
  Among strange victims
    The poet and amputees come sit together.

ARTHUR CRAVAN

Among Strange Victims

I

THE THIRD PERSON

It's unnecessary to start by describing the actions that make up my routine. That tedious list will come later. First, I'd like to state that my head floats about two inches above the top of my neck, detached from me. From that position, it's easier for me to observe the irritating texture of the days.

When it rains, I don't get melancholy. Quite the reverse. I simply have the impression that the weather is, finally, doing justice to the general grayness of existence. Good-bye, tropical hypocrisy; let the sun return to its corner of the galaxy and for once leave us to contemplate the unrelieved darkness that looms over us, sad mortals attired in fake Nike tennis shoes covered in mud.

I sometimes think it would be wonderful to draw diagrams that, rather than the usual preposterous and hyperspecific statistic, represent a dull, everyday state of affairs. Diagrams that tame the seeming disorder of things and help me to place myself among them. For example, a chart with the speeds, accelerations, and even the manias and minor defects of the passersby who file around this fountain. While I watch them from my disintegrating bench at one end of an oval gazebo, I try to imagine those variables, the columns and colors of that chart. The all-powerful statistics will summarize, in perfectly round numbers, the comings and goings of the pigeons. I'm not really sure how, but the fat man who is right now shifting his weight from one foot to the other and has a tiny mobile phone in his hand will be represented. The children running around their parents like small, feverish satellites will appear as relevant data, as will the couples oscillating around the bushes, looking for a patch of shadow in which to lavish indecent displays of affection on each

other. In the chart will be the aimless hobbling of the elderly pen-
sioner who, only a few moments ago, looked at me with a mixture
of suppressed rage and resignation as if envying the youth of which,
from the old man's point of view, I am not taking full advantage; and
the firm gait of the ice cream seller, who knows exactly what the
afternoon holds for him, will be there too. The chart will also register, by means of occasional footnotes, the exceptional cases: the
sudden stillness of the passersby when a screeching of tires, after a
barely perceptible silence, results in a crash; the collective haste of
mothers when the first raindrops fall from the sky.

And of course the chart will have a whole column, or a huge
portion of its round pie, for a detailed account of my meanderings:
if I take three turns around the fountain, the chart will know and
represent them in a special, phosphorescent color; if I allow my
steps to be guided by the perfume of a woman in a tailored dress,
the same will be true; if I decide to stop idling away the time in this
gazebo and walk slowly home, dragging my feet along the sidewalk
as the four-in-the-afternoon sun begins to lose its strength, as I am
now doing, the chart will know it too.

But there is no fanatical god of statistics who amuses himself
designing Excel tables on his celestial laptop, paying disproportionate attention to this region of the world, just outside the center of
Mexico City, so I have to keep walking and resign myself to the fact
that I'm the only person aware of the rhythm of my steps, the only
one who knows that I twist my left foot slightly inward and try to
cross the digits of my right foot, putting the big toe over the one
next to it, a custom thanks to which my foot begins to hurt after a
few blocks, and the soles of my shoes always end up splitting in
the same place, under the ball of my foot—objects are traitorous.
I'm the only person who knows me in such detail, and for that reason I'm the only one who can register this, even if it is only on the
ephemeral chalkboard of the memory, for the detail then to disappear, without warning, among thousands of other pieces of data
related to the rhythm and cadence of my steps, data no one will ever
consult with insatiable curiosity in the immensely vast annals of
a virtual library of nonsense. "Statistics doesn't recognize my true
value," I tell myself, in summary.

Fortunately, as soon as I enter my apartment, those slightly oppressive thoughts disappear at exactly the same moment I press the stop button on my iPod, take off the headphones, and switch on the living room light. In contrast to the bedroom, the living room is always dark, so I have to illuminate it, even at this hour: 4:17 in the afternoon.

The vista that is revealed isn't particularly beautiful, or perhaps I should say it isn't canonically beautiful. My furniture is old and each piece is slightly broken in some way, with the exception of a small red coffee table I bought two months ago; the fabric lampshade, hanging from a cable repaired with duct tape that sprouts from a hole in the ceiling, accumulates inexplicable stains that are projected onto the walls like cave paintings. Certain parts of the wall, afflicted with damp, have some sort of blisters of paint that eventually burst and cover the dark blue upholstery of my armchair in fine white powder.

But despite these signs of deterioration, to me my apartment doesn't seem completely squalid. I have some plants, a small black bookcase holding an encyclopedia of biology—the corner of a page turned down in the fifth volume marks the most exciting chapter: rotifers—and my two windows: the one in the living room, with a view of the interior courtyard of the building, and the one in my bedroom, looking onto a vacant lot. It's a strange arrangement of space. A sensible architect would have reversed the order, leaving the living room with an external window and the bedroom with a view of the courtyard; but maybe the architect was afraid someone would construct a ghastly, enormous building, with barbed wire everywhere, on that vacant lot, and so left the bedroom window, always less important than the one in the living room—a domestic agora—with that unfulfilled threat. Luckily, the vacant lot is still vacant.

Saturdays all, or almost all, go like this: I wake around nine, idle away the first few hours looking at the vacant lot or pretending—to no one—to read in bed; I prepare a simple breakfast and go out to take a walk around the neighborhood; I have something to eat in the street at lunchtime and, afterwards, I sit on the disintegrating bench in the gazebo to watch the people walking by. At about four o'clock, I go back home to try to do all those things I don't have time for during the week, things that for five days I swear up and down I'll get around to on Saturday. I do, in fact, try to do them, but I rarely succeed. Today, for example, with great effort, I've managed to organize the bills so that early on Monday morning, before work, I can pay the electricity, telephone, and water. Next Saturday, perhaps, I'll manage to get someone to come and give me an exact diagnosis of what is happening to my living room walls, even though, as I said, the damp doesn't particularly bother me. I won't do this for my own benefit but for potential visitors, the women out there waiting for me to talk to them and invite them up for coffee—"Sorry, I'm out of sugar"—in my living room—the domestic agora, as I said. But to tell the truth, I don't invite many people into my apartment. In fact, I've never invited a woman in, except for once, when a neighbor who doesn't live here anymore asked if she could use the telephone, and that wasn't even really an invitation, just, at best, a passive concession.

(Following the line of thought these last reflections timidly suggest, I never cease to be surprised that men in general, or so they say, have certain functional techniques for approaching women that to me seem outrageously aggressive, or at least impossibly audacious. I can't imagine myself under any circumstances inviting a stranger, or someone only recently met, to come to my apartment; I can't imagine myself explaining to her, while feigning distraction and opening a beer, the esoteric details of my boring job, let alone asking her about things that don't interest me—she knows they don't interest me—in order to get down, as soon as possible, to the hurried ritual of "getting acquainted" and then jump into bed, like in a Discovery Channel sequence. Thinking it over, the only way it would seem natural for someone to come to my apartment is if they had already been there before . . . oh, the paradox.)

The damp is, from the viewpoint of memory and its symbolic labyrinths, important to me, although I rarely admit that aloud and instead tend to complain about its detrimental effects on the upholstery of my armchair. One of my mother's houses, when I lived with her, also had damp, and there was no way, however hard we tried, to eradicate that architectural blight permanently. It was the same throughout the whole neighborhood, all twenty-seven blocks of it. There was even a story, probably apocryphal, about a woman on the eighth block who painted the whole façade of her house in proudly traditional fuchsia and, after the damp sabotaged her undertaking in less than a week, strung a noose from a beam in the kitchen and hanged herself. It's most likely that the two events–the rapidly rising damp and the lady's suicide–coincided in time but without any sense of cause and effect. Whatever the case, it's one more of the stories that mark my relationship with damp, and I now prefer to live peaceably with the moist blisters rather than carry on a vain battle against phenomena that are beyond human understanding.

My life is a repetition of one Saturday after another. What's in between deserves another name. Sundays don't count: they consist– I'm exaggerating here–of twenty-four wasted hours of which I will remember nothing the following day, and that following day, Monday, marks the beginning of the reign of inertia, whose only function is to carry me along smoothly, as if floating on a cloud of certainties, to the next Saturday. What's more, on Saturdays I masturbate twice. This latter action isn't a norm, but that's what generally happens, though I don't plan it: it's one of those indisputable recurrences of natural phenomena, I guess, like when the fireflies in an area flicker on and off together at regular intervals, synchronized by an invisible being. I masturbate once in the morning, when I wake up, and again in the afternoon, when I come back from my walk around the neighborhood. I usually do it while looking at porn on the internet, though I sometimes resort to traditional methods, like imagination.

The vacant lot my apartment overlooks is the reason I moved here. Fed up with the homogenous panorama of buildings surrounding my former house, I decided I needed a little clean air, a rest for the eyes that only vegetation and a certain rural ambience could provide. As neither of these was to be found at a reasonable distance from the museum, I looked for apartments next to vacant lots. This was the only one I found.

My job isn't particularly difficult, or particularly tedious. In fact, you could say that I like it. Three years ago, when I was out of regular work for almost four months, doing occasional commissions for various government institutions, I thought I would never find a place where spending eight hours a day would seem as pleasant as watching TV or looking through one of the volumes of my encyclopedia of biology. Then I got an offer from the museum and decided to accept it, so now I pass the day in an open-plan office with high ceilings, in an old building in the historic downtown of Mexico City, spending hours on end writing texts related to the site: press releases, salon notes, letters and speeches for the director, and so on. I also have other functions, which only occasionally require my skills, such as meeting and repelling the impromptu visitors who turn up to propose ridiculous exhibitions, or battling with the people in the printing department when there's an error in a catalog.

As there was no title for the post I occupy, or at least no one told me what it was, I decided to invent one myself, and now I sign official e-mails as the museum's "knowledge administrator." I got the idea from a billboard on the Periférico beltway advertising the new degrees of a private university. One of them was just that: Knowledge Administration. I loved it; I felt it expressed my deepest convictions. Considering what is known of the world, it's more than sufficient, I guess. Nowadays, the procedure is to administer knowledge in a way that makes people feel happy, or at least not constantly and irremediably miserable.

I'm not particularly happy. And, moreover, I don't think I'll ever study that degree program. In fact, I'm never going to study any degree program. In fact, I've never taken any course, at least not all the way through. True, I did spend four semesters doing English literature, but a deeply felt rejection of academic zeal made me stop in time, just before–hijacked by one of those diligent pupils who have an opinion about everything–I became convinced of the advantages of opting for a specific area of study, prepared to spend years dissecting the same, identical fragment of a nineteenth-century novel.

2

It must measure more or less 60 by 120 feet, but at night the lot looks bigger than it really is, and then I look out the window and imagine it's really a large thicket. When I was young I also lived next to a vacant lot, in Cuernavaca, that all the local kids called the Thicket. (It wasn't the damp house I mentioned earlier but another one, my father's.) In contrast to my childhood lot, this one has a wall separating it from the street, so you're hardly likely to be aware that the waste ground exists if you're only passing by with other things on your mind. For that reason, I went around noting every lot that might be overgrown with shrubs until I found an apartment for rent next to one. It took me months, but I wasn't in a hurry.

As I don't have many belongings or many visitors, I didn't mind that the place was really a small studio, and not in a very good state of repair. If I had more free time outside of work, I'd think about moving somewhere bigger and in better condition so I wouldn't have to spend hours listening to the downstairs neighbors' untimely arguments. But as I have little free time, I don't mind much, and have even come to feel a certain delight in listening to the disputes of those neighbors, who, late at night, make me feel that I'm not alone.

3

Today, as I was leaving the museum, I decided to walk home rather than take the metro for the four stops that separate downtown from the station nearest to where I live. I'd never done this before. I hadn't even considered the possibility of walking all the way here. I'd always imagined the various zones that make up this city, or the part of the city I know, as being unconnected on the surface, like islands that can only be approached from underground, on the metro. Walking, discovering that the pedestrian level is also a continuum, was a strange experience.

It's curious how a small, apparently innocuous detail like walking home from work instead of taking the metro—a good hour and a half on foot, at a brisk pace—can precipitate events or influence the direction of things in a way that is perhaps irreversible. I'm surprised, truly surprised, that the greatest concepts, and also maybe some of the most vigorous spirits in history, were, in essence, determined by a particular afternoon when a man decided to do something slightly different. On a smaller scale, that's how the decision to walk home now seems to me. I don't mean it has converted me into a twenty-first-century Napoleon, but I have the feeling that the order of something deep in my chest has been irrevocably subverted.

I avoided the main avenues and made my way along back streets, where the noise was more bearable and I could browse the shop windows. One place galvanized my attention, though I recognize that it was arbitrariness—or perhaps a paranormal force, inherent in urban development—which made me stop just there. It was a café that displayed its menu by means of laminated photographs from at least thirty years before. Jurassic omelets with avocado, hamburgers sampled by my forebears. The photos of the dishes made me, nonsensically, think of the stars, which are, according to popular wisdom and expert thought, testimony to a reality that no longer exists.

I went into the café and sat at the counter, next to a man who looked like part of the furniture. I ordered a coffee. A skinny man in a red shirt, on the other side of the counter, replied in a surprisingly brusque tone that they didn't have any.

"But I can offer you a cup of hot water for Nescafé, we've got that."

"You wouldn't have chamomile tea, or something similar?"

The man in the red shirt disappeared through a greasy curtain covering the upper half of a doorway (a hole, to be precise) in the wall behind the counter; on the other side of this curtain, I caught a glimpse of some family photos and, hanging from the ceiling, a chandelier with half the bulbs blown; under the light, a green table, and at it, a boy doing his homework. This was probably the home of the owner of the incompetent café, and that simple curtain divided his working and private worlds, if such a distinction made any sense in his particular case, which is questionable.

The owner–or the person I took to be the owner–came back after a while, carrying a packet of tea that looked as old as the photographs in the entrance.

"Yes, but it's normal tea. I couldn't find the chamomile." By "normal" he evidently meant black.

"Well, give me a cup of that then, and let's hope it doesn't keep me from sleeping," I said, seeking some sort of complicity with the owner of the café, though without really understanding why I was seeking that complicity or how such a state would emerge from a situation as trivial as the one that had united us so far. The man gave me a sardonic, scornful look.

"It's coffee that keeps you from sleeping, son, not tea; they give tea to the sick."

I had no wish to discuss the effects of theine and halfheartedly agreed with him. He put the cup of steaming water down in front of me and also left the whole packet of black tea on the counter. I extracted a tea bag, put it in the cup, and stared–transfixed by the way it soaked up the scalding water and sank like a shipwrecked barge–before I added a little sugar. I drank the tea in silence, not listening to the complaints the furniture–faced customer addressed to the three or four other locals. (His banality was disturbing and his ability to emit streams of foul language, prodigious.)

When I'd finished my beverage, I looked in amazement at the bag of black tea at the bottom of the empty cup, limp and useless as a newly sloughed skin. I can't explain exactly what I thought, but that uninspiring object seemed beautiful in its insignificance, so I wrapped it in my napkin and put it in my pocket. I was concerned that the owner or one of the customers, noticing my eccentric maneuver, might berate me, but apparently no one saw me. I paid and went out.

I am now in my apartment and the tea bag is on the table, in the center of a sodden napkin. The pocket of my jacket was also soaked, and if it hadn't been a dark jacket, I would probably have had to take it to the dry cleaner, because everyone knows that tea, as they say is also true of sin, leaves a permanent stain.

The tea bag doesn't seem as surprising now as it did when it was at the bottom of the cup, but I've decided to keep it, so I get my staple

gun from the toolbox, and, after a dull thud, the end of the string with
the label is stapled onto the wall, right in front of the bed, so that
this useless, vaguely obscene pendulum–aesthetically speaking, it
is something akin to a sanitary pad–will be the first thing I see in
the morning. The bag is still dripping slightly, and a tiny puddle is
gradually forming on the floor, plus an elongated brown stain on
the wall. I think the stain will add an interesting touch to the room
and perhaps, by accentuating the corrosive effects of the damp, will
end up being the decorative focus of the apartment. I think I like the
term "decorative focus," although I'm not completely certain what it
means. (On a wall covered in crucifixes, is God the decorative focus?)
I also think it will be pleasant to wake up every day and contemplate
the tea bag hanging on the wall, not just for its appearance–slightly
disagreeable at the moment–but because it will be a souvenir of that
afternoon, of that sudden, arbitrary decision to walk home from the
museum and have a cup of tea on the way. It's good to create souvenirs of authentic, minute moments of happiness.

   I listen to an argument in the downstairs apartment, related,
from what I can gather, to a video game; they are in their forties
and arguing about a video game, a Nintendo, almost certainly from
twenty years back. It's already dark and, in the vacant lot, almost
impossible to make out any detail. The plants merge with the
strands of rusty wire on the ground and the bags of garbage some
people in the street throw over the wall. Leaning out the window,
I look at the lot and try to imagine that it's a thicket, or the lot opposite my father's house in Cuernavaca, the one we used to call the
Thicket, or that cities don't exist and there's no point in distinguish-
ing between a thicket and anything else.

   The neighbors' argument has finished, or at least is smoldering,
awaiting a new spark. I close my eyes and the sound of the canned
laughter of a TV program comes to me from another apartment.
The insomniac's questions edge their way in: How much do actors
charge for false laughter? What–if anything–do they think of when
they want to produce it? Are there actors, in every corner of the
world, whose job it is to dub other people's false laughter into their
own language? Do these actors have conventions and conferences,
in towering hotels, to share the secrets of false laughter, to mutually

amuse one another, to overcome the sadness that stops them sleeping? Are there support groups for false-laughter actors? Are there help lines–1-800-LAUGHTER, for instance–you can call in the early hours so you don't feel alone, so you can laugh falsely again, talk about your childhood?

The laughter is muffled by a new argument between the forty-something neighbors and their mother, with whom they live. The old lady shouts, "Candy, Candy!" Candy is a small, gray male dog. It doesn't occur to them, apparently, to give their pet a name appropriate to its gender.

I think I'd like to smoke a cigarette at moments like this, to have something to do while I do nothing, but I've never been capable of acquiring the habit.

4

Tuesday, the inertia continues. On opening my eyes, in contradiction to what I'd predicted, it is not the tea bag I first see but the window overlooking the vacant lot. With my morning coffee steaming before me, while I wait for the computer to start up so I can take a quick glance at the day's headlines on the internet, I look out the window to see how the lot is doing this morning: if there are more or fewer garbage bags–every so often, without explanation, the bags disappear–if it rained during the night and the ground is muddy, if some vagrant has gotten in to find shelter and safety under the branches. Checking out the state of the lot every morning is a basic activity. It makes me think of people who live near a river, who, as soon as they wake, hurry to see what state the waters are in: "It's low today," they announce, or "It'll flood today."

The garbage bags haven't gone. There are no down-and-outs. But I notice a movement among the bushes in the lot. "That'll be a cat," I think. There have been cats on other occasions. Lost or exiled kittens, or kittens booted out, almost as soon as they've left the bloody womb, by happy but practical families who know they can't

live with animals everywhere. But it isn't a cat: a dirty hen appears
between the weeds, pecking at the ground in search of food. How
could that hen have gotten there? Perhaps someone has surrepti-
tiously installed himself in the lot and let loose his farm animals, for
personal consumption, as they say. But I can't see anyone, nor any
other farm animals, just the hen, which occasionally disappears
behind some car tire or scrub plant and reappears on the other side,
making that intermittent noise I never know the name for because
I've never lived a particularly rural life, except for that other vacant
lot, the childhood one we used to call the Thicket, which never had
any fauna besides the scorpions and spiders my father used to warn
me about when I went out to play with the other children.

No, I've always been eminently urban. Before this apartment, I lived
very close to the Zócalo, in one of those alleys where the street
vendors used to crowd together, shouting, until the city authorities
gave the zone a facelift and put them all in an enormous warehouse so
they had to suffer the penance of their own cries without deafening
the tourists, mutually punishing each other with their earsplitting
reverberations.

   And before I lived downtown, I was in Coapa, in one of those residential estates with identical houses that were once upper middle
class and are now inevitably occupied by hordes of teenagers accustomed to the cultural aridity of the periphery; teenagers who gather
in the green spaces to smoke pot and show off their skateboarding
tricks, and whose career ambitions are usually to work in a skateboard store or have someone pay them to set fire to vacant lots.

   I was one of those innocuous teenagers, I admit it, and not as
long ago as I'm ready to accept. I was, let's say, an aging adolescent
in Coapa, when I lived with my mother–in the damp house, near
the one where a woman hanged herself from a beam–and I pretended to go to the university every day, while in fact I'd already
dropped out and was convinced it wasn't necessary to study anything (as I am now, although maybe I was more belligerently convinced then). I used to go to the green spaces as well, and though I
didn't skateboard, I did smoke pot and bought acid tabs that I later
sold at a profit outside a state high school to make a little money
for books or pirate video games, bought in nearby Pericoapa–the

video games—or Avenida Miguel Ángel—the books. (I have a particularly fond memory of a book written by a French executioner from who knows what remote century and a video game in which, for the fun of it, you could kick your opponent when he was down.) I never had a dog or a cat, much less a hen, although once, during those horrible teenage years, bored and high on drugs, I bought a rabbit at the traffic lights and then treated it so badly that it attacked me viciously, making the most implausible gash on my arm, from which I still have a scar, and in moments of weariness, it seems to take the shape of a rabbit—as happens, they say, with the full moon, though I've never been able to verify that.

After the rabbit, I don't think I ever again lived with animals. At best I must have seen, out the car window on the highway to Acapulco, the agglomerations of sheep and the distant, iconic cows. And now—right under my window, in a central zone of a city for which, like God, the apt metaphor is the circle whose center is everywhere and whose circumference is nowhere—well, now I can see a dirty hen pecking the ground of the vacant lot. Do you say "crow?" No, that's cocks. The thing is that hens have their own sound, so inalienably their own, and I can't go on thinking about what you call that intermittent chirping, because it's Inertia Tuesday and I have to go to the museum to correct the letters the secretary writes incorrectly and meet—in a corridor; I don't have my own office—the unwelcome photographers who are proposing an exhibition on heroin users who live in the sewers, or women who live in the upscale suburb of Polanco and screw their chauffeurs when their husbands go to New York on business.

I've got it: it's called clucking. The sound the hen makes is called clucking.

5

My childhood, excepting the above-mentioned absence of pets, was pretty normal, if anyone's childhood can ever be normal. In Cuernavaca, in my father's house, I amused myself torturing beetles, tying their legs to watch how they flew in circles, burning them with a magnifying glass, or asphyxiating them with the fuel from a lighter. I also used to make waterways out of the PVC tubing I found in the Thicket, that other vacant lot that may have inspired me in the search for the one that now lies below my window. I would assemble long sequences of tubes, the joints perfectly sealed with Play-Doh, through which I would run the water and then throw in my toys. This ludic activity suggested the fruitful career as a civil engineer I had the good judgment to avoid, to the disappointment of some of my relations and the great disgrace of my savings account.

At school—it was a Montessori school—I liked lying down at the back of the classroom and falling asleep in the middle of the lesson, something that was perfectly allowable and even encouraged by certain ultramodern teachers. These same teachers, who had probably once, or more than once, gotten a divorce, and fancied themselves as artists—one painted in oils; still lifes, I seem to remember—had legs covered in hair, and staring at their calves was like observing the wild, impenetrable depths of the Thicket.

College meant a return to the capital, to my mom's house. Dad had fallen in love with a woman from Chiapas and had settled in San Cristóbal de las Casas, taking with him his modest workshop for the manufacture of "artistic aromatic" candles and its three or four employees. The designs for the candles included symbols like the yin-yang or Viking runes, and in a San Cristóbal, which—in the final years of the last century—was making its debut as the destination of choice for revolutionary tourism, those New Age details were well received by the floating population of Italians. My dad's artistic candle business flourished in this context, as did many medium-sized and small businesses that took advantage of a niche in the market produced by the neo-Zapatista movement (the woolen Subcomandante Marcos figures made by the indigenous people, the baggy T-shirts with slogans and motifs related to the struggle, the traditional medicine clinics, et cetera). With the passage of time, my dad got fed up with the candles and delegated the management of sales and manufacture to his wife, returning to academia, if only peripherally, to give a couple of classes in a forgotten political research institute in the center of San Cristóbal.

And as I said, I returned at the beginning of term to the capital, where I was received with hostility, as if the city were reproaching me for having left. Coapa showed its only–negative–side, and I had the misfortune to fall in with the most unsuitable people in the neighborhood. Very soon, at the age of just fifteen, the only conversations that interested me were those related to drugs. Unconsciously subverting the natural order of things, I first tried cocaine at the insistence of the older brother of a well-to-do close friend, and then pot, which touched something more intimate in me. However, my inability to take drugs in the company of others very soon became apparent: when I wasn't beset by completely unjustified paranoia, irrepressible laughter and sudden attacks of autism alternated in taking control of my nerves. From then on, I decided only to take drugs for purely experimental purposes, which in the end saved me from turning into a foul-mouthed addict like the rest of my neighbors and classmates. Experimentation, as I understood and practiced it, involved always looking for a completely new situation in which to consume: I swallowed a tab of acid in physics class on the day they were explaining the first law of thermodynamics–I've never since been able to forget it; I did coke on a school trip to a farm with cuddly deer; I snorted ground ecstasy pills before entering a natural sciences museum; and finally–my master stroke–I ate hallucinogenic mushrooms during a family dinner, under the quizzical gaze of my grandmother.

Despite all this, the resulting experiences were hardly worth mentioning, and if they truly marked my character, it was in making me understand that one of my strengths is an ability to enjoy the most trivial situations intensely, and not because they gave rise to an air of extrovert magnetism. It's possible that if it weren't for those experiences, I wouldn't now be an office worker, or so thoroughly enjoy such an obvious piece of stupidity as asking the museum's security guard about the previous Sunday's soccer match between two mediocre provincial teams. A match that, of course, I hadn't seen and had never had any intention of seeing.

6

Leaving home, on my way to work, I decide to buy a lottery ticket. "Yesterday I spent my money on a cup of tea, and now this," I think, absurdly, since the sum of these two whims is tiny in relation to the margin of whimsicality my salary allows. But I've always felt guilty about spending money on insubstantial things, as if an austerity chip had been implanted into me at the fetal stage. And on top of all that, last week I bought a shirt to replace another, very similar one that had been left unrecognizable by an accident with a dish of black mole sauce. Yes, I feel guilty about the expense, but then I tell myself the rent on my current apartment is a lot lower than what I used to pay for the one near Zócalo, so when you come down to it, I can invest the difference in small trivialities, like a cup of tea in the evenings and a lottery ticket in the mornings, and even more serious things (a trip from time to time, if I liked trips). On finding that fallacious arithmetical balance, I feel less guilty. I'm in the habit of seeking out the exact transaction to redeem myself. I choose the lottery ticket without giving much thought to the numbers, though I do manage to include a six, for which I've always had a particular affection.

In fact, and this is a symptom of a solidly middle-class childhood, monetary questions don't usually bother me much, apart from the guilt certain financial outgoings spark. Saving isn't so much an effort as a natural consequence of the life I lead, frugal and boring. My salary at the museum is meager, but it's regular, and the institutions I worked for before the museum still occasionally ask me to proofread the odd program or catalog, so I pocket a few extra pesos every now and then. If I've decided to buy a lottery ticket, it's not for any desire to become a millionaire, but because I know perfectly well that the simple fact of having a lottery ticket in your pocket stimulates the imagination, and that I can spend the day mentally hatching ridiculously dandyish plans, the extravagances I'll commit in the unlikely event that I win.

In the museum, I distractedly say good morning to Cecilia, the director's secretary, who tells me that Ms. Watkins won't be in till later because she's got a meeting in some restaurant or other in the south

of the city, a business or political relations–there's no difference–
breakfast. Without listening to the whole explanation, which seems
to me overly long, I sit at my desk in the same enormous room as
all the other desks, except for Ms. Watkins's. The designer, I notice,
is watching a TV series on the internet. On his screen, two women
are kissing tenderly; he feels someone watching him and gives me a
nervous smile.

Cecilia has renounced her love of conversation and is now sitting at her screen laughing, by which I surmise that she is either
chatting with some friend or watching the same lesbian series as
the designer. While my computer–a PC that takes ages to react to
the instructions I give it–is booting up, I go down to the courtyard
of the museum, one of those spaces surrounded by arcades that can
be found in all the colonial mansions in the center of the city. I sit
on the front steps and look toward the entrance to the museum. On
the other side, the hubbub of the city's historic downtown and the
suffocating heat of the asphalt seem to be at full force: vans with
loudspeakers announcing a deal on oranges, competing CD sellers
raising the volume of their speakers . . . all this under a sun that, however strong, can't disguise the ashen scaffolding of the atmosphere.

All the while, the thick stone walls of the museum and the courtyard overshadowed by a high canvas awning keep the air inside cool,
and the noise of the street seems to come from a parallel universe
that we silent inhabitants of this building can gaze at as calmly as if
looking into a fish tank, without any sense of asphyxia.

I calculate that my computer will be ready by now and that the
time idled away in rumination must have exceeded that needed for
a simple visit to the bathroom, and although the director is at her
breakfast meeting in the south of the city, I suspect her secretary,
Cecilia–as spiteful and cunning as they come–would be capable of
denouncing me for laziness if I spent too long away from the office. So
I decide to go back, if only to search the internet for the same series
that, it seems most likely to me, all the other employees are watching,
until someone with the minimum of authority–the security guard,
the bookkeeper, or, in a worst-case scenario, the director herself–
appears in the doorway and, pointing with evil intent to the sign saying Administration, tells us all we're not exactly in a movie theater.

While I'm pretending to write a press release, with the chess window minimized and ready for me to continue my game against the computer–I've never won–Jorge, the designer, comes up looking as if he's about to ask me an enormous favor that will undoubtedly, or so I think for a moment, make me unhappy. Getting ready to refuse, I swivel my chair around to face him. He says–feeling sorry to have interrupted me–that since I'm the "grammar expert," he wanted to see if I could help him write a reference for a friend, also a designer, he says, who has applied for a job in a cosmetics company. I say I will, that I haven't got much in my inbox, and that we should do it now before Isabel Watkins, the director, gets back, because when she's around, we'll have our noses back to the fucking grindstone.

"The fucking grindstone," that's how I put it. The expression feels odd on my tongue, and that strangeness appears to be mutual, as even Jorge looks astonished by a word that is, so he believes, so little in keeping with my usual decorum. I write the letter, and the profusion of his thanks makes me doubt his sexual orientation, as if it weren't possible to be overly nice and at the same time behave like a "real man." Jorge, the designer, goes back to his desk and leaves me thinking that those discreet genres, such as references and rejection letters, are undervalued areas of poetic expression but as valid and moving as any lousy Italian sonnet.

Later, without Isabel Watkins having returned from her now eternal breakfast, I'm suddenly, for no apparent reason, struck by a whiplash of lust, and resolved to give it free rein in a more private area of the building, I head for the bathroom. In the cubicle, I unfold the pornographic photo I keep in my wallet, together with a pocket calendar with an image of the Virgin, and holding the clipping in my left hand, I give myself up to an age-old pleasure with the right. Masturbating during work hours is, I think, one of those small delights the male office worker has succeeded in safeguarding from the omniscience of the system. The photo acts as a simple amulet, resting in my hand while, eyes closed, I imagine unspeakable perversions involving Cecilia, Ms. Watkins's unbearable secretary, and even Isabel Watkins, the still-absent director of the museum.

I finish with a rather unsatisfactory grunt. The semen, which in more propitious circumstances would have spurted out with a certain gallantry, seems to reluctantly dribble into the worn pouch of my tighty-whities. After this relief, the pornographic magazine clipping loses its magical powers, and now reveals its true ugliness: the model, who has a hairstyle from the late eighties–one of those gravity-defying perms that made such an impact–is lying in an uncomfortable position next to a pair of fishnet stockings that, if it weren't for the infinite number of creases in the clipping, would be a phosphorescent green, precursor of the garish chromatic disasters of the nineties, when the advantages of adding insane quantities of lead to any pigment were discovered.

I soak up the traces of sin with a little toilet paper, small fragments of which apparently were glued to my fingertips by the semen, a fact that later, on my return to the office, obliged me to bury the guilty secret in my pockets.

To the delight of us all, the day passes without incident and without Isabel Watkins returning from her appointment, which by this time–six in the evening–would be absurd to still call a breakfast meeting. On leaving the museum, I decide to drop in on the charming characters in the café without coffee, so I set out on the trek to the same greasy counter, at which I once again order a black tea that I prepare myself and, this time without any embarrassment, put the damp tea bag in my pocket by way of a relic or personal fetish. The furniture-faced customer is still in his place, and if he weren't wearing a different sweater, I'd believe he hadn't moved from his seat since yesterday. On this occasion, the owner of the café pays me less attention and seems resigned to seeing me among his regulars: I'm already the "cup o' tea."

When I get home, it seems to me logical to fetch the staple gun once again and, after the dull thud, contemplate the second tea bag, hanging next to the first one, like the marks a convict makes day after day on the worn paint of his rickety cot to keep a record of the length of his imprisonment. Although in my case, I tell myself, these tea bags are testimony to my two working days, the first two well-deserved days of my full exercise of freedom. A freedom whose chronological beginning was, it's true, arbitrary, but no less effective for that.

Emboldened by this notion, swollen with pride at my conquest, I look out at the vacant lot and watch the unsteady steps of the hen, clucking through the weeds.

7

Saturday. I've spent a whole week waiting for this moment. Saturday morning. I guess it's already late when I wake up, but I don't check, for the simple pleasure of exercising the free will I've been so proudly boasting of since my first incursion into the café without coffee. Rather than freedom, I'm now tempted to call this sense of uprooting "lack of inhibition." Regardless of the words used, the important thing is that I no longer perceive, as was my habit, the straitjacket of anguish that used to restrict my movements.

Still in bed, I contemplate the tea bags on the wall, now ten, one for every day since that inaugural Monday evening, excluding weekends, when I'm saved the walk home from work and so the obligatory visit to the café as well. Each of the bags hangs there with its small pile of tea, now dry, as if it were the tail of a comet. Each one like a trophy some government institution might have awarded me in a memorable ceremony to laud my nobility of spirit, to reward the constancy of my freedom, the self-assurance with which I exercise it: all this without renouncing my routine–as would a thoughtless libertarian–still focused on padding out Ms. Watkins's model letters despite the conviction that I could be doing something else. This is freedom, I say to myself: an eight-hour day that, if I so wished, could be seven, or even less. An affirmation of will, but without unnecessary upheavals. A distracted walk home, aware that it won't affect the general order of the universe one little bit if I stop to enjoy a cup of tea in a local café where I'm known. And yes, they call me Blacky in–hardly witty–allusion to the color of the beverage I invariably order: cup o' tea.

Saturday. At home I make myself coffee. Black coffee. I listen to the announcement coming from the megaphone of the gas truck, which is arriving, as it does every Saturday, to deliver the bottles. That makes me think it must be eleven in the morning, more or less, although trusting in the punctuality of megaphone announcements in this city is, to say the least, reckless. What a barbaric custom, receiving the most basic, essential services–gas, drinking water–by means of a raucous shout issuing from a truck in a worrying state of oxidation! Couldn't we inhabitants of this immense, beautiful city get the gas through invisible in-floor pipes, prudently reinforced with three layers of steel? No, such luxuries are always reserved for citizens of the First World, who–sons of bitches–can drink tap water instead of paying for demijohns, also sold from trucks with blaring megaphones. Everything at top volume here. In the future, I tell myself, we'll get electricity via blaring megaphones too. Even the most famous national celebration is popularly remembered as "El Grito," the shout. It's always a ridiculous occasion, and I have one clear childhood memory of it: the president comes out onto a well-known balcony and shouts. He shouts to his nation–shouts at the top of his voice and is, at the same time, paradoxically mute.

I switch on the TV just to feel its noisy presence, which seems to be adding backing vocals to the gas sellers' cries, confirming my theory about Mexico and the decibels of noncommunication. The picture is fuzzy: the rabbit-ear antenna has been broken for a couple of months. I make a mental note to do something about it later on, although I suspect, given my idleness, this "later on" could become several months. The sound of the television, in contrast, issues relatively sharply from the speakers. A woman with an unpleasant voice is announcing the winners of a competition and silencing any form of declaration on their part with her laughter of feigned enthusiasm. Despite all this, I leave the TV switched on and sit on the bed to look out the window, to watch the dark clouds looming over the vacant lot. Then it occurs to me that if it rains, the hen, that uncomplicated friend who has been clucking among the shadows for the last two weeks, will die of cold or the famous flu–the ailment that returns periodically to the front pages of the world's newspapers. It is indeed the first time rain has threatened in the whole year, and I can't let a storm do away with the local biodiversity, including its wildlife.

Disposed to save the hen's life, I decide to construct a shelter for it from a small wooden table I never use for anything. "Wrapped in plastic shopping bags, the table will make a good place of refuge for the hen," I think. When I've finished my task and the table is covered with the impermeable material, I realize I haven't considered the next step: how to get its new home, its planned refuge, to the animal. I dismiss the possibility of entering the lot in person since the distance from my window is too great—I live on the second floor—for me to drop down from here, and I don't want to get into arguments by climbing the wall from the street like some errant drug addict. Only one idea occurs to me: if I had a rope, a fairly long piece of rope, using the appropriate knots, I could lower the table from my window into the vacant lot and position it right on top of the pile of sand by the wall of my building.

As far as I can see, there are a two problems: how to get the rope back once the table is in place, since there would be no one down there to untie it. The other matter still to be considered is how to let the hen know it should shelter under the table when the rain starts. This second issue is the most difficult to resolve, as it involves a question my encyclopedia of biology doesn't address. I have little faith in the animal's instincts, and its mental powers don't inspire much confidence, either: the hen, while I ponder its means of salvation, continues as usual, walking around in semicircles and pecking the ground, possibly more quietly now, hardly giving a cluck, perhaps intuiting, via some not just avian but—to cap it all—feminine sixth sense, that her—she's female, after all—luck might change at any moment.

A third problem hinders my progress: I haven't got any rope. I've looked all over the apartment, and the only vaguely similar thing I've found is an electrical extension cord that isn't long enough. I should leave my Saturday seclusion and find a hardware store to buy a good four or even five yards of strong rope, but to tell the truth, the idea doesn't appeal to me, given the possibility that it's going to rain soon. So I decide to throw the table out the window, hoping it doesn't break on impact, then, from the sidewalk, climb the wall surrounding the lot, overcoming my fear of public opprobrium, and position the table in the correct place. If anyone sees me climbing into the lot, I can always say that, due to some difficult-to-explain mishap, a small table wrapped in plastic bags fell from my window, and I'm trying to retrieve it. However unlikely the story sounds, the table will be there in the undergrowth as undeniable proof of my tale.

I proceed as planned. I throw the table out the window and, to my surprise, it doesn't break. With this happy confirmation, and seeing how sturdy the table is, I think that maybe I should have kept or sold it. But no, the table is no longer a table but a fortified rainy-season refuge for hens, and it is my duty to go down to the vacant lot and position it correctly.

Outside, standing by the lot, I scan the street for cops or curious idlers who might shout out when I climb over the wall, but the streets are empty and only the noise of a distant airplane disturbs the charged air of this Saturday. "The rain will wash everything clean," I think. Before that, of course, I have to save the hen. I jump lightly up onto the wall (feeling myself infinitely more agile than I'd expected), and once perched atop it, I look down; I don't want the hen to be passing underneath when I decide to jump and, in my rescue bid, end up killing her (this possibility brings to mind Chinese sayings about the wisdom of immobility). But I jump down toward the weeds and land on solid earth. Now inside the lot, I decide to take a look around to get a detailed idea of all the things I've so far only seen from my window, so I carefully make my way through the shrubs, managing to step on the protruding stones and avoiding the areas littered with trash.

In a clearing in the thicket—to use the very widest possible acceptance of the term—in the middle of the lot, I discover a supermarket bag. The central location of this object seems to me deliberate, in contrast to the random placement of the ordinary bags people toss over from the sidewalk, so I go to inspect its contents. The bag is tied with a tight knot, but there's a hole in one side and I decide to examine it. Something seems to be leaking out, and as I peer into the hole I see that it's an organ, something like a cow's intestines, dripping blood and crawling with maggots. As if my sense of smell had, until that moment, been blocked, I suddenly note the strong stench of putrefaction and feel revolted. It's a repugnant sight, and everything becomes tinged in a violet tone, like in a splatter movie. My visual field registers a hyperbolic, astringent disquiet. I run back toward the wall and with the same agility, if not with equal prudence, leap. On the other side, across the street, two women under a flowered umbrella are staring at me in astonishment. My expression can't have inspired much confidence in them, because they drop their eyes, walk more quickly, and turn off at the first corner. I drop down into the street and, just as quickly, go back into my building.

Later on it starts to rain heavily. I think the table discarded in the vacant lot will be ruined by the water. I avoid looking out the window for the rest of the day. I also avoid thinking about the hen.

----------------------------------- **8** -----------------------------------

Since Saturday I haven't been able to get the image of the entrails poking through the supermarket bag out of my head. The strength of that memory, its persistent purity, is such that I haven't even felt like having my black tea after work, and my collection of tea bags stapled to the wall has stopped growing. And neither have I gone down to the bathroom in the museum with lascivious intentions to unfold my pornographic magazine clipping, nor listened to the clucking of the hen in the adjacent vacant lot. I imagine, mournfully, that she has died of pneumonia.

I write letters. I compose the speech Isabel Watkins is going to give tomorrow to a group of bureaucrats from the Ministry of Culture. Every so often I slip the odd exaggeration into the speech that will show up my boss before the most widely read in the audience but be, otherwise, simply epic, even worthy of applause. Things like "while we are working, we must not, for a single second, forget that the word *museum* should return to its etymological roots, evoking the Muses." I consider putting in something even more stupid but am afraid of being fired. I imagine Ms. Watkins reading the speech, her technical pauses, her expression of frustration and terror when she gets to a line that says, "And for this reason, we have decided to knock down all the walls, even if it means a lawsuit with the Commission for Historic Buildings, and convert the museum into a place of sexual diversion, over which I will preside as the Matron Superior." But no, I can't write that, nor can Ms. Watkins read it tomorrow to the bureaucrats, all of them prepared to be bored until she comes down from the platform and they're able to take a discreet look down her plunging neckline.

Rapt in these perverse thoughts, I don't realize that, momentarily, a grim smile has twisted my lips. Cecilia, the secretary, looks at me distrustfully from her desk. Her expression shakes me out of the state of deep abstraction into which I had sunk, and I feel as if a great noise has suddenly been silenced. I have the sense of having spoken aloud but can't say if that sensation has any manifestation in interpersonal reality. Apparently not, since only Cecilia has her disapproving eyes fixed on me, while my other colleagues are getting along with their routine tasks, almost without noticing me.

This happens to me sometimes: I come back—as if from a distant, parallel world—and have no idea if I've spent a long while in silence or absentmindedly speaking aloud. The sensation doesn't generally have a high enough level of reality to alarm me, but at times like this one, the fine line between what I imagine and what exists is blurred and I panic.

Cecilia has stopped staring at me because Ms. Watkins has called her into her office. To respond to this call, the secretary has to pass very close to my desk as the space is limited and I'm the one who is nearest to the director (physically, that is, because in relation to this institution's organigram of power, there are only two levels: Ms. Watkins and everyone else). As she approaches me, Cecilia turns as if to make sure no one is looking and leaves a folded note on my desk, giving me, as she does so, a suddenly complicit, deeply disconcerting smile. Wasn't she some sort of working-life nemesis, perpetually embittered and ready to do her all to ruin the day of any fellow employee, especially me? The note lies there before me on the desk, and Cecilia is already in Ms. Watkins's office, but I don't dare read its message.

9

At the end of the workday, when everyone was beginning to switch off their computers and give a distracted "See you tomorrow" from the door, I picked up Cecilia's note and slipped it quickly into my jacket pocket. I left the office with the same "See you tomorrow" and came home.

The note is here before me, but I still need to pluck up the courage to unfold it. Could it be an invitation to her house? An amorous confession? A raffle ticket? I go out to the corner store in search of cans of beer. The corner store, however, is closed, so I walk through the neighborhood as night falls, looking for somewhere else to buy beer.

Coapa was, as I now know, an inhospitable world. Coming out of college, all the students (or all the ones I remember, myself included) would enter a locality that was like a lost city and, cramming ourselves into a pokey room, silently drink beer. Ever since that time, I've liked the flavor of canned Modelo. Now, more than twelve years later, I open an identical can in my small apartment in a better area (that is, closer to the center) and take a couple of swigs of the same cold, almost transparent, slightly greenish liquid I've spent half an hour looking for. I drink three beers, one after the other, hardly pausing between swigs, and feel triumphantly drunk. It will be impossible, I think, to go to the office tomorrow. It is in this state that I decide to unfold Cecilia's note, disposed to satisfy my bloated curiosity. There are two words on the paper, and as soon as I read them I realize there has been a colossal misunderstanding. It is yet to be seen if it's an ultimately beneficial misunderstanding, insofar as the satisfaction of my concupiscence is concerned, or if the misunderstanding will end up being as much a burden as if I'd decided to carry a truck on my back for the rest of my nights. The words, written in an unsteady hand, have, for once in Cecilia's lettered life, no spelling errors; they are "I accept."

Accept what? I consider the possibility that it might refer to an ambiguous, human, metaphysical acceptance, the acceptance of things as they appear in our path as we file along the city's median strips; the acceptance of the sound of the cars and of the morning announcements of the men selling gas and water and other products, the utility of which is never made clear; a wholesale acceptance, without fissures, that embraces creation, its multiple faces, its most sordid corners; the continual scorn of her father, her post as a secretary, her humiliation at the hands of Ms. Watkins, the unbearable silence of her workmates. I consider all this as the possible reference of the terse message, but later I understand that it was the beer talking, and that Cecilia, the sly secretary, is probably alluding to something more concrete.

It then occurs to me that when I started working at the museum, they gave me a sheet of paper with the extensions of all the employees, and some, the most committed or the most indispensable, had included a home phone number in case some extremely urgent, work-related emergency necessitated their immediate localization–something that, it goes without saying, never occurred in that museum, with its slack work pace. Without much hope, I look through the untidy pile of papers in a drawer until I find the sheet of paper, and there is Cecilia's cell phone number. Thank goodness it's her cell phone, I think, otherwise it would be a real pain to call her house and have a male voice–unexpected and hostile–answer the phone.

"Hello," she says in an almost challenging tone, as if she had been waiting for my call.

"Hi Ceci, it's me, Rodrigo, from the office." I've never before used the shortened form of her name, nor heard anyone else use it, but her reply is concise and rapid, so I suppose she didn't mind my affectionate "Ceci" too much.

"I know it's you, I recognized your voice right away . . . So, what is it?" she asks, as if she doesn't know.

"How do you mean, 'what is it?' Your little message, of course."

"Ah, that."

There's an uneasy silence on both sides. I have the sense I should take some sort of initiative but don't feel up to it. An unexpected timidity has my throat in its stranglehold, and I think my voice will sound more high-pitched than usual. Eventually it is she who breaks the silence, and I have the strange sensation this lack of initiative on my part will have negative repercussions for me at some not too distant point in my life.

"Don't you think you should talk about the little message you sent me? That came first, right?" she says.

The misunderstanding is now clear: someone, either in error or out of malice, had left a message on Cecilia's desk, signed with my name or somehow insinuating that I wrote it. As her voice is friendlier than usual, and given that her response to the mysterious note was positive ("I accept"), I don't want to disillusion her by explaining the mechanisms of the cruel trick that has been played on her. I'm the sort of person who worries about the effects of my actions on others.

"Ah, my little message," I say, as if we were both not fed up by now with using that ridiculous term. "What did you think about it?"

"Well, to be honest, it was a bit weird of you to say it out of the blue like that, but I'd already thought, you know . . . and so I accepted. I just want to ask you not to say anything until I've talked to my mom and dad."

Numbed by the turn the conversation has taken, I decide to let things run their course, guided not only by my drunkenness, but also by a suicidal instinct that at times like this translates into inexplicable forms of behavior and a discursive fluency I'm normally lacking.

"Take as long as you need, Ceci, don't worry. I've waited for this moment a long time, so I can hold on a bit longer." The words come out as if from an answering machine that has cut in completely against my will. I can scarcely believe the nerve with which I'm playing my own dirty trick, but there's something impersonal about it all, as if the events were happening far, far away from me, in a movie I'm watching, in a world similar to this one but stranger, where Cecilia and I have an age-old friendship. She, luckily, interrupts my thoughts just when I'm at the point of speaking again.

"Rodrigo, one more thing. I'd like it to be in a church, just to please my grandma; she's ever so devout."

This last turn takes me completely by surprise. I suspect that it is Cecilia—the cruel secretary who has made my life impossible since I started at the museum—who tells Ms. Watkins when I leave the office to waste a little time in the courtyard; that it is this same Cecilia who is playing a slightly ridiculous, thoroughly bad-taste joke on me. My response is slow in coming, but I eventually agree in a preoccupied tone and splutter out some impromptu praise of the Catholic Church that she, I note, doesn't completely believe.

I hurriedly make a brief farewell, which doesn't, however, avoid the worst. "Love you," she says. "See you tomorrow at the office."

As I hang up, I'm overwhelmed by corrosive anxiety. What have I done? What am I doing here by the telephone, my hand trembling, having accepted and, apparently, even proposed marriage to the secretary I have always silently despised?

I decide to go to bed without dinner but can't sleep. I resolve that first thing tomorrow, I will unravel the enormous tangle that has resulted in me getting engaged, in Cecilia sighing tenderly, and, I imagine, some office jokers being doubled over with laughter of secret delight.

----------------------------------- **10** -----------------------------------

And such was, in fact, my intention: to clear up that bad joke, even if it meant doing irreparable harm to the unhappy Cecilia, and return to my routine of walks and cups of tea and vacant lots inhabited by clucking hens. But today turned out differently, as if, yet again, against my will.

I am now once more sitting by the telephone in my apartment, waiting to pluck up the courage to call my mom and give her the news of my wedding. I still can't believe the course events have taken since this same time yesterday, when I called Cecilia with a hint of lust, prepared to take immediate advantage of her enigmatic note.

I arrived at the museum quite late this morning, as if fearing the moment of finding myself face to face with the woman who was now my fiancée. When I entered the office, she was already at her desk, wearing three pounds more makeup than recommended by

health experts and gazing at me with an ingenuous little smile that
shattered something inside me. I thought she would be deeply disappointed if I didn't walk over and give her a good-morning kiss,
something I had never done in my life. Once I was close enough to
her face to hear her accelerated breathing and clearly smell that
mixture of perfume and cheap makeup with which she was gar-
nished, Ceci swiveled around and planted a discreet, restrained
kiss on my lips in response to what must have seemed to her my
invitation. I then heard behind me an uneasy commotion, a noise
like people whispering and purposely letting pencils drop from
their hands. I began to think I must have imagined that adolescent
reaction from my coworkers, because as soon as I turned around
toward them, what I noted was enormous indifference. And, having started along that route, I thought their imagined reaction
sprang from a profound impulse of my own: perhaps I was the
adolescent who turned in his chair while Rodrigo Saldívar, that
office worker of rigid habits, threw his existence off-kilter by kissing the museum secretary.

After the kiss, I moved, blushing and looking ridiculous, to my
seat and succeeded in keeping my eyes fixed on the computer screen
until lunchtime. There wasn't much work to be done, but I pretended
to be writing the salon notes for the next forty exhibitions, while in
fact I was robotically copying dictionary entries.

At the set hour, I stood up to go to the small restaurant where I
always eat. As soon as she spotted me, Cecilia abandoned her work
and caught up with me as I was disappearing out of the museum,
ready, she said, to accompany me.

"You're very shy, aren't you?" she remarked on the way there.
And before I could respond, she added, "That's what I really like
about you. You're not the same as the other men in the office, spending the whole day going on about their lap-dancing clubs and their
whores for all to hear."

Without being completely sure whom she was referring to, I said
I really liked Jorge, the designer.

"Yeah, but he's as gay as they get. They all used to say the same
about you, and that was why you and Jorge sometimes chatted at
your desk, but I always knew it was a lie. You're a real man, right?"

Despite the inconvenience of the whole situation, I felt offended, as if just the mere fact of questioning my manliness didn't sit well with me, didn't sit at all well with me, so I responded, with a degree of severity, that one didn't have to choose between being an idiot and being gay, and that you could be quiet and still be macho. That's what I said, *macho*, a word I obviously sorely repented later and one which would have made my belligerent, feminist mother violently strike out my name from the pages of her will.

My mother, whom I am at the point of calling to give the news (that I suspect no one, her least of all, will particularly welcome) of my imminent marriage.

Ceci and I walked to the restaurant. She told me she ate there too sometimes, but as we'd never seen each other, I interpreted her declaration as a gratuitous boast. I was silent, even crestfallen, responding monosyllabically to her infrequent demands. We sat down, and I ordered: soup, rice, diced beef tenderloin. She had the same. Then, suddenly infused with a strange power, I told her she had always seemed to me a very beautiful woman, and I knew she was hardworking as well, so that was why I'd decided to ask her to marry me. This declaration was, I have to admit, partially false, but only partially: I found Cecilia attractive, especially due to the haughty air that accompanied all her movements, as if implying that she, in spite of being a secretary, had us all, at every moment, firmly by the balls. It was this attitude that had, on more than one occasion, made me dream of dominating her, or letting myself be dominated by her toughness.

She smiled in an exaggerated way, as if trying, with her histrionics, to hide a touch of melancholy that was, nonetheless, easy to detect. I wondered if I should kiss her, but the smell of food on our breath and the memory of our clumsy kiss that morning put me off, so I left flirtation for later.

The rest of the day, spent sitting at my desk, passed without incident. I succeeded in avoiding Cecilia's little glances in my direction, and it was only when she passed near my desk, en route to Ms. Watkins's office, that I gave her a discreet, barely perceptible smile. I finally left the building and came straight home, without the long, liberating stroll or the cup of black tea in my beloved, perennially greasy café. That's why I'm sitting here, much earlier than usual, trying to pluck up the courage to call my mom and say, with my characteristic conviction, "I appear to be getting married."

<hr>

11

Isabel Watkins looks fixedly at me across her desk. She's holding a pink card, and lying before her is an envelope of the same color announcing, in gold lettering, the engagement of "Rodrigo Saldívar & Cecilia Román" in the eighteenth-century typeface Jorge, the designer, chose for us. On the diptych she has in her hand, Isabel Watkins reads her name—"plus one"—and the time and place of the event. Below this is the address of a party room Don Enrique, my future father-in-law, has booked against my better judgment. Isabel puts the sheet of paper on the desk beside the scented envelope and looks fixedly at me.

"I don't know what to say."

Silence.

After a moment, she continues. "When I employed you here at the museum, I thought you wouldn't last long, that within a few months you'd have found something better, on a magazine or in a publishing house, and that you'd have jumped at the opportunity to further your career. I also thought that you'd have wanted to rise up the cultural ladder, that you'd have politely introduced yourself to the minister at the first opening we held. And although that prospect annoyed me a little, I was also pleased to think you were a kid on the way up. But now you tell me you're going to get married to my secretary and . . . I don't know. It's just that I always thought you were looking for something different, that you expected something else from life."

"Yes, Isabel, I appreciate your sincerity. And I understand what you're saying. But to be honest, I don't expect anything, except that things happen to me."

That's what I say: "Things happen to me." The expression seems to exasperate Ms. Watkins, who quickly gets rid of me on some invented pretext, but with the menace of "we'll talk later," so that I'm on my guard for the rest of the day. It's Thursday, May 11. In two months, I'm going to be married. After numerous chats with Cecilia's parents, and Cecilia herself, I've convinced them all that the best thing would be for Ceci to move into my tiny apartment "while we're saving up to buy someplace." The promise of owner- ship dazzles them, and they all concur with me, though, in essence, the only motive for my proposal is staying near the vacant lot. During these last three weeks since the engagement became offi- cial, I've clung to the waste ground as if it were the last possible salvation from the arbitrariness of things.

Mom, against all odds, very quickly washed her hands of the affair, as if she were giving me up as a lost cause.

"And might I know whom you're going to marry?" she asked sharply over the phone.

"Ceci, you remember her. Ms. Watkins's assistant at the museum."

"An assistant?"

"Yes, you met her once, at that opening of the exhibition on social movements in the capital I invited you to about a year ago."

And she, after a silence pregnant with reproach, "The secretary?"

"Yes, that's the one. But she's like Ms. Watkins's personal assistant, not the secretary. She does a lot of different things in the museum."

"Ah, I'm happy for you, Rodrigo. Let me know when you've fixed a date so I can book the ticket early; you know how it is with the planes—there are only two flights a week, and they're always packed."

Maybe if my mother had been indignant. Maybe if she'd shaken me out of this lethargy, this frame of mind that makes me yield to the secret designs of fate, turning up disguised as the most absurd acci- dents: a note given to a woman who is suddenly in love with me, or says she is; a café that becomes a haunt because I come across it one fine day on my way home; a growing collection of tea bags that occupies more and more wall space in my bedroom, remind- ing me my wedding day will soon be upon me, and I'll have no time to prepare myself psychologically before the babies and the diapers and the smell of shit become the ritornello of my nights . . .

Maybe if my mother had warned me, in her wisdom–as blind as it is immense–that getting married is one of the most serious blunders anyone can make . . . Maybe then, well, I would have woken up to a different reality, one in which entering into a marital contract with a woman I don't respect would mean the complete demolition of my self-esteem. But that wasn't the case. My mother limited herself to asking about the date of the fateful incident, and we ended the call with a nominal kiss that, for her part, signified simple pity. Pity and compassion.

In the same distant, disillusioned tone employed by my mother, Isabel Watkins called me into her office this morning to tell me she had received my message and didn't understand the reasons for this unexpected piece of news. Despite the fact that both Cecilia and I come to the office every day, we sent her invitation by mail, a week ago now, at the insistence of my fiancée, who seemed to believe it was bad taste to deliver it in person–but not, for example, to use cheap, pink, scented paper for the invitation to our engagement party.

What I find most impressive about the situation is that never before has Ms. Watkins spoken to me as an equal; I'd never noticed the least sign of empathy in her or seen the smallest gesture of kindness toward us, her unhappy subjects. Diligent, professional, hysterical, she had always treated me with the remote coldness of political figures; but this morning, as if I'd confessed to her that I had prostate cancer, she spoke to me with sincere, unforeseen friendship. I'm disconcerted to think she had hoped to see me rise up the boring pyramid of bureaucracy. I'm disconcerted, but also moved. I imagine myself as the deputy director of cultural heritage or undersecretary for national celebrations or head of the institute for the preservation of her fucking ass.

I leave work and walk home without stopping for tea in the café without coffee. A few days ago I bought a packet of Lipton's, and now I prepare the infusion myself, so my collection of used tea bags continues to grow at the rate of one a day–if I drink more than one cup of tea, I throw the residue away.

When the discussion about the matrimonial residence began, Cecilia, in the presence of her parents, proposed that she should move in with me immediately, even though it was still a couple of months to the wedding. Don Enrique silently granted his daughter the right to live in concubinage for a while so long as we married at the end of that period. I roundly refused: I intended to respect Cecilia's dignity until our wedding day, I said.

The resulting situation was equally uncomfortable for us all, and I would gladly have avoided it if it had only been up to me. Don Enrique, with slightly alarming knowledge of the cause, informed me that Cecilia–there present–was not a virgin and added that for such a right-minded person as me, that was a disadvantage. As if that wasn't enough, Don Enrique said he thought it was normal for me to want to "know" Cecilia before the wedding, and added that he wouldn't disapprove of our moving in together right away. Finding myself cornered, I argued that it was "a matter of principle," and independent of the state of my future wife's hymen–I didn't put it like that, of course–I'd prefer to wait for the proper moment, to give the ceremony greater meaning.

My decision received Don Enrique's approval and was particularly welcomed by Carmelita, Cecilia's mom. My fiancée, meanwhile, distanced herself from the negotiation of her sullied virginity.

12

There's the hen again. I don't know how, but she's survived the frequent storms. She didn't show herself for several days. Now she's pecking the earth in the vacant lot, and I suspect she knows I'm observing her. There's something flirtatious about her I've never noted before. She's making a less unpleasant noise–cluck–than usual, more tuneful, you might say. It's half past seven on Friday evening, and the setting sun shines on some of her feathers, making her more beautiful. She almost seems like a noble animal, a Paleolithic hen, capable of perching high up in an oak tree, a holly oak, and emitting a melodic, tuneful song.

I go to the kitchen for some grains of rice to throw to her. The hen understands what I'm doing and stands just below the window,

moving her tail just as gracefully as she can, which isn't very gracefully. I think about bringing her into the house, going down and
fetching her or lowering a basket full of delicacies into which she
will climb, sure of her good luck. Bringing her to my bedroom or
leaving her in the living room to surprise Cecilia when she comes
to visit me tonight to go over—once again—the details of the wedding.

But the hen isn't mine, I think. She must have a careful owner
who purposely leaves her in the lot so that she doesn't have to live
shut up in an apartment like mine, and so the kindly neighbors
and the filthy worms feed her, saving the owner the expense. And if
she doesn't have an owner, the hen is, as are few creatures in this
city, in this world, her own mistress. She does just as she pleases,
unaware of the precarious situation in which she lives. Tomorrow
they could start building on the lot or declare it a parking lot,
and the hen would probably be violently evicted, left in the street,
vulnerable to the passing cars, alone in the whirlwind of legs of
a cloudy afternoon. But in spite of this threat of danger, the hen
doesn't lose her wits, or whatever wits she might have, but continues pecking the ground unconcernedly. The hen is free. Maybe, it
occurs to me, because she was never in a uterus. She never dribbled
inside a mother or was attached by a fragile cartilage to someone
else's belly. She was born from a limpid egg. A smooth, white egg,
devoid of notable features, that opened up for her and left her beak
exposed to the harsh Mesopotamian sun. Ah, the oviparous animal,
what a model of behavior and temperance during its birth!

To be honest, I've never seen a hen being born, or any other
bird. Once I found the body of a newly hatched turtledove on the
sidewalk, but that's as far as it goes. Despite this, I like to imagine
the birth process of birds—something I must have seen on TV, now
that I come to think of it. If not, how do I know a bird is born from
an egg? Could someone, without having seen it or heard a detailed
description, imagine how birds are born? And mammals? Would it
be possible to think up the idea of a little calf covered in blood coming out of the rear end of a cow if there were no visual antecedent of
such a traumatic event?

It's as difficult for me to imagine, based on a complete lack of
information, the birth of a calf as it is to think of what marriage will

be like. I've never had close experience of it. No one around me even considered marriage as a possibility. In my life, it appeared next to other myths belonging to some remote era of which even my parents–divorced since time began–spoke of, in a tone of prudent reserve, as something that had now been superseded. I thought of other, almost magical situations that sounded to me contemporary with marriage: the maize field to which a young servant goes at daybreak every morning to soak the grain in water and lime before making that day's tortillas; the black-and-white television announcing a contretemps between the gringos and the Russians; the firm belief that a group of students can change the world once and for all. All those things I used to hear my mother and her friends commenting on; things my father never wanted to have to mention again. And among those situations, marriage, like an enormous unknown that, in idle hours, I fancy to be perverse.

Now, in just two weeks' time, I'll also be one half of a married couple, a perverse husband who will do everything he can to retain the secret of his deepest passions: the Franciscan love I profess for a stray hen, a propensity for making collections of arbitrary objects, my tendency to recall a dull, Coapa-lysergic adolescence as a dark, dusty corner in my history. An office-worker husband who will shut away his pornographic clipping from the eighties and his used tea bags in a desk drawer, together with his photo of his only trip to an island–Cozumel, at the age of sixteen, with a girlfriend who gave every sign of brilliance and ended up selling handicrafts on one side of the main square in Tepoztlán–and the piece of yellow paper on which a potential lover scrawled her telephone number with a pink pen so they could arrange a date in a pay-by-the-hour hotel on the Tlalpan highway.

Yes, because that's the type of husband I'll be. If I get married (and it's not that I've made up my mind yet; it's not really up to me), it won't be to lovingly accept Cecilia's fashion sense–she uses the excuse of it being Sunday to wear her favorite T-shirt: faded cotton with a ridiculous slogan in the center (it says something like "Coco Loco," "Sexy Austria," or "University of Cars," an impossible conjunction of words that must have sounded vaguely prestigious in the nineties). No, that's not why. And neither will I get married for the pleasure of her company in a silence laden with ingenuous emotion. Nor to dream of taking her to Acapulco on the first possible occasion. No.

13

The wedding was reasonably successful. My mom came to the capital, arrived at the ceremony on time, and left early for a hotel I'd booked in advance. The next day she flew back home to Los Girasoles. I didn't tell my dad because we have a relationship that is friendly as long as we don't talk to each other, and I thought it would be a bad idea to change things. What's more, he lives in San Cristóbal and, in contrast to my mother, doesn't have enough money to buy a return flight on short notice: as an uncle of mine once informed me, my dad has two other children, both very young, and what with the habitual costs of paternity and the caprices of his wife, the meager profits from his candle factory are eaten up, along with his even more insignificant salary as a second-rank academic.

Cecilia was more excited than ever in her white dress with ten thousand flounces that cost me exactly ten thousand pesos. I was moved. And she even–although I find it hard to accept–inspired a sentiment close to love in me.

The religious ceremony took longer than I'd expected, and it was only possible thanks to my having bribed the priest of a modest neighborhood church, revealing to him that I'd never been baptized and explaining that my fiancée's family mustn't know as they were very Catholic. The priest showed himself to be understanding, or perhaps greedy, and accepted the second financial incentive I offered, pretending, despite this display of nerve, that he was saving my soul by bringing me back into the fold. A fold to which I had, in fact, never belonged.

Then came the party proper in the excessively ornate venue my father-in-law had booked. Don Enrique very quickly got drunk and gave an awkward, unintelligible speech that everyone applauded.

Carmelita attempted, but obviously didn't manage, to drag my mother down into a spiral of tears. Jorge, the designer from the museum, was radiant throughout the whole reception, endlessly repeating the same mantra: that he'd watched us fall in love, that he'd been there from the beginning. I abstained from asking him, given his role as a key witness, to provide some explanation of what was happening in my life. Isabel Watkins had hit the bottle too, but she disguised her drunkenness by hanging from the neck of her companion, a photographer ten years her junior whose work had recently been exhibited in the museum.

The honeymoon—a couple of nights at a Guerrero beach—turned out, in spite of our continued state of intoxication, to be pleasant. Cecilia asked me to take her standing up, resting her weight on the window ledge of a cheap, semi-rustic hotel, with her wedding dress bunched up on her brown back. I admit that in the nude, she was more beautiful than she seemed when dressed, and I enjoyed making her tremble by stroking the skin around her anus, a zone privileged by her nervous system. (But I also have to say that I was not, for all this, a notable lover.)

The festivities lasted a weekend, and then we returned—having taken the Monday off for her to move into my apartment—to our respective posts at the museum. I am now sitting at my desk while she looks at me, and I can't get my head around the idea that the secretary, Cecilia, that woman who wiggles past on her way to Ms. Watkins's office, is my legally recognized wife, whom I have to watch from my uncomfortable wooden chair while typing letters to no one.

When we leave the museum, we walk hand in hand to the metro. In the carriage, we stand in shy silence, and I pass the time looking at the faces of the other travelers while my hand rests on Cecilia's right buttock. She seems grateful for this slight contact, which, from her perspective, saves her from the ignominy of being single, so she smiles secretly and, when the crush becomes oppressive, rests her head against my chest. When we come up from the metro, we walk along the less busy streets in the neighborhood. We stop off briefly at the corner store and buy a sugary treat for after dinner. (I have a suspicion that this custom, repeated over decades of wholesome matrimony, will result in consensual diabetes that we will both accept almost without complaint.)

That's the way it's been for a whole week. Today is, at last, Friday.

The apartment is a bit small for us, so I'm glad to have never bought large furniture, except for my wooden bed and the chest of drawers that holds my clothes in a knotted mess. Cecilia brought a flat-pack wardrobe from her parents' home and many boxes with holiday souvenirs, which we've put in the tiny storage room on the roof. (That space, I have to admit, was her discovery. I was scarcely aware I had the dirty, peeling storeroom, full of cobwebs, that now holds my wife's boxes of Veracruz key rings.) She also brought some kitchen utensils, inherited from her mother: a frying pan, two saucepans, a Teflon spatula, and a pewter spoon. There were hardly any wedding gifts; I was very explicit in that respect. Instead, I asked all the relatives—both hers and mine—to give us cash, to add to our savings so we could eventually move to a decent residence. Of course I don't have the least intention of leaving my apartment, my vacant lot. I put the money we received in a metal box in the wardrobe Cecilia brought with her, keeping it for a rainy day. The office, I realize, makes one humiliatingly prudent.

Cecilia, for her part, hasn't taken a single look at the vacant lot. I doubt if she has even noticed its existence. While she's sitting in the living room, battling with the rabbit-ear antenna on the TV in order to watch her game shows, I go to the bedroom, on the pretext of reading, and look out the window at the lot. Now, for instance, I'm scrutinizing it in search of the hen. But she doesn't appear. The muffled sound of the television filters through from the living room, mixed with Cecilia's laughter, which leads me to suspect she's managed to tune in to some program where the contestants are constantly humiliated.

Just as I'd predicted, Cecilia forcefully suggested we take down the tea bags I'd stapled to the wall opposite the bed. After a short exchange of words on the matter, I gave in, resignedly. I bought a couple of pints of whitewash and painted over the brown stain left by the tea bags until it disappeared. In place of my tea bags, Cecilia hung a hideous still life, the only wedding present that didn't comply with my request: some purple flowers in an earthenware vase, a clumsy imitation of Diego Rivera's essentially despicable creations. The painting was given to us by one of her aunts, who considered my idea of asking for cash to be–as she expressed it–in poor taste.

Apart from that elderly aunt, embittered by stereotypical widowhood and rancor, my in-laws have treated me well. Don Enrique, being old-fashioned in his ways, considers being married to his daughter an enormous sacrifice on my part (and he's not completely wrong), and so is continually making me aware of his profound gratitude. One of the ways in which he believes he is repaying the favor is by showing me how to do repairs around the house: during our wedding day, he started explaining how to deal with a leak if you can't find the valve. I, feigning interest, asked if he knew how to get rid of damp, which must have been a moment of pure joy for him since he immediately assured me he would take on the task of sorting out the problem, especially as his daughter would now be living with me in the apartment. So on Saturday morning, instead of walking to the gazebo to sit contemplating the various speeds of the passersby, or dedicating the morning to pampering the hen with special seeds, I'll have to wait for my father-in-law to stop by to assess the state of the walls.

Cecilia is twenty-nine, two years my senior. Nevertheless, we both look older. My total lack of a life plan and my haste to be a grown-up left the stamp of frustration on my features. My wife, for her part, comes from a family environment in which passing twenty-two without having at least one child is a sign of ingratitude–I don't know for what–or a lack of Guadalupian virtues. She was, at twenty-nine, the black sheep of a multitudinous family that understands marriage as an early rite of passage into adult life. It may be that the pressure from her extended family, in that sense, is responsible for the fact that she perpetually has a slight look of disgust–a haughty upper lip. Even now, when she's laughing her head off in front of the TV in our living room.

Little by little, I'm losing all those small details that, until recently, I'd considered to be indispensable, all those minutiae I'd come to count as features that matched my slightly grubby character: the tea bags, the damp in the living room, the laudable undertaking to

walk back to my apartment, and the dead, inane Saturdays in the
oval gazebo, dreaming of impossible statistics that depict me as
the center of the universe. All this, which until just recently could
be considered a protean identity, a fluctuating but almost organic
extension of my own body, is now at the point of extinction. In
exchange, I have the DVD player Cecilia bought to watch her pirate
videos on, and sexual activity I don't have to pay money for (at least
in the short term) and which I can enjoy almost anytime I want,
excluding the hours devoted to TV and, for now, the office.

I evaluate the advantages of this apparently irreversible trade-
off and decide I didn't do too badly: when you come down to it, I can
store my collection of tea bags in my chest of drawers and staple
them up again in around ten years' time when Cecilia will have
completely given up on the idea of modifying my habits.

Perhaps the most serious thing this pact entails—except for my
wife's sour breath in the mornings—is the great, and now insuperable, distance that has opened up between my mother and me. In
the past, despite her explicit repudiation of my major decisions, my
mom retained a filament of enthusiasm for having given birth, just
over a quarter of a century ago, to a relatively functional son. Now,
given that a deceptively golden wedding ring adorns my finger,
tying me, like a prison tattoo, to a way of life she disapproves of, her
expectations have been notably devalued. We don't speak so often
on the phone now, and when we do, her voice acquires the same
tired tone she used when I was a boy and she, taking refuge in a
migraine, would send me to my room, giving rise to a sharp pang of
sadness inside me.

She reproaches me, of course, for not having studied something.
And not just anything, naturally: a profession with demonstrable
social utility would have been her choice for me. A lawyer, a rural
doctor, or even an economist, just so long as I opted for a project
that would include the most vulnerable communities. Anything, in
fact, that would demonstrate I was concerned about giving continuity, during my lifetime, to her now-diminished desire to change
the world. My mother holds youth in very high esteem since hers
was intense and madcap, very much in keeping with the times.
She therefore hoped my youth would act as a culture medium for a

sensitive, decisive character, and not be a fleeting preamble to obesity and tedium. From her point of view, ingenuousness is a concept to be defended during at least the first thirty years of existence, and for a couple of years more that characteristic should translate into a sustained interest in changing the world, even if you then relinquish that desire. The fact that I, from early adolescence, and once my flirtation with drugs was behind me, had begun to exhibit a prebureaucratic attitude as if affiliating myself to the most insipid strand of character, causes my mom a sense of disillusion equivalent to dishonor. My marriage to a secretary—even though she, my mother, would never dare admit it—is the last straw.

14

I have a few thoughts of a general nature about marriage and the limits that should be imposed on it to preserve, as far as possible, some notion of personal decency. First, never, under any circumstances, will I allow Cecilia to defecate while I'm taking a shower. This incontrovertible point cannot be refuted by watertight folding doors or blue patterned shower curtains—it's a crucial, life-defining question. Second, it should be clear to both parties that I had no expectations of or genuine enthusiasm for the future before getting married. I don't want such a fundamental aspect of my personality to be relegated, over time, to a collateral effect of the marriage into which we have contracted, taking all credit from my phlegm, so stoically overcome. Third, allowing that I'm willing to yield to many things—using ridiculous pet names when speaking to her: "my cute little piggywinks," for example—nothing can convince me of the need to be sincere to my wife. (A parenthesis is needed here. At what inalterable juncture, at what hour, did sincerity and communication become related elements? Nothing is further from spontaneous intuition, popular wisdom, historical experience: communication is, precisely, the avoidance of sincerity in order to reach agreement.)

Displaying a composure that, even to myself, seems astonishing, I attempted to elucidate these and other theoretical aspects of marriage in the company of my adored wife, talking as one adult to another. As soon as I said I found the idea of showering while she was shitting repugnant, she gave me a furious look and flounced out of the apartment. She returned half an hour later with a pack of cigarettes, a lighter, and her mascara streaked. "I'm going to start smoking," she said. She's now smoking in the living room while I get ready to take a shower.

That was our first argument, and her reaction was heartening: instead of confrontation, a new vice. Instead of sorting things out and endlessly talking them over, a protracted, voluntary death. Assumption of pain. Metabolism. (Sorry, I was digressing.)

Mexico City is lovelier than ever. Two days ago, when Cecilia and I were on our way home from work, in a passage of the metro, a woman began insulting a policeman, explaining, with ample smatterings of "idiot" and "shut up," that her usual station had been closed and she'd had to walk to that one. Unperturbed, the policeman gave her a scornful look and quite rightly replied, "Well, stop voting for the PRD. It's all the democrats' fault . . . Up the PRI!" and then he repeated his slogan for the onlookers: "Up the PRI, ladies and gentlemen, up with the Institutional Revolutionary Party!"

I spoke to Cecilia about the possibility of looking for a different job, citing the opportunities for professional development and the need to augment my savings. Obviously, those are not my reasons at all: seeing my wife eight hours a day, only four desks away, then going home to find her overpowering mug on the other pillow, at the table, everywhere, has become a form of torture. We don't even have recourse to that thoroughly middle-class ritual of asking each other how our days were. Even if the answer to that question is always the same, I suspect there is a deeply calming pleasure to be found in asking it each evening over a microwave dinner.

On the other hand, I find the very idea of leaving the museum, abandoning Ms. Watkins, painful. Ever since she showed her unexpected talent for empathy, reprimanding me for marrying beneath myself, I see her almost as an alter ego: a woman conscious of the general grayness of existence who has let herself be dragged along by the inappropriate speed of events. Although, of course, there is a crucial difference that forms a breach between us: Ms. Watkins still retains the basically romantic belief that the string of accidents determining us can finally lead to the sort of destiny we were, against all odds, made for. I couldn't disagree more: the pencil that draws the line of my biography can only trace out an insipid figure, oblivious to even the discreet sumptuousness of geometry. If I were able to choose that figure, the final perimeter that represents, once and for all, the collection of vicissitudes I've lived through, it would be a dick. Yes, a penis: iconic, puerile, the kind teenagers draw on the chalkboard to annoy the teacher. A simple, unadorned prick that evades all psychological analysis and reclaims its original potential for insult. That would be my ideal figure, the embodiment of all the blunders that make me up. That or an ass.

Maybe I'm saying this because, during the last few days, a ridiculously dense cloud, a lugubrious mood, has been hanging over me. I'm surprised to find conventionally important events—a wedding—happen to me as if to a second cousin, scarcely affecting me. I get news of my life, but I don't feel it. And it's not that life is, as some would wish, to be found elsewhere, but that it's been reduced to a weak, heterogeneous set of associations: a hen walking around a vacant lot, a lottery ticket with the number 6 printed on it, a collection of used tea bags. Every so often, one of those details of my most intimate cartography is erased without any great fuss and a new one appears, substituting it.

In the end, the only thing that matters to me is conserving enough clarity to be able to articulately criticize what I see; if some illness stopped me from doing this, nothing would have meaning anymore. I'm not worried about physical degeneration, the whitish drool dribbling onto a shabby suit, premature baldness, prostate cancer. I'm not worried about them so long as I can go on complaining about what I see. I don't seek the permission of the Fates to find a soul mate with whom to deploy my melancholy; I can be alone, really alone, but I do ask the god of neural functions to let me retain this faint line of voice that crosses my cranium, allowing me to laugh at the world around me. This is the only grade of intelligence I aspire to, and it makes me immensely happy that it doesn't depend in the least on books or people.

(I say all this at the risk of sounding *maudit*; that is neither my intention nor feeling; otherwise, I would be oozing highly profitable mauditism in the modern salons of pomp and circumstance.)

15

The hen appears in and disappears from the lot at completely unpredictable intervals. Sometimes she's there all night long, and at others there's no sign of her for several days. I've turned the matter over in my mind, but I can't crack the code of the bird's irregular life. The topic is beginning to have pathological importance in relation to my daily routine, and I'm aware of it, which makes it even more disturbing.

Cecilia finally noticed the lot.

"Why did you move to a building next to a piece of waste ground, my love? It must have so many rats, you know."

The exaggeration of her warning irritates me. I tell her there isn't a single rat in the lot, just a hen. Long silence. I feel I've betrayed an enormous secret. Cecilia looks puzzled and gives a, for me, repulsive laugh: the sort of laugh emitted by teenagers who don't have control over their extremities. She asks how there could be a hen there. Plucking up my courage, I grab her arm, drag her to the window, and point to the mound of earth where the hen is usually found. Nothing.

Cecilia gives me a worried look, and I, in the mood for a leg-pull, insist, "Look, there's the hen. So, believe me now?"

Cecilia extracts herself from my grip–I'm probably hurting her–and goes to the kitchen. I stay here alone, looking at the lot, leaning against what some would call "the sill." This is our second attempt at an argument after the one when Ceci took up smoking. I wonder what new vice she'll acquire this time. Hopefully it won't be coprophagy or getting her nails painted with whole landscapes–I wouldn't tolerate either.

Then the hen appears from behind some bushes and climbs to the top of the mound with Tibetan calm. I look at her enviously and don't even contemplate the possibility of calling Cecilia and showing her I'm not out of my mind. Instead, I decide to hatch a plot for discovering every detail of the feathered creature's life-style: I'll call in sick, even act out a serious illness so Cecilia won't suspect anything—Would she, at this stage, be capable of report-ing me to Ms. Watkins?—and rather than going to the museum, I'll spend the whole day in the vacant lot, following the hen's every movement.

While I'm hatching this dishonest scheme, the bird moves back into the bosky shadows of the lot. I sit on the bed and open the drawer in which I keep the used tea bags. After contemplating them for a while, I decide I need a new project, something as ambitious as that collection, one that completely absorbs my intellectual capaci-ties, that aligns my ideas in a single direction, in just the same way as a magnetized metal bar aligns iron filings.

That's what I need: a Project. The other possible solution to overcoming the lethal sense of dissatisfaction into which I've sunk (for how long?) would be to find something like a Community: a close bond with a group of people who understand my interest in collecting tea bags, for instance, or my irrepressible desire to live next to an empty lot. But I suspect that no such groups exist, and that I have steadily dynamited all the communities I ever belonged to—the drug addicts in the gardens near the house in Coapa, the girl-friend I went to Cozumel with, and even Ms. Watkins, that secretly friendly boss who, despite all, believed in my abilities for a while. Dynamited them to the point where I've ended up more alone than a chili in a maize field, as my grandmother used to say, living with a woman to whom nothing except neutral Newtonian space seems to unite me.

16

It's Monday. The minute I woke, I uttered an exaggerated groan that frightened Cecilia more than I'd expected.

"What's wrong?" she asked in alarm. I invented a complex stomach ailment that would keep me in bed for at least forty-eight hours. Cecilia didn't believe me, but even so she agreed to tell Ms. Watkins I couldn't come in. She's less unpleasant now that she's my wife. If I'd missed a day at the office while we were simple workmates, she would have hurried to Ms. Watkins to vehemently demand my dismissal. Luckily, I never missed a day during those three years.

So, I stayed at home. The first thing I did was leaf through, without seriously reading, a newspaper from last week. The classified ads occupied my attention more than any other section, and within them, most particularly, those relating to sexual encounters. I amused myself in this way until my imagination sparked up, encouraged by the indecent messages of seek and capture, and I slowly masturbated on the bed, unconcerned about the possibility of ejaculating onto Cecilia's pillow, which I did. After that, I watched TV for quite a while and once again tried to think up an Important Project that would give meaning to my haphazard existence. Two hours later, resigned to my fate, I resolved to go into the lot to find the bird's secret hiding place, to decipher the reasons behind her actions. That was to some extent an Important Project, even if it wasn't really one. It was to some extent because it related one of my most authentic obsessions, the hen, to the need to understand her mechanisms, her minutiae, her little animal decisions that, without being decisions, made up a strangely fascinating, ordinary existence.

And here I am now on the other side of the wall, my shoes half sunk in the mud. I walk carefully through the undergrowth, searching for the hen and attempting to attract her with a sound I feel would be familiar, exciting: the equivalent of the sex-wanted ads in the newspaper, but in clucks. "Seeking a female with dirty feathers and loose morals," I cluck to her.

After walking across a couple of rotting planks, I reach the darkest, wildest core of the waste ground, that part that can't be seen from my window, toward which the hen is usually walking when I lose sight of her. The first time I entered the lot, with the frustrated intention of enticing her toward the table that was to serve as a shelter, I didn't get as far as this remote, overgrown region. I can hear the hen clucking in the bushes, but although she's close by, it's difficult to get through the dense vegetation to the place where the sound is coming from, and I have to make numerous detours to avoid nettles, thorny branches, and pieces of barbed wire. When I'm at the point of locating its origin, the clucking stops; nor can I see any movement among the leaves. The hen has disappeared. I desperately search all around but don't find a single feather. On the other hand, I do uncover a plastic bag just like the other one that, a few months ago, made me back off and run out of the lot, the bag full of viscera. The possibility that this bag might also be stuffed with intestines in an advanced state of putrefaction horrifies me. Not just because of my disgust and revulsion, my profound and, you might say, fainthearted dislike of blood, but also because finding a second bag during this second incursion into the lot would imply a pattern, a wink of complicity, a recurrence of–for god's sake–grotesque, abhorrent things; it would imply the lot is a place of perversion and death, a place where you could, with astounding impunity, dump the corpses of large mammals, thinking mammals, mammals with skirts.

Confronted with these pure possibilities, I feel overtaken by events. I have the sudden intuition that it wasn't my liking for things rural that led me to move next to the plot, but a propensity for catastrophe and a tendency toward the sordid that goes beyond my conscious undertaking to convert myself into a mediocre, spineless man. So I decide to take a roundabout path through other shady areas of the lot to avoid contact with, or simple closeness to, the bag possibly full of intestines. I stoop to pass below a branch that hangs, as if brought down by lightning, over a heap of trash. And as I move into the darkness, with the foliage of the lianas and the general vegetal disorder covering my body, I feel a blow on the back of my neck. And I fall. I fall as if going beyond the ground. Like Alice when she falls while following the rabbit. The rabbit whose form can be clearly made out in the scar on my arm, and on the moon, so they say. The rabbit that, in my case, is a stray and–who knows?–even imaginary hen, let loose in the weeds of my inertia.

─────────────── **17** ───────────────

I'm woken by a beautiful ray of sunlight falling directly onto my face and the cackling presence of the hen, who is pulling up worms a couple of feet from my ear. I pass my tongue over my lips and discover the taste of dust. I can also sense the dryness of the earth on the skin of my arms, the palms of my hands, my eyelids, my whole body. I'm lying faceup. I received a blow to the back of the neck, and I'm lying faceup, covered in dirt. I probably fell on my front and took the opportunity of an instant of consciousness to turn on my own axis, like a predictable planet.

Pain. Pain very close to the back of my neck. The blow wasn't exactly on the back of my neck. It was on my head, to one side, a few inches from the ear now listening to the clucking of the hen. It was a blow on that part of my head where the infestations of lice always started in my childhood. In the finest, most vulnerable hairs through which I would run my hand to feel the gritty lumps of blood, the pain. Pain and confusion.

I can't have been lying here for long. One or two hours at the most. Cecilia hasn't left the museum, and the sun is still high, so it's somewhere between midday and early afternoon. Two hours maybe. Not more. A few short hours disconnected, absent, lying faceup in the lot–my beloved waste ground next to my building– accompanied by the intermittent clucking of my wardress, by the pain of her victims, the worms. Worm pain. Neck pain. I sense and look at my grimy body. I extract a twig from my mouth. I wipe the earth from my eyelids with the right sleeve of my shirt, which is less dirty than the rest of me. My slow efforts to stand don't seem to surprise the hen, whom I've never before seen at such close quarters. Now I can appreciate the dull opacity of her plumage, the unhealthy look of her legs, the food fighting for survival, wriggling in her mouth. Worms.

Once on my feet, I'm overcome by a slight dizziness, accompanied by the precise sensation of blood flowing and veins pulsing in the area around the wound on my head. I check that my belongings–keys, wallet, cell phone–are still in their usual places– left pocket, back pocket, and right pocket, respectively–and as they are, I discount robbery as the motive for the aggression to which I was subjected, if that's what it was, and not a falling branch or a stone or a piece of drywall someone threw over from the street, imagining the lot to be empty as usual. Maybe I saved the hen from that very same blow that, I say to myself, given the size and fragility of the bird, would have been lethal.

Though it seems more likely it was a calculated attack. What was I hit with? A bat, a piece of rusty pipe from the lot, a tree trunk struck by lightning, the perpetrator's own wrath? And what was the motive for that sudden, unjustified attack? Simple rage; jealousy; the defense of a particular territory; incomprehensible, naked, unshod Evil?

Pissed off, I make my way back to the wall.

18

From the very moment I start ascending the stairs of my building, while I'm rummaging in my pockets for the key that keeps my meager belongings relatively secure, I suspect something is not as it should be. On the other side of the door, I can hear noises that, though not loud–barely perceptible in fact–only add anxiety to my heightened sensitivity. Despite having ascertained that the wound on my head is more shocking than serious, I can still feel it throbbing, and I think I'll have to invent something to explain the presence of the crusted blood on my scalp to Cecilia. (The truth is unthinkable: I could never explain why I went into the lot, why I followed the hen, why I was hit.) I'm distracted from my thoughts and my future excuses by the sounds on the other side of the door as I'm about to open it. Lo and behold, just to make a frigging awful situation worse, some burglar has, in his wisdom, broken into my dwelling with impunity to commit some outrage that, in my anxiety, I imagine to be not so much robbery as licentious acts involving my underwear and the pink lipstick Cecilia uses when she wants to project an air of elegance.

Prepared to frustrate the perverse siege, I enter the apartment and, with great presence of mind, shout out in as deep a voice as I can manage, feigning heroic, baritone, burglar-proof manliness. But at least in the living room, there is no burglar or anyone of a profession akin to that. I head for the bedroom with a crepuscular presentiment but on opening the door don't immediately see anything out of the ordinary. But this apparent calm masks a more serious perversion: in the geometric center of the bed lies a coiled piece of shit. A perfect turd on the tiger-striped bedspread.

II

FUNDAMENTAL CONSIDERATIONS ON SOMETHING

Marcelo Valente was sitting on the balcony of his Madrid apartment, marking the final exams of the academic year while mentally running through the objectives of his trip. And although he wanted, at all costs, to escape from that pallid tableland, he also knew he would end up, however unwillingly, missing many of the things that were just then triggering a profound sense of boredom.

This wasn't to be just any old year. Despite having dedicated as many as four consecutive months to academic tourism (exchanges, conferences, symposia, periods of research in Eurozone countries), he had always traveled with the notion of a quick return in mind. In contrast, he knew his stay in Mexico could become almost indefinite, and spending a year in a remote third-world university, traveling around small, out-of-the-way towns, at the mercy of the sun and the narco wars wasn't the same as, for example, having breakfast on a comfortable Parisian terrace and walking tranquilly to the small, confined office he had been assigned.

He had only been in Latin America once before, in Buenos Aires. His time in that city had left him favorably disposed toward the whole continent, which had perfectly satisfied his expectations of moderate quaintness, somehow gratifying his vanity and reining in his belief that it was possible to know a little about everything. A three-month stay had been long enough to cover the entire spectrum of the emotions a city could inspire in him, from the blind enchantment of the first weeks to the final relief of watching through the plane window as Ezeiza Airport grew smaller, plus a number of intermediate stages: the shameless wooing of a married woman, the embarrassing bout of drunkenness in a stranger's home, and the untimely shove given to a dean of philosophy (with the accompanying cry of "Not everyone in Spain is a pompous ass!"). In short, a story he wasn't sure he could be proud of.

This was something that seldom occurred to him in relation to his past; his usual procedure was to brag, on every possible occasion, about the versatility of his CV: arrogantly list the nationalities of his lovers and the ideological diversity of his thesis advisors, many of whom had asked him, a posteriori, to contribute to books they were editing. The perfect mixture, in short, of an unresolved inferiority complex and a pretty face, which rather than getting uglier with age was becoming more interesting. Marcelo Valente was, even in the words of his friends, "a cretin with a PHD."

He was aware that his personality inspired not a little reticence. He was no longer on nodding terms with more than one professor. The academic staff of the philosophy department were on the whole, by comparison, much more serious-minded: elderly, blind seminarians who were tangled up in the thousand and one proofs of the existence of God, hangover Marxists who organized independent study groups and papered the chapel of the law department with pro-Chavist leaflets, jaundiced mathematical logicians who put their faith in the advent of the cyborgs and, to some extent, anticipated that arrival with their own mechanical existences. Marcelo didn't belong to this realm. He had, in fact, studied art history, and only after a PHD in aesthetics at the Sorbonne had he definitely switched departments. For many academics that showed, to say the least, a lack of respect.

Part of Marcelo's misunderstood charm consisted of treating everyone with the same effusiveness, as if turning a deaf ear to rebuffs. This technique of overpowering friendliness ended by softening the hearts of his declared enemies. They once again invited him to congresses on the construction of aesthetic thought during the frenzied interwar years, the only area of study in which he displayed relative assurance—and disproportionate pretensions.

Marcelo had an emotional relationship with his object of study that made him stand out among other philosophy professors. While some—the majority—dedicated themselves to the tediously monotonous repetition of anyone else's ideas, Marcelo was convinced that thought could be used to know something new about the world, even if that world was the limited field of the aesthetics of the avant-garde. His was not the optimism of the ignorant but that of the egomaniac, though anyone who didn't know him could easily confuse the two.

Marcelo Valente's story—as should be kept in mind henceforth—has two strands: his love life and his theoretical enthusiasms. These two spheres, in his case, cannot be separated. Any attempt to narrate his Mexican experience without taking this into consideration will be unsuccessful.

B

In December 1917, Edmund Belafonte Desjardins—poet and boxer, boastful jewel thief, con man, art dealer, serial deserter, Australian logger, light-heavyweight champion of France, Canadian challenger in Athens, Russian exile in New York, stowaway, teenage orange picker in California, exhibitionist, Irishman living in Lausanne under a false identity, fisherman, conference lecturer, editor of a five-issue magazine, ballet dancer, dandy, boxing coach in Mexico City's Calle Tacuba, expert on Egyptian art, buffoon, lover, liar, front man for nobody and for himself on innumerable occasions, nameless shadow, witness, minor personage in a time brimming over with great names, friend, wretch, brute—convinced Beatrice Langley to join him in Mexico, where he was scraping together a living under a pseudonym that would make him celebrated and despised, in equal measure, in the artistic milieus of Montmartre and New York: Richard Foret.

Bea arrived in Mexico in early January 1918, and twenty-four hours later they were married. Richard had already had enough of the city, the adjoining towns, the constant altercations with gringos and locals. He had had enough of that country full of thugs where he had, due to the painful process of missing Bea, plumbed the deepest abysses of his melancholy. He had been in Mexico for just six months, but he had had enough. He was mistaken for a spy wherever he went. In San Luís Potosí, the caudillo Saturnino Cedillo had held a gun to his head, threatening to shoot if he didn't confess whom he was working for. His muscular physique, his accent, his tattoos all made him untrustworthy: who was going to believe he was an eccentric writer waiting in Mexico for his wife—an English poetess residing in New York—who would be coming by train to rescue him, to save him from himself? They listened and thought he was insane. And for this reason he began to feign insanity, to exaggerate it to the point of losing himself in it, convinced that only in that way could he survive in a country of gunmen and anarchists.

He had reached Mexico after a journey full of mishaps, fleeing the Great War, and found himself faced with another war, equally incomprehensible, equally cruel, although luckily, thought Foret, a little less rational, a little more from the gut, or at least so it seemed to him. And this was, when you came down to it, what mattered. In Paris he had battled, with his own guts, against the castrating intellectualism of the Apollinaires, the soulless Cubists, the Marinettis of this world. Where in the work of these people was love, the unmoving motor of all the stars, fixed point and vertex of the actions of men of real daring? Nothing of that was left, only the pantomime of art, and Foret shat a million times on art. (He would express it in those very words in his *Considerations*.)

In New York, as an illegal immigrant, he had received his draft papers and had started out on a two-month trek through Quebec until he found a schooner bound for Mexico. The United States was, by that time, too dangerous for him, especially after the trap laid by that son of a bitch Marcel Duchamp, the calculating, sham-timid pig who had deliberately gotten him drunk and put him up on a stage, like a circus monkey, in front of two hundred people, just to have a laugh at his expense. He should have floored Marcel with one of his powerful jabs. After all, it was that lecture that had brought him to the attention of the u.s. draft board, in whose view he was a strong soldier and an undesirable alien, a man worth more in the trenches, shouldering a bayonet, than sleeping in parks and stripping down in front of upper-middle-class ladies. But Foret feared the war because of his height; he used to say he might at any moment forget where he was, stand up in a trench, and get a bullet between the eyes. The war was for short, inconsistent people, he said. For dwarves convinced a weapon made them powerful. He was powerful without the use of arms, even if the smell of gunpowder in a small theater was one of his secret pleasures.

With Bea in Mexico, he at last felt calm. When he was with her, he regained the conviction that he could do anything with his life. Write poetry, for instance, and hang up his gloves for a time to dedicate himself to reading and trying to articulate his emotions. Bea had brought him a chest of books from New York: not only *Childe Harold's Pilgrimage* by Lord Byron, which Richard had explicitly requested, but also a pile of offerings from Bea herself that would reveal to him a whole new world: James Joyce, the poetry of Ezra Pound, Eliot, and Williams in grubby magazines. Foret had never been a great reader. His references were scarce, though very intense.

If there was one disadvantage to Foret's tender savagery, thought Bea, it was his jealousy. Mention of Marinetti and his manifestos was banned in the house; in New York, Bea had hidden them under a mattress and had, to avoid arguments, decided not to bring the books with her to Mexico. Bea had been Marinetti's lover during the time she lived in Florence, and that, added to the fact that many of her Parisian colleagues constantly compared the two men's impassioned natures and tendency to violence, was enough to make Foret feel persecuted by the famous Futurist. Aside from jealousy, the comparison offended him: Marinetti's passion was cold, haughty, mathematical; Foret considered himself to be a gentleman of the old style, the last emissary of spleen in a world proud of its unthinking iconoclasm. Even his violent character was misinterpreted: Foret had spent years escaping from the war, that same war to which Marinetti composed odes.

He had, however, not read Pound. For him, the world of literature ended with Rimbaud; everything afterwards had been imposture. He knew almost nothing about u.s. literature. The only things he respected in North America were the locomotives. But anything Bea gave him was sacred, so he sat down in a corner of the room to browse through one of the new books. Bea watched him tenderly: her *enfant sauvage*, her great big little brute, her sensitive boxer.

Outside were the sounds of ambulances, street sellers, packs of warring dogs, the usual noises of the center of Mexico City on a sunny afternoon in 1918.

──────────────────────── **A** ────────────────────────

In Argentina, Marcelo's personality was more jarring than usual. In general, he considered his Buenos Aires experience to have been a failure. Except perhaps for the vaguely tragic liaison with that married woman, Romina, in a house on the delta of the River Plate, where they had spent a whole week eating apples and hoping the husband's return would, for whatever reason, be delayed.

It was a rather predictable love story, seasoned with every cliché of the Argentinian character: Italian family, hysteria, an almost genetic tendency for orgasm. From the very first, Marcelo set out to attract her: he invited her to dinner, took her to a small apartment near Retiro that a professor at the University of Buenos Aires had lent him during his visit, and uttered outrageously imprudent words. Romina, faced with all this, feigned resistance to his Madrid charms, professing a sense of remorse that in the hours dedicated to the bedchamber and its delights made no appearance whatsoever. Until the inevitable occurred: Romina began to utter words possibly even more imprudent than Marcelo's, mentioning future trips to Finland and Venice. That was when he returned to the path of virtue; subtly, he suggested to Romina the possibility—however remote—that none of those plans would come to fruition since they shouldn't forget she was married to a man of strong character, and he, Marcelo Valente, would soon be returning to Spain.

The breakup and related emotional outburst took place on a train taking them from Retiro to Tigre: they both shouted, Romina cried, and a pair of down-and-outs threatened Marcelo in an argot he found incomprehensible, promising to crack his head open if he didn't leave the lady alone. Obviously, such was exactly Marcelo's intention at that moment, so he left the lady alone and got off two stations early, to then take the next train in the opposite direction and never see her again.

Romina was, for Marcelo, the embodiment of a stereotype that was not merely Argentinian but, thanks to his willful ignorance, Latin American. In his imagination, the entire subcontinent was a place populated by women like that, capricious and laxly Catholic, determined to "give pleasure" to the men in their lives. Perhaps for that reason, with the prospect of living in Mexico for a year in view, Marcelo Valente clearly sensed every drop of blood in his body flowing to the tip of his cock.

B

In a person with such varied interests as Richard Foret, it would be impossible not to find contradictions. While reason is confined to a monosemous logic, and the most sensible people choose their actions based on cause-and-effect calculations—thus acquiring a certain continuity and direction in their lives—sentiment, as is well known, is at the mercy of climatic changes and tends to move between one extreme or the other with a naturalness that only the most valiant of men would call their own. And there is no doubt about it: Richard Foret was a valiant man.

If we are surprised by the absurd plurality of the lives he lived in so short a time, if the list of his occupations, nationalities, and hazardous deeds sounds ridiculous, it is because a degree of rationality greater than his beats within us, a stronger desire for identity. Only for those who exist between two separate forms of life, for those who accept fluctuation, is it possible to approach the life of Richard Foret without being absorbed by it. If our preference for reason is absolute, seamless, then we will never hear his name, never know anything of his greatest love, never—even by mistake—read the string of absurdities that make up his work. We will live in another universe, a universe where Richard Foret has no place, where the Richard Forets who have lived in the world don't exist.

A midpoint has to be found for Richard Foret to matter for us without our being blown away by the hurricane of his dementia. His is a personality—as many of those who suffered the vehemence of his friendship know—capable of sinking any story.

In the end, the only way to approach Foret without condemning his changeable nature is to speak of his relationship with Beatrice. In Bea Langley, Richard finds the axis mundi he is lacking. He organizes his obsessions around a woman with whom he lived for barely a few months, and she appears to return his feelings. The merit for this obsession does not only rest with Foret: Bea had already captivated other lovers of undeniable spiritual vigor. Forged in the fire of a love triangle with Marinetti and Papini—a triangle that sparked the enmity between the two Italians in the years before the Great War—Bea Langley's attraction belonged to the realm of terrifying love: falling in love with her meant, if one didn't have the determination and misogyny of a Futurist, that all the intellectual and emotional activity of the lover would, sooner or later, be centered on her gray eyes.

The relationship between Foret and Langley is the definitive point of inflection in both their lives. His, after Bea, comes to an abrupt end; hers, after Foret's death, traces out a path increasingly distant from worldly passion. Bea, dedicating herself to the creation of a form of free verse stripped of punctuation, becomes an ethereal woman who, until the sixties, divides her time between the England she had renounced and the Paris she loves. He destroys himself, hounded by all the wars, among strange victims, with the grace of a seagull hunting for fish, sinking his head in the rough sea.

It is a commonplace to talk of an impossible love that, notwithstanding its impossibility, achieves success and yet, in its passage, destroys the agents of that attainment. But although some historian or person of letters, carried away by cliché, may have attempted to understand it in this way, Foret and Langley's love was something different. Her confidence, the strength of her protofeminism, makes it impossible for us to imagine a tragic end for Bea. Richard, in contrast, had just such an end tattooed on his brow, and his life consisted of the uninterrupted search for a death worthy of his megalomania. That he may have found in love the detonator of his katabasis should surprise no one: the most timid lover feels his chest swell and the most circumspect becomes epic; in someone like Foret, such an emotion could only exacerbate a nature that tended to be extreme–in the sense where the adjective is used to describe a climate that alternatively scorches and freezes, without any neutral point. Perhaps the only surprising thing is that Foret had not fallen in love before, that he had survived to the age of thirty-one despite the mark of his condemnation, that he had written an incomprehensible book–*Fundamental Considerations on Something,* composed of not always illuminating notes–and a couple of good articles on art criticism. It seems improbable that such a hyperactive spirit could have found time to sit down and write, in solid prose, an indictment of the *Salon des Independants,* but this unexpectedly sane exploit is typical of our hero: his lives were several and parallel; this is the only way to explain how he could have been capable of having a German prostitute on either arm during a memorable night of debauchery and at the same time editing a literary magazine, written by himself alone, under a variety of pseudonyms.

And this is another important point: for all the pseudonyms, the multiplicity of carnivalesque masks he invented for himself, Foret had, against all odds, a consistent *style.* This isn't a Pessoa on amphetamines, capable of mutating in his writing like a chameleon walking over a Newtonian wheel. Foret's pseudonyms allowed him to change genre, to flirt with the fictional chronicle and return to the familiar space of satire and from there back to poetry, but all these texts have a certain something in common; the violence of the opinions is the same, as is the demoniacal gratuitousness of his inventiveness, which shines through in his *Fundamental Considerations on Something,* where it is unconstrained by any form of textual coherence.

As is the case in a large part of the avant-garde in the early twentieth century, during the years before the Great War, Foret oscillates between frenzied humanism ("Tell me where my fellow man is before I amputate my leg") and a vicarious enthusiasm for great machines ("Give me back that locomotive, you great son of a bitch. It belongs to my spirit.")

When war broke out and his mobilization seemed immanent, Foret embarked, with forged travel documents, on an adventure that took him to Paris, Greece, then Barcelona, and finally New York. His rejection of the war cannot be read as pacifism (a stance that is rare among the artists of the period) or simple fear of death: he felt it beneath his dignity to be dragged hither and thither by an army; in his freedom of movement—epitomized by his love of railways—Foret found the moral sticking point beyond which he would not cede to society's desire for control. The erratic nomadism he practiced was the end point of his discussion with totalitarianisms: he was unimpressed by any frontier, not even coastal ones. His submission to other norms is debatable, but his love of movement was incorruptible.

---------------------------- **A** ----------------------------

Marcelo couldn't help but identify with the objects of his study, like a child who, during a movie, is unable to stop himself from producing a noise when he sees an explosion. As his career would suggest, his writings ranged from the typical anecdotes of art historians to lingering descriptions of the avant-garde environment and highly intellectualized conclusions: impenetrable paragraphs on the aesthetic project of Futurism, the political drift of the movement, the penetration of art by technology.

Obviously, his was not a comfortable role, and not only philosophers but also historians derided his work, which seemed only to be enjoyed by the wider public—a couple of his monographs had been rewritten in more amenable form by some anonymous copy editor and were now available in Spanish bookstores as mere novels. This circumstance delighted Marcelo. He was able to pride himself on being a "writer of the people," on having escaped to the uncouth language and loudmouthed autoreferentiality of the crudest form of academia to become a "spreader of profound thought," as he put it.

His figure had gradually begun to take on that air of celebrity only granted to two or three professors in each department. First-year students, unaware of Marcelo's complete lack of vocation for teaching, would get up at sunrise on registration day to put their names down to be included in the small group able to take his elective class: The Aesthetics of the Avant-garde and the Birth of Postmodernity. It would be no exaggeration to say that over the preceding years, a number of students had changed majors–from philology to philosophy, for example–at the last minute with the ambition of becoming belatedly postmodern writers under Marcelo Valente's tutelage.

The face of Spanish fiction was finally, against all predictions, changing. After decades of polished, correct, and boring prose, the return of the idea, of experimentation, of the essay, was timidly show-ing its face. In this tessitura of rapidly changing fashions, Marcelo's pallid work had undeservedly acquired cult status. Of course he didn't read a word of contemporary fiction, and he couldn't have cared less what his students did with the knowledge he plastered over them like mud, just so long as they retained a degree of devotion to his words and continued to recommend his *Duchamp: Mysticism and Lies* (Ediciones Canela en Rama, 2007) to their friends.

It is fair to say that Professor Valente's sense of self-esteem didn't rest on that single professional and ultimately superfluous conquest, but on his success with women. At the age of forty-five, Marcelo had attained the dubious of pleasure of "not tying himself to anyone" and carried his bachelorhood with the same air of self-sufficiency with which he defended his vegetarianism.

"It's a question of ethics, Pombo; there's no hidden scam. Nowa-days the European man can get by without meat, and in his decision to do so, he is affirming himself as the heir to a tradition of renun-ciation whose roots can be traced back to Augustine of Hippo, the motivation for which is simply the recognition of personal finitude."

"Finitude doesn't get it up for me," responded Professor Pombo while chewing on a pork bone.

Naturally Marcelo didn't believe the half of this. A famous Asturian gastroenterologist, a family friend, had told him six years before that his extremely delicate digestive system would not be

able to withstand the negligence involved in his taste for roast suck-
ling pig much longer. And although the doctor had not suggested a
radically vegetarian diet, Marcelo had taken up the cause as one of
the few modern preferences he would allow himself the luxury of
incorporating into his lifestyle just before reaching forty—the age at
which, in his view, a man should have a well-defined, immutable
character—so he had for some time been living on an abundance
of green vegetables and pulses, with the occasional lapse he didn't
mention to anyone. He was, in general, a person of firm, if arbitrary, principles.

Marking exam papers bored him, but he occasionally had to
laugh at the notions that occurred to his students, whose little brains
appeared to be as lost on the paths of contemporary aesthetics as
their bodies were on the plains of Castile, rambling without rhyme
or reason through the corridors of a department that displayed a
portrait of a king in every classroom. (Marcelo, a man who managed
to have an opinion about almost everything, didn't care one way or
the other about the monarchy. In his younger days, he had been a
fervent defender of the Republic, without this—in his megalomania—
stopping him from identifying himself with His Majesty, perhaps
because the tabloids of the heart had taught him that He too was
a man tormented by a multifaceted passion. But after a certain
moment, he had lost interest in the king. Now Marcelo was one of
those few Spaniards who felt themselves, as he himself expressed it
whenever the occasion allowed, "closer to Europe than to his native
soil," and in the subtle clockwork mechanism that kept his convictions ticking, this was sufficient reason for pretending to ignore the
Great National Issues.)

The exam papers he was marking were truly pitiful. He had the
feeling none of his students had understood, not just the general
sense of the module, but even his writing on the whiteboard. The
majority limited themselves to repeating, with imbecilic exactitude,
odd phrases extracted at random from the list of required reading,
out-of-context fragments that could as easily pass for irrefutable
maxims as pieces of graffiti scrawled on a bathroom wall. One
more original student attempted to explain—without ever coming
to the point—why Surrealism and its theoretical consequences led,

unhindered, to the legitimization of female circumcision. (Marcelo predicted for this student a notable future as a newspaper columnist and gave him a top grade: he always tried not to be hard on the most idiotic ones, absolutely convinced they would go far.)

Faced with the flagrant stupidity of the new generations of philosophers he was supposedly educating, Marcelo Valente felt depressed. Who, in that future filled with the derision of thought and cellular phones with an increasing number of functions, would make the effort to understand the greatness, the originality of his essay on Richard Foret? Marcelo had put the last scrap of enthusiasm in his career into this project. Afterwards, it would be all total indifference, the inane repetition of the same old class for thirty years, the acts of homage to this or that departing dean in the university auditorium, the tranquility and shame of knowing yourself to be protected by your tenure and a right to the professorial freedom you do not exercise.

But this would all come later. For now, the project on Foret was taking shape. Individualistic, uncouth, a stranger to the theoretical pretensions of his peers, Richard Foret embodied a version of the avant-garde Marcelo related to the spirit and ambience of his own youth back in the eighties, in a Madrid to which punk had arrived belatedly, violently, hand in hand with heroin and bad taste, to modify the face of Spain forever. Punk was, in a certain sense, Foret's cold vengeance, his raised fist seven decades on, and his posthumous triumph over Surrealist sentimentality and the innocuous eccentricity of Dada. Foret was, moreover, the architect of the Grand Trick, the first avant-garde artist who had managed to gather, in a final act, the dispersed threads of his life and work and weave them together in a gesture that made him immortal: his disappearance.

Foret had spent his last days–of which very little is known–in Mexico and had written letters to his wife, Bea Langley, that indicated a clear loss of reason. Marcelo was convinced he could, for once, set aside the speculative nature of his work for a year and dedicate himself to finding, in Mexico, Foret's unpublished writings and the records of his final months to add the finishing touches to his intellectual biography of the eccentric author and, with this done, compose a paper that would refer to punk as an artistic avant-garde and interpret Foret's disappearance as the *triple salto mortale* that closes the pages of a text with a paragraph that is not final, but leaves forever open the roads that lead from the life to the work. Marcelo had something like that in mind.

Maybe it wasn't very original or very exciting, but it was a research project like any other, and he had already gotten in touch with Professor Velásquez at the University of Los Girasoles in Mexico to tell him how much he admired his work: his monograph–"with its sparks of brilliance," as he put it, in a momentary fit of banality– "on the crazy avant-garde artists who ended up in Mexico" and a short chapter on Foret were to some extent along the same lines as his own interests, so he would now have to go there and occupy a pigeon-infested office (the only one available, according to Velásquez) while following to its finale the not completely justified impulse that had led him to fix on Richard Foret as the guiding light of the next year of his life. And he went to Mexico.

B

Beatrice Marjorie Langley. Daughter of Thomas Langley of Birmingham, a robust man with a frank mustache and a perhaps overly ingenuous gaze, a lawyer and humanist who died in London at dusk on the seventh day of 1905.

Beatrice M. Langley. Divorced. Mother of two children whom she abandoned in a boarding school in a country at war, and to whom she writes occasional letters, heavy with guilt, pretending they are having an exciting adventure. Letters that receive no reply other than a brief telegram from the headmistress reminding her it is time to pay the fees.

Bea Langley, formerly Bea Burton, formerly just Bea. Daughter of Elizabeth Langley, née Boyd, Francophile, unhappy, tyrannizer of servants, collector of Chinese porcelain, resident of London.

Beatrice: marked by a name that evokes the pain of a lover who descends into the underworld, a name she scarcely conceals with the "Bea" by which her father, her beloved father, called her as a child.

Bea, with the thin lips, dark eyes, and the wide hips that make her see herself as even tinier than she is. With the impossible hair her mother used to comb with more anger than discipline during her entire childhood, complaining all the while that her daughter, her only daughter, had not inherited the silky hair of the Boyds, but that thick mane–a Langley trait–Bea bore all too happily. "Don't smile so much, Beatrice, you look stupid."

Beatriz, the cosmopolitan poet and mediocre depicter of fairy scenes. The woman who would later have a daughter, Ada–indisputably her favorite–with a square jaw, like her dead father. Bea, the Mexican, the Londoner, the Parisian, resident of Buenos Aires, of Brooklyn, the desirable but unattainable woman for whom free love didn't include allowing the same brutes who, two years earlier, had proposed marriage to her on bended knee to touch her breasts. The liar who would so often say "I'm fine" during the twenties with suspicious conviction; the woman who, in the thirties, would vainly attempt to reinvent herself as a writer of light comedies and would end up, in the forties, writing the only thing she could write, what she should always have known she had to write: the story of her most alive, most dead lover, the story of her most monstrous suffering, of her fall.

Bea, the woman who, in the fifties, would find peace, or at least an attempt at oblivion that was perhaps the product of her years. The woman who has grandchildren she silently watches over each summer in her apartment in Montmartre. The Bea, Beatrice, Beatriz Langley, B. Langley, who will go on signing letters to a defunct lover with all those variants of her name. The one who will tear up the letters. The one who will hide the secret of her frustration in order to write poems dictated by pure, simple reason, the reason of dazzling insufficiency, timid reason.

Three events from her life before 1918 in some way sum up those thirty-three years. The scene is this: 1901; a melancholy, teenage Bea, with thin limbs covered by a fine golden down and painfully budding breasts, is crossing Europe with her father, alighting from the train in the cities he considers essential to the sentimental and artistic education of the child. Elizabeth, the mother, resentfully imagines, from her bedroom with heavy curtains in the high-ceilinged house in London, how the complicit relationship between father and daughter becomes closer as they visit continental castles; a complicity in which she has never been included.

In a small station, the train is scheduled to stop for longer than usual, according to the ticket inspector. It is a large town or minor city in the north of Italy. The father remembers having heard that a very good wine, made from a native strain of grape, is consumed in the region, so he proposes having an early dinner in some trattoria and coming back to the platform before the train departs. But Bea isn't hungry. She is very quiet and is looking at people with her eyes half-closed, a characteristic she inherited from her mother that makes Mr. Langley nervous. The father leaves her in the care of one of the servants and gives her a stiff-armed wave from the platform; she watches him, undaunted, from the window.

Bea continues looking out the window for a long time. A man and a woman, both elegant and with an English air, are sitting on a station bench with a pair of suitcases before them; they seem to be arguing, although their voices are inaudible to the young girl, who invents an ingenuous love story for them. The woman, watched by the man, suddenly stands and straightens the brim of her hat, which the breeze had disarranged. Bea silently spies on the scene as the woman takes a suitcase in either hand and stamps off down the platform to a distant point on the right of Bea's line of sight. The man watches the retreating woman, takes off his top hat, and places it at his side on the bench; the man looks at his hat as if it were a friend he is asking what he should do next. Bea believes she understands what is happening: an amorous snub. The woman does not turn her head to see what her forsaken lover is doing. He slowly gets to his feet and pulls out a pistol from some fold in his overcoat: a long, slender gun that makes Bea think of her father's study, of the leather-bound books, of the curtain rails and the candelabras of her London home.

Beatrice Langley, at the age of sixteen, watches the scene in silence from the safety of her anonymity within the train carriage.

The pistol rises in slow motion until the barrel is perfectly hori-
zontal, following the line of the man's arm. It is an extension of his
body, a rigid finger pointing to and condemning the fleeing woman.
Bea has to twist around to see—at the end of that line that will soon,
following the trajectory of the bullet, cease to be imaginary—the
woman moving away, suspecting nothing.

Bea isn't sure if she heard the shot. It seems to her that a sharp,
painful whistle has occupied her head from the moment she saw the
pistol to when the man, kneeling on the platform, all his elegance
giving way to desperation and pain, is detained by the local police.
The woman does not seem so much dead as to have disappeared,
as if by magic, among the many folds of her dress, which spills over
the platform like an octopus whose insides have been emptied out.

After the bustle has died down and the curious onlookers have
moved on, after the corpse has been removed to the morgue, Bea
continues to watch, as if hypnotized, the silent dialogue between
the top hat, still lying on the bench, and the bloodstain, ten or fifteen
yards away.

A

None of the warnings about the ugliness of Los Girasoles had prepared Marcelo Valente for what he would find there. The town was
dull to the core of its streetlights; the members of the academic community, perhaps a little more isolated from the real world than he
had noted in other such institutions, were in the habit of generating
unfounded rumors at lightning speed, and the reigning endogamy
was so deeply entrenched that—as Professor Velásquez informed
him—he had hardly even arrived before the aesthetics department
was abuzz with speculation about the immediate future of his single
status. Velásquez gave him a quick, politically incorrect summary of
the physical virtues of each of the female professors, laying particularly irritating emphasis on the size of their respective breasts and
the fact that he, Velásquez, had been married to two of them. ("But

the record's held by Porter, a miserable little gringo professor who's been here for six years and has already been married and divorced four times, each to a different member of the female teaching staff," added Velásquez with an undisguised tinge of jealousy.)

Velásquez, despite the great romantic deeds he boasted of, was not a handsome man: short, potbellied, with graying hair on some areas of his scalp and the round glasses that had gone out of fashion three or four decades before. The prototype of the absentminded academic who manages to shine due to an unjustified confidence in himself and a glibness, not lacking in humor, that had to be–thought Marcelo–one of his most positive attributes.

The flight from Madrid to Mexico City had been easier and less tiring than Marcelo had expected; nothing like the multiple stopovers–Houston and then Lima–that had made his journey to Buenos Aires torture two years before, on a flight the university had gotten for free but that had cost him his mental equilibrium for two weeks, at the end of which he had promptly met Romina.

Descending into Mexico City, just before landing, he had been impressed by the interminable sea of small lights streaming up hillsides and along avenues like an inexhaustible flow of electricity. He had, nevertheless, expected more in the way of architecture; his idea of a metropolis was closer to Manhattan or a movie version of Tokyo: glass skyscrapers stretching to infinity, their façades mirroring the crisscrossing layers of cumulonimbi that darkened the afternoons with their threat of rain. In contrast, he discovered, from the descending plane, a sprawling city with low houses and the lines of the avenues emulating a nonfunctioning, disorganized sanguineous circulatory system.

In the airport, he had felt intimidated by the hardness of the local faces, the gaze–somewhere between humorous and scornful–of the customs officials, the friendliness of the unlicensed cabdrivers that masked a scam. He was to spend the night there in the city, close to the airport, and the next day Velásquez, who was in the capital on some personal business, would pick him up and drive him to Los Girasoles. It was, he was told, a six-hour journey, seven if there was traffic.

In Mexico City, Marcelo breathed air that, while foul and containing large quantities of lead, still held the glow of some ancient past. The dirty yellow line on the edge of the sidewalks, viewed from the cab, seemed to him a metaphor for just about everything, although he couldn't say exactly why. A tone of violated legality hung over things, leaving an ample margin for nameless atrocities, but also, paradoxically, for the construction of an untroubled, dissipated style of life. Everything had two sides. Marcelo thought he would have liked to explore that city for several more days, even months: a blind pilgrimage over the pedestrian bridges, along the boulevards with their sad eucalyptus trees, and through the rich, noisy bustle of the itinerant markets. But he would come back later, he thought, when he would have time to get properly acquainted with the Distrito Federal's sordid quaintness, the "defective" and the pure and simple "defect" of that blackened basin.

The hotel, a few minutes from the airport, was a mound of reinforced concrete and reflective windows with a neon sign at its apex. The sign alternated, according to the whim of the circuit breaker, between the words *hotel* and *otel*. The building overlooked the junction of two immense avenues, a noisy spot that promised to be constantly busy. Marcelo had asked the cabdriver at the airport to take him to any cheap hotel, reasonably nearby, since he had arranged to meet Velásquez for breakfast the next day in a restaurant in the same airport and then leave for the university town of Los Girasoles, where he was to fix his residence for the following year. The driver dropped Marcelo at the main entrance, and the moment he saw the place, the professor thought it showed no sign of adding anything positive to a first night in a city "charged with energy." That was how he had formulated it to himself. Marcelo reconsidered his phrasing and was ashamed to find himself a doctor of contemporary rationality who was capable of uttering such an ambiguous cliché, an expression that, beyond the high-voltage cables running from pole to pole along the roadside, didn't relate to anything in particular. But perhaps it wasn't necessary that it did: the tangle of cables, exposed to the vagaries of the rains and the whims of earthquakes, was enough to leave one feeling no longer just concerned, but even deeply disturbed in one's innermost being, attacked in that fraction of the soul one reserves for things that cannot be explained. This being the case, Marcelo went into the hotel as if affected by a premonition related to the energy resources of the nation offering him accommodation. None of that, he thought later, made any sense, but one does not select the weapons with which to assault one's peace of mind.

The bed had a metal frame, and the sheets had circular burn marks. Marcelo feared there would be scorpions or enormous cockroaches on the walls—a friend had told him a dismal story about bugs in Mexico City—but after a cautious inspection, he decided he was safe. He thought that perhaps the cabdriver had misunderstood his instructions and, on hearing he was looking for a cheap hotel, had decided what the Spanish passenger wanted was prostitutes. The hotel certainly did look as if it were normally used on a by-the-hour basis. The decor in his room was rather ugly: two Chinese jars of fake porcelain (they were plastic to the touch) on a painted wood-veneer table. And between the jars, as if standing guard, a small TV.

That night, he dreamed that Richard Foret came into his room dressed as a boxer and, without saying a single word, handed him the notebook in which he had recorded details of the perambulations of his final months. A so-far undiscovered notebook that he, Marcelo, would rescue from oblivion for the benefit of mankind.

The next day everything went as planned: Marcelo handed in his hotel key in the morning, asked at the reception desk for a cab, and returned to the airport. He quickly found Velásquez in the restaurant where they had arranged to meet—he had seen his face on the University of Los Girasoles' website—and sat down to breakfast with him. Velásquez seemed excited. He spoke rapidly, and some words were lost in the spiel, but what was important was not the detail but the torrent: he passed agilely from recounting the story of his catastrophic relationship with his second wife to glossing—with added insults—a talk he had heard in San Diego on the Surrealists and Mexico, then to recommending a cantina in Los Girasoles that served the only good bourbon to be had in the country—"the owner of the bar is a wetback who drives his truck full of bottles down from L.A. every two weeks," babbled Velásquez, pausing only to take a sip of coffee.

Marcelo listened patiently, wondering if he would ever manage to understand all those strange turns of phrase the New World was continually spitting out at him. He was particularly fascinated by the diminutive in the phrase *ya merito*, which he roughly translated as "any second now," and attempted to describe the spirit of the expression by referring to an essay by Roland Barthes; luckily for him, Velásquez pretended not to hear this display of his prowess and continued with his unstoppable cascade of verbosity.

During the drive to Los Girasoles, Velásquez quieted down a little and Marcelo felt, for the first time, that he might become his friend. The professor was a proficient driver, taking frequent puffs on a cigar that he held in his left hand and communicating with other vehicles through deft use of the horn. They crossed through such a diverse range of climates that when Marcelo surfaced from a torpor of several hours' duration and took a good look at the surrounding landscape, he thought for a moment they must have been on the road for more than a day and had already crossed over the frontier to the United States. But no, they were not so far north, not by a long way. Outside, the verdant forests and steep cliffs had disappeared, and now a wide plain stretched out around them, replete with shrubs, prickly pears, and yellow earth.

Los Girasoles was a town of some fifty thousand inhabitants in the middle of that plain. Before the university came, there had been nothing to justify a visit from a foreigner. Like all such towns, it had a rectangular main square with its church and government palace and, surrounding this, a not very extensive area of colonial buildings painted brick red. But beyond the center, the town lacked color: everything merged into the dry air of the plain. Houses with corrugated metal roofs, soccer fields dotted with stones, pedestrian bridges from which hung banners singing the praises of the administration of the moment. ("The Government of Los Girasoles is working for you: more pedestrian bridges for pedestrians.")

Velásquez asked Marcelo if he wanted to be taken to the house he had rented through the internet, near the University of Los Girasoles, or if he would prefer to get something to eat in the center and settle in afterwards. Marcelo had taken a liking to Professor Velásquez, even before meeting him, when he had written from

Madrid announcing that, according to his agreement with the Madrid institution he had the opportunity–and, in this case, the desire–to spend a sabbatical year in the sister, albeit third-world, University of Los Girasoles. But however much this liking for the plump, aging Mexican might make him feel like having a meal in his company, in some traditional restaurant with hot, spicy food, the urgent need to find himself finally alone after the car journey was stronger, so he declined the offer to get to know the center of the town and, after summarizing the reasons for his weariness, asked Velásquez to drop him at his new home.

What was no surprise to Marcelo was that the internet–and, in general, the malicious use of the technology–was an infallible tool for successfully committing fraud. The house he had found on a web page, and for which he had paid six months' rent up front, was a sad and painful confirmation of this axiom. The online advertisement found on a site for academics described it as "a little tropical paradise just ten minutes from the University of Los *Jirasoles*" and stressed its "excellent view, magnificent location, and excellent price." The only thing that was true had to do with the financial side: the place was cheap, although only in comparison to the exorbitant cost of rented accommodations in Madrid, and taking into account the huge advantage that Marcelo was still being paid in euros despite the fact that he was living in a "little tropical paradise." The small house was almost an orphaned apartment, as if it had been wrested from a parent building, and also an inferno: it was located in a residential estate that stretched like a biblical plague along an immense hill of bare, rocky earth, raising its water tanks to the sun like an army of Cyclopes.

The residential estate known as Puerta del Aire was some fifteen minutes' drive from Los Girasoles, on a road connecting the town to the university. The plan for the distribution of the small houses seemed to have been made by a blind man. The bathroom fixtures, which didn't appear in the promotional photos, were of a chromatic spectrum ranging from lilac with silvery glints to bile green. The house came furnished and, on the internet, the furniture had looked brand-new and reasonably tasteful. The reality was different: the armchairs belonged to different living rooms, none of them were handsome, and on the wall was a painting of a Christ figure and various decorated ceramic plates, attached by some irreversible process. Marcelo knew he would not be able to spend very long there.

He dumped his luggage in the bedroom—painted a mind-boggling red—and went out to look around. The environment was not exactly welcoming: the planners of that estate, in alliance with the corrupt local administration that had tendered the contract, had neglected to put in any sidewalks. Luckily there wasn't much traffic on those cracked concrete streets: the whole neighborhood gave the impression of having been uninhabited for some time. Outside a house identical to his own, about two hundred yards away in a parallel street, he saw a parked car: a gray pickup with Texas license plates from which, due to the heat, seemed to be rising a fine mist, or a mirage in the process of formation. Marcelo felt dizzy: he had not drunk any water during the entire journey from Mexico City, and the implacable sun of that hillside, which would beat down on his house from seven in the morning until the curtain of the fiery night fell, was, in conjunction with the inevitable jetlag and a night in a fifth-rate hotel, beginning to wreak havoc on his feeble, desk-bound anatomy.

When he first heard of Los Girasoles, he had expected the place to be a sort of colonial retreat, a town founded by the conquistadors to guard their maidens in pools of warm water and to return to from time to time to rest from their battles. He had imagined the university would be an old building, a former hacienda or disused monastery with stories of dark virgins and poet-nuns in voluntary reclusion. He had thought there would be an abundance of rivers and waterfalls nearby, and that the old people would trudge along timeworn paths to sell fruit in a neighboring town. Sunk in his autistic imagination, Marcelo Valente had not bothered to do in-depth research into the topic. Violently drawn on by his desire to get away from Madrid for a while, in his plans he merged fantasies about the last months of Richard Foret's life with the almost nonexistent information he had about Los Girasoles. Now he was paying the high price of disillusion for that blunder.

There was no bottled water in his new home, and Velásquez had warned him all too clearly about the negative effects of the tap

water–a unique mixture of fecal material and toxins–on the health
of a European, so he decided to walk a little way to the estate's security booth and ask where he could buy a demijohn of drinking water.

The guard spotted Marcelo in the distance, making his way
along the sun-drenched street, and sardonically thought this must
be the new foreigner they'd all been making so much noise about.
The owner of numbers 34, 35, and 36 had told him a Spanish professor was going to occupy 34 for a whole year, to work at the university. After this announcement, he had heard other members
of the teaching staff–number 59 and number 28–commenting
that some guy was coming from Europe on an interuniversity
exchange to nab the few straight female professors they had.
Jacinto, the guard, had seen a lot of gringos like that one file
through Puerta del Aire. He had seen them move into number 44,
number 60, numbers 70 and 75, and had seen every single one
of them throw in the towel before the fight was over: return to
their respective countries, go to DF, spend the night in their tiny
offices . . . None had survived Puerta del Aire for more than six
consecutive months, and this tall little Spaniard with ruffled hair
wasn't going to be any different, you could see that from a mile
away. As a zealous, conscientious army officer, Jacinto was proud
of the level of desertions Puerta del Aire had achieved among the
foreign population. The estate was, in his nameless fantasy, a
smaller but worthier version of the country as a whole, a territory impermeable to the evil intentions of gringos, badass and
independent from the steel beams of its houses to the dirty white
dust of its streets. And in this country, made to the measure of his
ambitions, Jacinto ruled the roost.

Marcelo arrived panting at the security booth and, once in
the shade, had to take a number of deep breaths before asking the
guard where the nearest store was. Jacinto was slowly and silently
chewing a segment of a mandarin orange while his hands were
employed in peeling the rest of the fruit; a thread of juice trickled
down his dark chin.

"You're the Spanish guy, right?"

"I suppose so. Well, I don't know if I'm *the* Spanish guy, but I'm
Spanish and I'm a guy. Were you told I was coming?"

The guard insolently ignored that last question and continued to concentrate on his orange. Marcelo Valente was sweaty and found the guard's attitude slightly maddening.

After a long pause, Jacinto spoke again, returning to the initial, and for Marcelo, more pressing question, "Well, there's no store around here . . . You'll have to drive to the outskirts of Los Girasoles . . . or the other way . . ." Between each linguistic outflow, Jacinto appeared to be savoring the anxiety he was provoking.

"The other way? Where?" asked Marcelo, intrigued, seeming to remember Velásquez had said the road came to an abrupt end at the university, five or ten minutes away. Was Jacinto trying to say he could buy bottles of water at the university?

The guard took off his blue cap bearing the logo of the security company and put it on the table, which, together with a portable radio and some sheets of paper with prestamped signatures, was the only object visible in the booth. He appeared to think this over for a while, wiped the trickle of mandarin juice from his chin with his sleeve, and then went on, looking Marcelo in the eyes for the first time. "No, the store's farther off if you go the other way, señor. You'd be better off waiting for Señora Ridruejo to come . . ."

Señora Ridruejo was the owner of numbers 34, 35, and 36. And she was the person responsible for the untruthful internet advertisement that now had Marcelo boiling with indignation. The professor, however, had completely forgotten the owner's surname, and in the security guard's mouth it sounded even stranger than before. He oscillated between surprise and exasperation. He was thirsty, he didn't want to talk to any Señora Ridruejo, and he was beginning to regret not having stayed at the (h)otel a few days longer.

"Are you saying that if you don't have a car, you can't buy a bottle of water?" Marcelo asked bluntly, letting his growing anger show.

"No. Well, to get to the store you do need a car, but not to buy water. You asked about the store, not a place where you can buy water." Jacinto's response was as mysterious as it was irritating, and his unwillingness to say things plainly made Marcelo think his stay in Mexico was going to feel like a very long one. Openly impassioned, he rebuked the guard, consciously bringing into play that brusque Castilian manner that was to cause him so many mix-ups.

Jacinto went on the defensive: "Keep your temper, eh? I'm not some errand boy here to go looking for stores for you . . . What I do is watch, so that they don't bump you off in the night," he said, maintaining his tone of indifference, in spite of the harshness of his message. "If you want water, you can knock on the window of number 9. They sell things there . . ."

Marcelo thought he didn't know a more exact definition of "store" than "a place where they sell things," but he kept that semantic reflection to himself to avoid further argument and held out a hand to the guard in farewell. "I'm Professor Marcelo Valente. I'll be living here for some time. A pleasure to meet you, and thank you for your help."

This courteous gesture softened the other's manner; he shook Marcelo's hand firmly, introducing himself as "Jacinto Nogales Pedrosa At Your Service." Marcelo left the booth and immediately felt the sun beating down once more on his neck. He walked along the main street until he saw the number 9, leaning to one side over a door, and gently tapped on the window with his knuckles. Since no one responded and no movement was to be seen inside, Marcelo had the sudden suspicion Jacinto Nogales Pedrosa At Your Service had been pulling his leg, sending him off to one of the many empty houses. Luckily, before Marcelo could knock again, the door was opened by an elderly woman, anchored to the floor by a pair of pink slippers, who sold him a demijohn of water with a speed and efficiency that, for the first time, met the urgency of his situation.

Back in the house, Marcelo sat down on his orange two-seater sofa and drank straight from the bottle. Once his thirst was quenched, he began to feel hunger pangs, and he thought he would never manage to do anything until he had a car of his own in which to escape from Puerta del Aire. It was by then almost six in the evening, and Marcelo Valente hadn't had a bite since the meager bread roll he had eaten with his coffee in the airport before setting off for Los Girasoles. To cap it all off, his moral vegetarianism made things difficult since it was improbable, in this region famous for its cattle, he would be able to find a decent meal of vegetal origin. He then told himself he would eat the first thing he saw. In any case, he thought, none of his colleagues at the University of Los Girasoles would discover him slicing into a filet steak at this hour, so it would be possible to maintain the ethical rigor of his character intact, if not that of his person.

B

The second event to mark the life of Bea Langley, now Bea Burton, occurs thirteen years later, in 1914. Her father has died; her mother is living in London, embittered and reclusive, like a dried-up piece of fruit someone has left in a drawer. Bea is now Beatrice, as her husband calls her, and Mama, as her children—a boy and a girl—call her, in an accent that mixes the uncertain tone of five- and seven-year-olds with the insecurity of living in an almost excessive state of linguistic diversity. Their house in Florence is not exactly a villa, but it has a pleasant courtyard where the Burtons receive any foreigner who passes through the city, in addition to their English expatriate friends, who spend their time complaining about Mediterranean manners but can't go to London without becoming immediately depressed.

A week before this second event, Bea exhibits some of her most recent drawings in the Florentine gallery where her friend Heather acts as a consultant. Matthew Burton, her husband, is an aspiring art dealer and travels frequently to India, Paris, and the United States, buying and selling pieces on which he makes a marginal profit. They depend, in fact, on Bea's inheritance. During her husband's travels, Beatrice lives—according to the gossip among the British community in Florence—an unconventional life. If Marinetti is in the city, he stays at her house, in the studio furnished for visitors on the other side of the courtyard. At night, his hostess slips out to the Futurist's bed. She has also, judging by the candor of the letters still in existence, enthralled Giovanni Papini, although it's unclear if she allows him as many liberties as she certainly does Marinetti.

The Italian spring dissolves, amid rumors of the imminent conflict, into the most stultifying of summers, and Bea's lovers ditch her to write pamphlets against their country's neutrality. The Archduke Franz Ferdinand and his wife fall time after time in Serbia, brought down by bullets, with every conversation in the Burtons' courtyard describing their death.

Matthew is an insensitive husband who attempts to make up for his total lack of empathy by lavishing Bea with advice of an academic timbre on her painting, something she finds deeply and justifiably irritating: "Try to achieve less sinuosity in your forms, my dear; I think it would do you good to spend more time in the Galería degli Uffizi; something tells me Giotto's brushwork would refine your eye." Bea listens with manifest embarrassment and casts long-suffering glances at her friend Heather, who laughs silently.

Matthew writes to Bea from London, where he is closing a deal, saying he intends to postpone his return to Florence until the war fever dies down. The poor man does not suspect he will have to sit there waiting a historical eternity for this to occur: the war fever would never die down. The letter is written in a cold tone, and at the end, in a cramped hand, a phrase shatters Beatrice's equanimity: "Give my best wishes to your friend Marinetti, you slut." Bea remembers, more vividly than ever, the top hat and the pool of blood on the platform of that station in Piedmont. That image, which has stayed with her like an ill omen for thirteen years, is added to one of her principal thematic obsessions: The Battle of the Sexes. She has even written a manifesto and shown it to Heather, who extolled the virtues of Bea's prose. But Bea is not interested in prose; she is interested in the battle of ideas that exemplifies, or perhaps keeps alive, the battle of the sexes. Marriage, for her, is a sweetened version of murder. A top hat and a pool of blood united forever in the gaze of a young girl. A dress like an octopus whose insides have been emptied out into a stone sink.

This second episode is less dramatic than the first. There are no gunshots or platforms, no father to leave her alone to face the brutality of the world. It is more like a silent revelation, the inkling of a truth that will shed light on her present. Men, she says, are predatory. While her alliance with the Futurists might tell her sex is a dance of pistons, she knows there is another, less obvious reality:

a fatal attraction of opposite poles, a mechanism that makes vaginas and penises seek out and yearn for each other in a deeper way. The ghost in the machine. The steam that, expelled from locomotives, becomes consciousness, expansive will, the aspiration to be ether.

A

The small office he had been assigned was, indeed, full of pigeons. The birds lived in four cages piled one on top of the other, blocking the only external window. Velásquez explained that the office had belonged to an agronomist who, one fine day, had declared himself to be ill and never returned. His students had received the news with complete indifference, and no one had made any effort to discover his whereabouts. After a few months he had been dismissed, and the caretaker confessed that the agronomist had left him in charge of a number of pigeons. Marcelo suspected, and voiced his suspicion, that the pigeons could have infected the agronomist with some strange disease. That his illness, his disappearance, maybe his death, were related to those pestilential birds. Velásquez, who had never considered that possibility, promised to talk to the administration about having the cages removed before Marcelo installed his books and laptop in the office. But the rhythm of the institution didn't appear to be very different from what Marcelo had observed in other aspects of that Mexican province, and it took a week for the administration to remove the cages and put down, donate, or liberate the pigeons. In the meantime, Marcelo also took things calmly: he would arrive at the university at any hour he pleased and sit for a long while in a small garden in the courtyard, pretending to read the collection of essays on the work of Foret he had brought with him. After that, he would go to Velásquez's office and, seated on a filing cabinet, chat with his colleague for a couple of hours, both of them waiting for the canteen to serve the menu of the day (from which Marcelo, of course, only chose the salads and the noodle soup). Their topics of conversation were always the same: women, a comparison of their respective teenage years in different countries, jibes aimed at the university teaching staff in Spain (Velásquez had studied for one semester of his master's degree in Barcelona and knew very well what Valente was talking about when he criticized the monotonous, pedantic way of speaking of his fellow academics). They also talked about their respective families, but in this, as in questions of music (Velásquez's only preference was for romantic Bachata songs), the gulf between their experiences was so pronounced that they soon bored of the topics and returned to areas of equivalence.

Velásquez had been born in Mexico City in the early sixties; Marcelo was born in the second half of the decade, but this statistically negligible difference opened like a wide breach between Velásquez's gray hair and ample waistline and Marcelo's arrogant slimness and fierce elegance. It amused them to find chronological correspondences, weave their own parallel lives—each equally insipid in the eyes of the other, but, as is natural, deeply moving to themselves.

"Wow, so when you were screwing around drinking coffee and discussing the dehumanization of art," Velásquez would begin, referring to the stories Marcelo told, which located him, wearing a turtleneck sweater, in a pretentious tertulia at the Café Comercial, discussing Ortega y Gasset. "I was right there in my baseball period, setting up the famous Tlacuaches de Xochimilco," he would go on to say, summarizing the exploits of that unsuccessful team, whose name he had chosen for euphonic reasons since they didn't train in Xochimilco but Ciudad Satélite, on the opposite extreme of DF.

In 1985, Velásquez was studying journalism, but the vision of horror in the days following the September earthquake had confronted him with a latent theoretical doubt that, misinterpreted, led him to enroll in philosophy. By December the horrors had evaporated, and Velásquez had absolutely no idea what he was doing in philosophy. In spite of everything, he had stuck with the major, promising to redress the balance during his master's, studying a specialty that would reconcile him with his original vocation. This didn't occur: he ended up specializing in aesthetics and then made the leap to literary theory and wrote his doctoral thesis on the French writers who had passed through Mexico.

In that same year of 1985, Marcelo Valente enrolled simultaneously in philosophy and art history. He buried his nose in books and threw himself into the Byzantine discussions on the neo-Kantians with a devotion only equivalent to that he felt for Glutamato Ye-Yé, a rock group of the counterculture Movida Madrileña whose extreme levels of absurdity ("There's a Man in My Fridge" is the title of one of their most notorious songs) helped him survive the dose of rationalism he was subjected to morning noon and night. He hung around with a number of completely unrelated groups: his school friends, in whose company he experimented with cocaine and bisexuality, the fundamental adornments of the era; his fellow students in philosophy, with whom he shared a naïve desire to change the world by means of the exhaustive analysis of the works of the Frankfurt School; and, finally, other university students in art history, of whom he really only knew two: a sometime girlfriend called Sixi–Remedios in real life, though no one called her by that name–and Guillermo, a misfit cousin two years older than himself, who seemed predestined to sell soft drugs for the rest of his life, a destiny he would fulfill with singular diligence until it landed him in prison seven years later.

In 1989, Professor Velásquez had a son with a girlfriend he had met through a distant cousin. At the time the child was born, they had just moved to an apartment in Copilco overlooking the University City. She taught math in a secondary school, and Velásquez had become closely involved in editing a magazine that earned him fame but no money. Two years later, she took their son back to her hometown of Toluca, and Velásquez decided not to protest since he had confirmed that, as a father, his performance was pretty poor. He had continued to see his son every couple of weeks until he was offered the research position in Los Girasoles; after that, they only met during holidays, and with increasingly less frequency.

While this was going on, Marcelo Valente finished his two undergraduate degrees in record time–though with unspectacular grades–and, having dazzled the wealthy faction of his family, went to London–partly sponsored by an aunt–for a whole summer with another, also sometime, girlfriend called Lucía.

Marcelo and Velásquez could spend hours like that, analyzing from year to year the tenuous coincidences in their lives and happily laughing at the differences.

After wiping the plates of his three servings of salad with a piece of stale bread, Marcelo would return to Puerta del Aire. Velásquez had introduced him to someone from the university's administrative department who was anxious to sell his car, and Marcelo bought it, convinced he could resell it with equal ease at the end of his sabbatical year. So now he had a car.

Back at his house, he dedicated himself to light reading–war novels for the most part–that he found in the only non-university bookstore in Los Girasoles. He had brought very few belongings with him, and the only books he had were related to his research, so he would have to wait for his next trip to DF to stock up on his bibliographic resources and even a couple of box sets to kill time. After reading for a while, he'd begin to feel irritated by his surroundings, the ugliness of the furniture, and would set out again– "I'll be back later, Don Jacinto," he'd call to the guard–on a drive along the four central streets of Los Girasoles. In the only café that merited the name, he had become a familiar face since his second day, and it was there he sat to leaf through the local newspaper and ignore the indigenous people from other lands offering him multicolored craft items.

The waiter was a lean, diligent man who liked to discover the tastes and manias of his regular customers. He already knew he should serve Marcelo an espresso with just a drop of milk and not bring sugar or sweetener or anything similar. He also had to bring the newspaper from the bar, if it was available, and if not promise he would be the next customer to get it. Sometimes, but only if Marcelo requested it, the waiter served a glass of mineral water with the espresso, but that only happened on very hot days.

Marcelo always greeted the waiter by name and gave a substantial tip when he left the terrace to take a couple of turns around the square with its pavilion. From the café, the professor could be seen taking that ritual, circular walk and then disappearing down one of the streets leading to another, smaller square, only to reappear after a short time in his noisy car, which had been left in a public parking lot two blocks away. He sometimes stopped off at the supermarket on the road to Puerta del Aire. This was, to cut a long story short, his average day.

Later on, Marcelo planned to visit the nearby towns on the weekends. The nearest was Nueva Francia, which appeared in the newspapers every three or four days, together with the words *narco* or *shoot-out*. In the last six months, Nueva Francia had changed its mayor three or four times. Killed, arrested, or politically ousted, the mayors who left the post were never again mentioned in the press or during conversations on public transportation. An omnivorous silence devoured the names of those defunct functionaries, a silence that passed with giant steps through the ranks of the dwindling population. One day, three beheaded corpses. Another, five individuals tied at the wrists, showing signs of torture. Yet another, a soldier, with his hands cut off, lying at the roadside.

Given these reports, Marcelo postponed the moment of getting to know Nueva Francia and, for the time being, contented himself with visiting the smallest, most distant towns that were featured in the *Globetrotter's Guide* he had brought with him from Madrid. While driving, he listened to Glutamato Ye-Yé on the car stereo, recalling the good times of the eighties and thinking nostalgically of all the women he had been with. Those uncultivated plains, those winding roads pitted with potholes were perfect for remembering the most important moments of his life, to the rhythm of an outdated style of pure rock that gratified the deepest depths of his memory.

"The only thing missing here," Marcelo would say to himself, "is a woman to help me get through this sabbatical year." The female staff members Velásquez introduced him to—all flat-chested—had looked at him with an eagerness that put Marcelo on his guard: just as in a cartoon, he believed he saw gold rings and wedding dresses in their black eyes, plus European passports and a life far distant from their offices in Los Girasoles and the executions in Nueva Francia. They were calculating women, academics who delivered their classes any old way and published articles in second-rate journals to gain points and so receive federal bonuses for top-class research. Marcelo knew them because they were the same the world over: in the Inalienably Autonomous University of Madrid,

in the University of Buenos Aires, in the Pontifical University of
Anywhere At All. It wasn't just the women, of course; in terms of
calculation and mediocrity, there was no possible discrimination:
all the researchers were of equal worth. But now Marcelo was
polishing up his misogyny because it was the women who looked
at him with lascivious desire, drawing an inelegant equivalence
between the foreignness of the newcomer and the social redemption of his hypothetical partner.

No. Marcelo needed a different woman, a Mexican with an
air of extreme wisdom who would show him the paths of the
national mystique and force him to part with his first-world prejudices. An intense, implacable woman who wouldn't allow him to
be distracted from his principal mission: to write a book on Foret
in Mexico, or rather on the sudden, inexplicable disappearance of
Foret in Mexico, on disappearance as the absolute aesthetic experience of the avant-garde—in the sense, that is, of Paul Virilio, but
more frivolously. A woman who would open doors for him and
explain the codes of conduct in this barren place, who would carry
him away from Puerta del Aire to a cool, shady, wooden house in
some grove, in some oasis that would isolate him from all the surrounding hostility.

———————————————————— **B** ————————————————————

The third episode to mark Bea Langley's life and put the finishing
touches to the mold of her character takes place in New York. It
is 1916, and Bea is a woman in her prime—with thirty-one springs
behind her—who won't change substantially, except for the degeneration of an already well-formed character. She has abandoned
her husband—who, eaten by jealousy, refuses to give her a divorce—
and her two offspring await, optimistically, the return of their
mother in an English boarding school a few miles from Florence.
The war is a frequent topic of conversation, and Richard Foret, of
whom Beatrice still knows nothing, or not much, is crossing the

Atlantic to New York on the liner in which, by chance, Trotsky is traveling into exile.

Bea is received with moderate enthusiasm by New Yorkers. Her exploits alongside the Futurists (the rumors of her affair with Marinetti) don't soften any hearts since the general opinion is that Futurism is overvalued, just a boorish bustling of loudmouthed, hirsute people. And neither has Bea's art had a positive impact: she is branded as a naïve painter, and the adjective is correct. Her poetry, by contrast, has better luck. Alfred Kreymborg, a dapper defender of free verse, invites her to contribute to his magazine, *Others,* and the poems published there are praised in circles she believes to be important, although their leading light, a young man with a pleonastic name, is, in fact, a small-town doctor from New Jersey: William Carlos Williams.

After being initially dazzled, Bea is, in a sense, disillusioned by New York. The people are pretentious or simply imbecilic, and no one has serious conversations about anything. They are all cynics, and erecting a wall of indifference between themselves and all things human is a fashion that coexists with the most ridiculous of hats. Her friend Heather, who has been in New York for a year, avoids her, offering risible excuses, and is only to be seen with a group of famous lesbians. Bea concentrates on her political writing, now more detailed and better argued than in her Italian period. In relation to her poetry, she is unaware that what she does can be justified so elegantly: the battle for free verse contributes to her theoretical redemption.

On an evening when Bea is returning to the apartment that also serves as her studio, having just left one of those salons where the dilettantes take great pains to shock by dressing like standard lamps, she is stopped by a down-and-out who brusquely asks her for money. Bea is accustomed to walking alone and has learned to avoid all manner of altercations. It is not unusual for men to follow her when they notice she lives by herself, and to make indecent proposals in the most sordid streets. But she is a tough woman and knows it is essential to keep smiling and reduce her aggressor to the size of a child, looking derisively at him; they usually leave her in peace.

This down-and-out, however, is persistent. A man of about fifty with a pockmarked face, dressed in stinking rags. He walks with a stoop, as if carrying a heavy load on his right shoulder, and has a long beard that does not completely hide the gauntness of his features. At some point he steps out in front of Bea, blocking her way. It is a narrow street, almost deserted at this twilight hour. Bea impatiently looks the undesirable in the eye and asks permission to pass. And then it happens: she recognizes the eyes and forehead of someone glimpsed in the past. She hesitates an instant longer, with time standing still around her, rummaging in her memory in search of such a face. When she finds it, she pales and her jaw drops in a gesture of surprise that will remain there for several days. The vagabond is none other than the murderer in that Piedmont station, the man who, fifteen years before, in a fit of spite, fired at a woman who was abandoning him in slow motion. Now Bea meets him again, on another continent and with a very different appearance, but it is undoubtedly the same person. She remembers in fine detail the pain on his face when the guards arrested him; under the gray beard, the man's expression is now identical: he seems frozen in that instant, as if it were impossible to feel any new emotion after that last, definitive one.

While Bea is thinking about the strange trajectories life traces out, the man continues to try to wheedle some money out of her, claiming hunger, but he becomes increasingly desperate and his words of entreaty less sweet. The destitute man pulls a rusty knife from his tattered overcoat and waves it before Bea's face. His movements become jerky and his voice, now shrill, demands that Beatrice give him everything she has, including her jewelry. But Bea stands motionless a few seconds longer. When aggression seems almost inevitable, when she becomes aware that the man is advancing on her, determined to get what he wants, Bea, in her most elegant British accent, pronounces the magic words: "You shot a woman in Italy fifteen years ago, in a train station."

The effect is instantaneous: the vagabond's expression suddenly changes. Starting in his neck—the tendons strained—a look of terror ascends his face and even seems to change the color of his uncombed hair. His right hand swells, and then opens with visible impotence, dropping the knife, which falls to the ground making much less noise than Bea would have supposed. The vagabond takes four steps back, his eyes wide open, then turns and runs.

At that moment, completely alone in the by then absolute darkness, Bea has a first inkling of the meaning of destiny.

A

The weeks passed. Having exhausted the list of nearby towns he was interested in driving to, Marcelo finally decided to visit the dreaded Nueva Francia. Out of prudence, he invited Velásquez to accompany him, but that weekend his friend had at last managed to arrange a meeting with his son, whom he was to pick up from the interstate bus terminal.

"You go, dude," he said to Marcelo in a tone of sincere intimacy, "but be really careful over there. Nueva Francia isn't exactly at its best right now. You'll have to go through a whole heap of military checkpoints, so take your passport and university ID with you. If they see you're a foreigner and a professor, they won't search you as often . . . unlike me. Even though the fucking sons of bitches know who I am, they make me empty my pockets every time. Oh, and don't miss Los Insurgentes cantina–it's the nearest thing Nueva Francia has to a tourist attraction."

Marcelo took his friend's recommendations on board and set out in his Renault at eleven in the morning with a bottle of water and several forms of identification, which he did indeed have to show the soldiers at the first checkpoint he came to, just over a mile from Los Girasoles. Other checkpoints followed the same pattern, and as he got closer to Nueva Francia, the sense of danger increased and the stony military gazes became more accusing, more difficult to avoid. At the fifth checkpoint, and despite the fact that his credentials gave him a certain advantage, they asked him to get out of the car and open the trunk. Marcelo, who was used to trusting the forces of law and order, was annoyed by the notion that the military was essentially bad. But everything pointed in that direction: these men spat, tended to be high-handed, and an emptiness in their eyes suggested sudden, gratuitous violence. At this last, fifth checkpoint, they asked him more precise questions, silently laughing at his answers and keeping their fingers on the triggers of their assault rifles.

When he saw Nueva Francia, Marcelo lost a little of the contempt he felt for Los Girasoles: this town was much worse. If the streets were dirty in Los Girasoles, and the road surface merged into the surrounding dirt every few yards, in Nueva Francia the inhabitants seemed to have been living in the same shit for the last thirty years, with the additional aggravation that a trickle of progress–the only one that had reached its dusty rurality–had provided them with the most up-to-date weapons, carried casually and proudly, not only by the people from the cartels, but even by the ordinary citizens, corrupted to the point of being unable to distinguish between one dead body and two hundred.

Marcelo parked the Renault on one side of the square. On a couple of benches, without even a single tree to relieve the harsh effects of the sun on their faces, two drunks were taking what looked to Marcelo like their last siesta. A policeman, standing in the corner, looking uncomfortable in a bulletproof vest and carrying a rusty rifle, was fanning himself with his blue uniform cap, sweating like a pig abandoned in the Sahara. As there was no one else in sight, Marcelo walked over to ask the policeman for directions.

"Excuse me, officer, do you know where Los Insurgentes cantina is?"

The policeman looked at him in surprise, as if he didn't even remotely expect anyone around there to talk to him. He gave a long, noisy, mucus-filled sniff and then spat a green substance onto the asphalt. The sun would evaporate that phlegm in a few seconds, and both Marcelo and the policeman would begin to breathe it in if they stayed as they were, regarding each other from close proximity.

"An' why the fuck d'you wanna go there?" asked the uniformed officer.

"A friend told me I had to see it, that it was *cool,*" Marcelo ingenuously replied in his Madrid accent, clearly displaying his foreignness and confrontational ineptitude.

"It's on this street, 'bout three blocks ahead," conceded the policeman, pointing slowly and vaguely in the general direction. Marcelo walked down the street, staggering with incomprehension under the fierce sun.

There was no sign over the entrance. If Marcelo realized that shady place was Los Insurgentes, it was because he thought, quite rightly, that nowhere else in the desolate town would be open at that hour. Near the door, barely protected from the sun by the shadow of the cantina, a one-legged man holding out a small box offered products for alleviating bad breath.

Inside, the decor was spare: a wall of bottles behind the bar–as if it were a legendary saloon in some Western–a few posters for music concerts on the opposite wall, and a photograph of Emilio Zapata on the bathroom door–there was no door for women. He ordered a beer. A couple of guys were having a lackluster discussion about soccer, leaning their weight on a tiny round table. From the bar, the manager of the joint added his voice to the argument, alternatively supporting one or the other of his customers. No one took much notice of Marcelo, despite the fact that the fashionable elegance of his clothes was clearly out of tune with the place. Perhaps making too much of their indifference, Marcelo thought this must be one of those touristy anti-tourist spots where foreigners inevitably end up, thirsting for something traditional; a Mexican equivalent of those bullfighting taverns in Hapsburg Madrid that sell decadence as their principal–possibly only–attraction.

But the impression of witnessing an elaborately staged scene immediately evaporated when a new customer appeared in the doorway of Los Insurgentes, a woman wearing a jacket and pants, over fifty but not looking it, with long, curly black hair, who walked confidently to the bar and asked for a dark draft beer, calling the manager by his first name. The woman had a sober, elegant style, and her manners showed an education level superior to that of the other drinkers. Marcelo thought her attractive, interesting to the point of weakening his already well-proven predilection for younger women. She didn't initially notice his presence, but–elbows on the bar, wrapped up in her thoughts–offered him, before a smile, the not-to-be-disdained landscape of the back of her well-cut pants.

Marcelo, for his part, pretended to be unaware of the newcomer and, before heading off to continue his tour of the hostile terrain of Nueva Francia, ordered another beer–this time dark and from the barrel–and it was then that he managed to draw from the woman a first look of interest. But that initial glance was not enough to substantially modify the circumstances, at least not immediately or perceptibly. The look would instead have to remain buried, latent, awaiting the moment in which it would provoke a notable change in the course of events, events that until that moment, and taking Marcelo's decision to come to live in Mexico as the point of departure, had turned out to be much less interesting and much less intense than he had originally supposed. And this noteworthy disillusion, this unfavorable comparison between expectations and actual events, didn't have so much to do with the expectations themselves or the events–generally neutral and all equally dispensable–as with the bored, opaque gaze of the person who was experiencing them, the dulled sensations of the person who played out the grotesque comedy of the events without really getting the message, without being changed by it, moved in his depths. Because Marcelo's depths were the cause of all his tedium, of all the slowness that filled his extremities and dulled his synaptic transmissions, and it was the slowness of Spain, and the slowness of Europe, and the slowness of philosophy that circulated phlegmatically inside him, so that a conventionally intense experience, like living in Los Girasoles and, one morning, visiting Nueva Francia, became an insipid outing in hostile, devastating heat, a ridiculously predictable outing from whose meanness he would not even be saved by the interested look of an attractive woman in a lugubrious cantina.

And in spite of the fact that slowness and opacity and tedium had been the elements of Marcelo's perpetual, irremediable emotional state for as long as he remembered, he had the sensation things had not always been like that. He suspected that at some moment, the entire pantomime of his enthusiasm for life had been sustained by an authentic feeling. It was somewhere in the remote past, before adulthood, that he located the spring of jubilation and creative vigor from which–in a later version, and according to him–he still drank. In the same way, he had the sense of an intensely creative future, always at the point of emerging, in which he would once again live with enthusiasm and plenitude, fully savoring each detail of everyday life. The perpetual postponement of that moment caused him periods of deep discomfort, but his extreme self-satisfaction impeded him from recognizing that the problem was, in fact, structural, and not a simple question of stages and processes.

Marcelo stood up, ready to make his way home. His excursion to Nueva Francia was beginning to seem like a mistake, an idiotic idea whose spores were spread by the primary inoculum of Professor Velásquez, with his huge propensity for tacky acts of exalted localism. True, he had not yet seen anything of Nueva Francia, apart from this incomprehensibly famous cantina that would leave him one single memory. But that single memory, the woman with curly hair, spoke to Marcelo just as he was preparing to leave.

"You're not going to Los Girasoles, are you?" she asked with what seemed to Marcelo almost authentically Castilian brusqueness.

B

There is among Richard Foret's eventful wanderings a chapter that eludes simple interpretation. The few students of his uneven work know this, and so prefer to leave it to one side or play down its importance in the offhand manner academics habitually reserve for anything they consider incomprehensible. This episode is, moreover, fundamental in terms of Foret's biography since it coincides with the writing of his most intriguing work, the *Considerations,* and the first suspicions, on Bea's part, that her lover is as mad as a hatter.

Richard and Bea, as all accounts indicate, met in New York at the beginning of 1917, although their mutual fame may have conceded them a brief glimpse of the other's personality (in the form of gossip) while Bea was living in Florence and Foret reeling drunkenly between Berlin and Paris in those epic years before the Great War. But it is generally agreed that the rumors flying across Europe were not strong enough to awaken in either of them a particular fascination for the existence of the other; yet the scraps of information they did obtain would form a firm basis, in the New World, for embarking on a first conversation that would, as the hours passed, become an enthused monologue on the part of Richard to which Bea listened with a smile of equal parts complicity and sheer delight.

When Foret reaps the same hatred in New York that he harvested in France, his few friends turn their backs on him, and Duchamp, as has been said, plays a joke of questionable innocence that attracts the attention of the draft board to him, or so the boxer-poet records in his bissextile magazine, perhaps pursued by more profound ghosts. And so his flight recommences (his whole life had been one); his unfounded hope for a home switches from the illuminated New York night to the muddy streets of Buenos Aires, the city toward which Foret sets the needle of the impetuous compass that could have pointed toward any other place. But despite being an indefatigable traveler–or perhaps precisely because of this–his understanding of world geography is somewhat dreamlike: Foret persuades himself of the convenience of making a discreet stopover in Mexico City before going on to Buenos Aires. Later he would discover to his great disillusionment that, given the distance and the paucity of the marine schedule, to get to Argentina from Mexico, he would either have to pass through Spain or embark in Florida, with the great risk of being either recruited or going out of his mind due to ridiculous suspicion.

But let us not get ahead of ourselves: that has yet to come. For now, Foret departs from New York disguised as a cadet on leave and, incomprehensibly, tries to reach the northern frontier. The reason: he wants to go to Canada in order to leave behind as soon as possible a country that, in his frazzled consciousness, is pursuing him with the intention of sending him to his death. His plan is confused, but from his letters it can be deduced that he intends to board a ship bound for Mexico at some point on the Canadian coast.

This is where matters become complicated. From the moment Foret first meets Bea until he flees to the north, only three months pass. Months that are definitive in the history of nations (the United

States enters the war), and months in which Foret and Bea cohabit, it can be assumed pleasurably since, from that point on, the letters between them reveal a plan in which their lives are entwined.

For Foret, those three months are enough for him to decide he wants to be with that woman forever. And Beatrice cannot ignore the evidence that something great is happening, and that if she wants to be true to the paths fate is laying out before her, she has to sacrifice the stability of her New York life to follow that madman wherever he leads. Yet in spite of that reciprocal conviction, Foret undertakes a delirious journey that separates him from Bea for a period of eight months.

During his first days in Canada, Foret travels around Quebec because he believes it will be simpler for him to mingle with the French-speaking natives, that being his first language, and so easier to find work as a merchant seaman on some ship bound for Mexico. But putting those plans into action takes two months. On his first afternoon in Montreal, he takes part in an antiwar demonstration, gives a spontaneous speech (he is expelled by two guards), and fornicates in a park with a prostitute. He then spends a week in an alcoholic stupor, sleeping in the room of a psychic. After that, he makes an effort to regain his lucidity and writes to Bea every day. Little is known of his actions for the following month and a half because his letters do not include anecdotes. In them, he attempts to sketch out for Bea his most personal creed: there are paragraphs of great theoretical density, many of which reiterate themes philosophers have already addressed, but which Foret has not read. (Some scholar or other has established a forced parallel between these scribblings and Spinoza's concept of *conatus*.)

These letters, written to Bea from Montreal, are the origin of *Fundamental Considerations on Something,* which Foret began to write at that time and continued to compose without interruption until his disappearance in Mexico a year and three months later. A fragment of the *Considerations,* which also forms part, literally transcribed, of a letter sent to Bea on July 19, 1917, is unusually autobiographical and offers a detailed narrative of the "elusive chapter" of Foret's life that his researchers generally prefer to ignore. In that fragment, the author tells of a walk through the port area of

Montreal, in the shade of the factories, and his meeting with a person he christens Mr. X, who spontaneously sits down next to him on a bench to talk. This person, whom Foret compares to "a sly fox," immediately says he knows the conflicts that are disturbing Foret's soul. The latter expresses his incredulity, and Mr. X softly murmurs the name "Beatrice." Livid, Richard asks if he knows her and if he has been sent to give him some piece of bad news about his lover, but Mr. X calms him, explaining there is nothing to fear, that he is just doing a favor for a mutual friend. On asking the name of this friend, Foret receives only an evasive gesture, so he decides to allow the strange character to say what he has come to say.

And that is where the problems start. According to Richard's letter and the earliest manuscript of the *Considerations,* Mr. X tells him a fictional story, clarifying that he only intends, by means of allegory, to share a "moral discovery." But the "innocent" story–as Foret transcribes it–summarizes in broad brushstrokes the political history of Europe in what remained of the twentieth century (remember that we are in 1917), including the Great War, the Weimar Republic, the rise of Nazism, the Holocaust, the Cold War, the student protests of the sixties, the Berlin Wall and its fall. Of course this is all narrated as fictitious speculation, without names or excessive detail, almost in the manner of a fable, and although Foret is impressed by the man's strange alienation, he doesn't believe a word of what he hears, nor extract any moral lesson from it. He merely assigns it to his letter and to the note that will later form part of the *Considerations.*

With the passage of time, after Foret's death, Bea will remember this letter, take it from her dark trunk in the iconic year of 1945, and be stupefied to see the absolute correlation with the world at that exact moment. Bea will, quite rightly, fear she would be taken for a lunatic or a fraud if she shows the letter to anyone, so she does not. As for the identical paragraph in the *Considerations,* there was not much chance of its being read as a timely prophecy: after a first edition in 1920, the book falls into an oblivion, only relieved by the death of Bea toward the end of the sixties, when Foret's first readers in five decades, believing the false prophecy to be a posthumous addition of the widow or the editors, refuse to credit such an absurdity.

Mr. X does not reappear as a character or reference in the rest of the *Considerations* or in Foret's letters to Bea. His prophecies, taken by many as amusing apocrypha (which they may be), leave Foret in a state approaching a trance, and under this influence he writes some of the most celebrated sections of his *Considerations*, or such is suggested by the chronology of the letters. Bea dies, taking with her to the grave the secret of the authenticity, or otherwise, of Mr. X's prophesies.

Traditional scholars of Foret's work, fearful of the consequences, pour fervent scorn on the affair. It's impossible to know what they think at night, away from their offices, their classrooms, and their university publishers, when doubt or suspicion or irrational vacillation seep through their sleepless eyelids. None of them have written anything on the subject.

A

An intensely white smoke, issuing from some branches burning without any visible flame on the side of the street, rises into the equally white light of Nueva Francia, in the middle of which Adela's untidy black hair darkens a precise area of the town.

Marcelo Valente walks a little way behind her, responding laconically to the questions about his status and origins.

"From Madrid."

. . .

"Yes, at the University of Los Girasoles."

. . .

"A whole year."

. . .

"I got here about a month ago."

. . .

"No way. What made you think I was a historian? Do I look like a historian?"

. . .

"Ha, ha. And what are European historians like?"

. . .

"No. I'm in the aesthetics department. In philosophy."

Adela is a strong woman. While Marcelo is driving his noisy car, alert to the possible military checkpoints, the possible roadblocks organized crime has prescribed for the community, she stares at the semidesert landscape of Nueva Francia, her mouth twisted in an inscrutable expression. She also works at the university, although Marcelo has never seen her there. This is explained by the fact that she has a free term with no classes, only a couple of consultations she can do at home. She lives right in the center of Los Girasoles in, she says, a colonial-style house with an interior patio. In this patio live her adored cacti and the odd aromatic plant.

Her field is not particularly clear: she did an undergraduate degree in law, has a master's in human rights, or something similar, and a PhD in history, though no one can understand how it was conferred. She gives free legal advice to women harassed by the "patriarchal system of the administration of justice," which, after a series of prudent but interested questions on Marcelo's part, turns out to mean she gets women out of prison—women who grow poppies for the drug trade, or the wives of the men who grow poppies for the drug trade, or the wives of the narcos imprisoned for abetting the growing of poppies. (Marcelo isn't clear about the nuances, but whatever the case, it has to do with deeply real areas of human existence his Madrid theoretical outlook will never manage to comprehend.)

Adela also asks questions and learns things about Marcelo Valente's life. That he was born in Madrid, that he lived in the center of that city and then, later, somewhere on the outskirts, that he studied philosophy in the first years of a democratic Spain. The post-Franco opening up arrived at the peak of his twenty-something fervor, but he was one of the few members of his group of friends to free himself from the irreversible rigors of heroin, punk, and other similar temptations that abounded at that time.

Marcelo speaks quickly, tripping over his words in his haste, as if nervous about the idea of having a new friend—someone more visually pleasing than chubby Professor Velásquez—with whom he can surely have good times during his stay in Los Girasoles.

When they reach the town, Adela gives Marcelo directions to the door of her house. The professor's car stops in the shade of a jacaranda tree, and Adela, before getting out, hands him a slip of paper on which she has scribbled a number (hers). They make their farewells with a kiss on the cheek that lasts a little longer than necessary.

Marcelo doesn't think of her as a potentially great lover until that night in his own bed, when he lingers over the details of Adela's figure outlined against the bar in Los Insurgentes, in the horrific Nueva Francia. According to her story, she had driven to that small town in her own car, but it had broken down and she had decided to have a drink in the cool of the cantina before sorting out her means of transport. She would come back the next day, in the pickup belonging to her trusted mechanic, to rescue her vehicle from possible Nueva Francian shoot-outs.

B

Mexico City was, for Foret, an ideal place, at least at first. No one knew him there, and he could indulge his excesses sheltered by the general brouhaha of a revolution he didn't completely understand. Foret's Spanish was rudimentary, sprinkled with French expressions he pronounced with what he thought to be a Mexican accent. Nevertheless, he felt comfortable in the language. French seemed to him a decadent tongue, and English too laconic; in contrast, Spanish was made to the measure of suffering. Only in Spanish could he miss Bea before she came to Mexico, and feel his words, full of open vowels, matched his emotions.

Of course, the students at the boxing school couldn't make head or tail of their eccentric teacher's babbling, but they sensed a vague authenticity in Foret's enthusiasm and allowed themselves to be guided by him, copying the ridiculous movements of his feet.

The owner of the gym very quickly realized Foret was a complete imposter, but he left him alone since he thought the teacher's foreign name added a touch of elegance to his business. What's more, Richard had lost a celebrated battle, two years before, against the world champion, which at least gave assurance of his bravery and the efficacy of his contacts in international boxing.

Bea arrived, as has been said, in January 1918, and they were able to resume their love affair as if they had only been separated for a few hours. They didn't even mention the heartbroken letters Richard had sent her with religious punctuality during those months, flirting at times with suicide as a form of emotional blackmail to draw her into his arms.

Mexican legislation was chaotic, not to say inoperative, and no one bothered to investigate Bea's earlier love life—as she had never divorced her first husband, she couldn't legally marry Richard. But they did marry, without really taking matrimony seriously, without any pretense that its official status substantially altered their life together.

They had, perhaps, too many plans, and Foret had acquired the bad habit of dreaming of a perfect city and projecting his hyperbolic desires onto an enthusiastic Bea. Buenos Aires continued to pulse within his cravings with a mystic resonance, the justification for which was unclear to anyone.

They lived in the center of Mexico City, in a hotel a few blocks from the boxing academy. Bea would spend the mornings working on a long poem, which she prudently lost at a later date so as not to be tormented by the memory of the joy that had been wrested from her. Richard went out early; he would pass the first hours of the day at the gym or in the Bosque de Chapultepec, doing the regular physical training that helped him calm down and temporarily expelled the darkest shadows from his head. Afterwards, three times a week, he trained the young athletes in the Tacuba school, and in the afternoon returned to the hotel, where he existed on a diet of maize, rice, and beans; Bea's inheritance, administered by her late father's attorney and normally sent to her every three months, ran the risk of disappearing in a country like Mexico, and they had yet to find a means of receiving the money without putting their lives at risk.

Fortunately the owner of the hotel had allowed them to take up residence on indefinite credit until they resolved their problems, placing more confidence in Bea's manners than in her husband's menacing physique and imperfect Spanish.

They were, as the cliché goes, poor but happy. But behind Foret's happiness was a constant threat, a cord stretched to the breaking point, an overinflated balloon that could burst at any moment. His joy was always incomplete, like a sort of addiction that in seeking satisfaction, constantly required greater stimulus. Although, for the first time in years, his life seemed to have become a little more settled, there was an elemental haste inside him, a desire to reach the next state, even if this might signify the collapse of his present tranquility. Bea accepted this haste and dissatisfaction as fundamental traits of her new husband's nature, although she was always aware of their problematic side. If she'd had her way, they would have either stayed in Mexico until their economic difficulties were resolved or awaited the end of the war there before going together to London, Paris, or wherever. But at the time, Richard had not correctly diagnosed his thirst for mutation, his propensity for change, and the tyranny of his own will: he believed that behind every plan was a concrete reality, and that Buenos Aires would really be the place where they could finally form a family. And he wasn't willing to put anything off.

By June, before they had even been married for six months, the situation had become unsustainable. Richard talked without respite of the marvels awaiting them in Buenos Aires, but he had also begun to propose parallel or, according to his humor, mutually exclusive plans that left Bea in a whirl. If it were raining, he would enthusiastically argue in favor of London. He would enter the country under a false name and shoot himself in the leg to avoid recruitment. Bea would be able to take charge of her inheritance and even bring her two children to live with them. Practical considerations (the impossibility of living together without Matthew, Bea's first husband, bringing a lawsuit, for example) were set aside with childish arguments or even more complex, makeshift plans to fill the gaps: they would both live in anonymity, or he would have Bea's first husband killed, and if he did so, they could then settle in Australia.

Bea was overtaken by a sense of unreality and absolute fragility. She imagined Richard's constant references to other lives to be
expressions of subconscious regrets: perhaps he would prefer to be
somewhere else, to return to his nomadic existence and the brag-
gart bachelor status some–she had been warned of this in New York,
when they tried to dissuade her–considered his dominant trait.

Caught up as he was in a whirlwind of confused and unachiev-
able futures, Richard didn't notice the deterioration of his present.
Not only was Bea's anxiety growing, but he himself had neglected
his work. In the gym, it was as if he were somewhere else, or he
would tell his students labyrinthine stories about his past or future
life, sometimes in languages the young pugilists had never heard
before. One day Señor Ortueta, the owner, called Richard into his
tidy office and said he couldn't go on paying him. As any good
Mexican in those years, he laid the blame for everything on the
revolution, and he fired Foret, with the only consolation being that
he could continue to use the splintered club facilities for his personal training. Foret naturally refused this offer and challenged him
to a duel. Luckily his bravado didn't bear fruit.

For Bea, Richard's working life debacle was the end of an era. It
was not that her instincts were telling her to put distance between
them until he calmed down, but that from a financial viewpoint, she
found herself forced to do so. She, therefore, suggested a two-stage
plan: she would go immediately to Buenos Aires, where she could
pick up the money that had been accumulating in London and find
a decent place for them to live while he stayed in Mexico for a few
months longer, until he could make enough money to cover their
debts and buy a passage to Buenos Aires. It might also be simpler to
get money to Richard from Argentina than from London.

Bea, who was much more practical than her husband, discovered it was possible to travel from Veracruz to Cuba and, from there,
to Buenos Aires, and had made inquiries about the dates: she would
sail in two weeks. The news hit Richard like the blade of a guillotine.
He went around for several days with a corpse-like face, tramping
along Calle Tacuba until the traders became suspicious. Bea tried
to calm him, to explain the practical advantages of the plan she had
outlined, but it was all in vain: the very idea of being separated from

her again weighed down on Foret's tattooed shoulders like a cedar wardrobe. At the same time, he was, at heart, conscious that the decision had already been taken. He knew Bea was a determined woman, and he also knew financial problems worried her in a way he would never understand. For her, it was important to establish herself in Buenos Aires and have a home, not a pokey hotel room in a city full of bandits (a situation that was more tolerable for him).

The day Bea set off for Veracruz, Foret cried like a baby. He clung to her with occlusive force until the driver of the car that was to take her to the railway station completely lost his patience. Bea's arrangements were quite clear: she would solve the problem and be responsible for ensuring that Richard arrived in Buenos Aires as soon as possible. There, they would live happily among other European immigrants until the war was over, and they would have hordes of children and both write unbearably beautiful poetry. This was the mantra Richard repeated to himself, even though he was convinced it would be the last time he touched Bea.

Maybe if he had not been so moved, so immersed in his own feelings, Richard would have noticed, during that final embrace, Bea Langley's slightly swollen belly.

On the day following his wife's departure, in despair at being suddenly alone, Foret repented having given in to Bea's pressure, having allowed her to leave, and abandoning all his possessions, he boarded a goods train at nightfall, hoping to arrive in Veracruz in time to stop his beloved from sailing.

A

Marcelo Valente lies very uncomfortably on the bed, looking at the ceiling of his small house in the Puerta del Aire residential estate. Beside him, recently abandoned on the rumpled sheets, lies the book *Fundamental Considerations on Something* by the admirable Richard Foret. He has been reading the whole day, snacking on grated carrots and turnip (a simple culinary discovery he is addicted to), and later he will go down to Adela's house in the center of Los Girasoles to have dinner with her.

He looks over the sections he has highlighted in fluorescent yellow in the Foretian *Considerations* and thinks they are an impossible collection of incoherent, hallucinatory axioms:

"The person who talks to himself knows the First Person does not exist."

"I warn you, my scant readers, that I have perceived a blossoming of my social concerns. At least once a week, I get the impulse to go out and plant bombs."

"When you begin to judge days according to the consistency of your excrement, you know you have done something bad in your life."

"My inclination toward murder, while impressive, is below average."

"All things are moving, only some of them move too slowly."

"I am surprised not to have written more frequently about sex, that elephant in the room of my head."

"The sea is for those who are far away."

"The person who talks to himself," Marcelo Valente says aloud, "knows the First Person does not exist." And he takes a short nap before leaving the house.

---- **B** ----

Foret, as his notes confirm, arrived in Veracruz too late. Bea had sailed three days earlier, and it took Richard quite some time to understand that there were sixty hours, of which he had no recollection, missing from his life. He had been robbed of the last of his money, his shirt was covered in vomit, and he had absolutely no memory of where he had obtained the hat he was wearing. He talked to strangers in the street and had the fevered gaze of those who have watched an era collapse around them.

Little is known of those final days. Bea Langley's later reconstructions suggest he was employed in a brothel, ejecting impertinent drunks in exchange for room, board, and a limited dose of violent entertainment. He had left a hefty bill behind in Mexico City, and the owner of the hotel would soon be sending someone to look for him; this was one of his main worries. He started to suspect an international conspiracy to discover his whereabouts; he imagined the u.s. draft board was in cahoots with Duchamp, with Marinetti, with his creditors in Germany, Paris, and Barcelona. They were all plotting to keep him away from Bea, to bury him at the bottom of a trench, to drive him mad.

Pursued by these and other visions, none of them realistic, Foret lived like a vagabond, trying unsuccessfully to pass as a seaman, for almost two weeks. But impatience was one of the crosses he had to bear, and he convinced himself of the immediate need to go to Buenos Aires, where Beatrice would greet him with kisses and exotic fruits. He wrote a couple of letters to his wife, telling her of his latest plan: to sail single-handed to the coast of Argentina in a sturdy boat. But he had no address to send the letters to and had to content himself with keeping them in a wooden box one of the prostitutes—driven by irrepressible tenderness—kept for him out of sight of the brothel keeper.

One Sunday afternoon, as if to gild the lily of a week of excess, Foret staggered to the port. He picked out a small boat that could be handled with a crew of one. He had some knowledge of sails, knots, and winds, and thought it would not be too hard for him to set out to sea and come ashore on the southern coast of Argentina. He imagined himself arriving in his boat at the very door of the house Bea would have prepared for their future life together, a house that would look directly out to sea or onto the River Plate. He stole the boat.

But as has already been mentioned, Foret was man of fluctuating interests. He had not been long aboard when he decided it would be simpler to head north, to Florida, and take an actual cruise ship bound for the south. He came to understand, perhaps late in the day, the complete impossibility of his original undertaking: no one could reach Argentina in a small boat. Florida sounded more plausible.

When he set the prow to the north, it was already a dark, moonless night, and the clouds were gathering above him.

III

THE SHRUBS OF THE TERRESTRIAL SPHERE

---------------------------------- **1** ----------------------------------

A year of economic crisis. The newspapers, the analysts, and the man on the street all make exaggerated complaints about the probable advent of the Apocalypse. There were enormous cuts to the culture budget. A wave of layoffs crashed down on the museum. I saw the effects of the stock market collapse approaching like a domino that, lined up with others, foresees its inexorable fate in the fall of its fellow tiles. Jorge, the designer, was the first to go: they said that in a few months, when everything was better, they would take him back on a freelance basis. Then it was the security guard's turn, in what was, to my mind, an accurate assessment on the part of the authorities: even in times of crisis, no one steals exhibits from a small museum. Finally, they decided they could manage without my wisdom. Though not without the docile flattery of Cecilia, who lives on untouched by the surrounding tsunami, not registering the effects of the crisis. At least, I think, I won't have to see her in the office.

The episode with the turd was a one-off. Maybe if I'd found another, identical one on the table a few days later, the image would have become less vivid. Instead, it remains as an incarnation inaugurating a new era: a personal Christ. Before and after the shit. Before: time killing, the nine-to-five consistency, the modicum of freedom, and the almost involuntary marriage of a person who only wants to reach old age, or not even that. After: unemployment, the idle mornings and their result–judicious reflection, the "things would be better if only . . ."

Cecilia comes back from work and, as in a bad South American film, reproaches me for my idleness, the constant procrastination.

"I've got a job interview tomorrow," I say, just to calm her for a while. She's beginning to break my balls . . .

Nowadays I offer insults more frequently. Since I don't have a job, I'm allowed to; I'd even say it's expected of me. I insult the institutions, my wife, the people–always invisible, although presumably close to power–who are to blame for the aforementioned crisis. My preference is for gratuitous, unexpected insults: "Frigging damp." (The complaint is, in reality, aimed at my father-in-law: he never got rid of the damp in the walls.) My father-in-law, of course, likes me less. He says he can get me a little something with one of his friends, but I say no. I imagine, and not without reason, that any job he could find me would make me unhappy for the rest of my days.

I've given up collecting tea bags–"See how I'm saving money, honey?"–and for some time, I've managed not to think about the vacant lot. The hen clucks like a bird possessed. I suspect the crisis has hit us all, except the worms, the twigs, except anything frigging domestic fowl like her eat.

Frigging seems to me a wonderful insult, being indefinite. It is the human equivalent of the hen's clucking. *Frigging* is one of those words that evokes the unspeakable, that's the only way to explain why this country is always in such a bad way. Now that I'm no longer concerned with the ghosts of progress, I contribute to the proliferation of disaster: "Frigging damp."

"Stop saying that, Rodrigo. My dad told you it's not damp; he said you can get rid of that with the damp-proofing paint he gave us."

I couldn't give a fuck about your dad, I think, but cautiously hold my tongue, clinging by my fingertips to the last morsel of common sense I've retained.

Common sense: a happy dodge. I imagine it as a chip inserted into the brain at about the age of seven. Or a vague presence, half magical, that murmurs answers in your ear. If it were a person, Common Sense would be very much like Ben Affleck, that North American parody of a hero who appears in the movies shown on interstate buses.

I haven't said a word about the shit. Not to Cecilia or anyone. I can't discount any suspect, and until my investigation into the situation is complete, I prefer not to speak about the affair. It could have been Ceci, who had perhaps not gone to the museum and was hiding behind a door to see what I was doing with my sick leave. Maybe she decided to take revenge when she saw me ejaculating on her pillow; or she went to the window, saw me walking around in the lot, and was overtaken by an urgent need. Though she would never have sullied her tiger-striped bedspread. Before doing that, just to screw up my existence, she would have defecated on the collection of tea bags I keep in a drawer in the dressing table. Or just on the floor. Anywhere but on her beloved bedspread.

Although I hate to admit it, I've discovered that in contradiction to my earlier convictions, I'm also excited by the idea of watching Cecilia shit. I've tried getting into the bathroom after her, but she always locks the door. "I'm in here, my love." "Come on, let me in." "No, Rodrigo, you're making me nervous. What do you want?" I leave her in peace. The shit on the bedspread has unleashed other deviations. (I can't call them by any other name.) I also, for example, imagine the type of crap passed by all the people I see in the street, as if divining their intestinal secrets would constitute some form of profound psychology. Now that I'm unemployed, I should put these obsessions to good use in some way or other. Setting up a business, for instance. There are businesses for every taste. There's a company in Santa María la Ribera that offers its clients random numbers. They mail them a slip of paper with a number of varying lengths. The customers open the envelope, read the number, consider it, fold the slip of paper, and put it somewhere safe until the next number arrives, two or three months later. Then they throw away the first slip of paper. At least that's what I'm told the company does. But thinking it over, there must be something in the whole process that I'm missing. Something significant that converts the number service into a matter of life or death. Anyway, what I mean to say is that there are all sorts of businesses. I could set up a deep psychology company. A company for intestinal secrets. For shit analysis. A detective company.

In any case, what makes me uneasy is to think that the suspect was still in the room when I entered the apartment. The sounds I heard from the door appear to confirm this theory. Also the fact that, in a moment of weakness I shouldn't have allowed myself,

I took longer than usual to enter the room, giving the crapper the chance to escape through the window, leaping like an athlete into the shadows of the lot. Maybe the intruder was there, getting ready to commit burglary, or just calculating the damage his excreta would cause my daily life because he knew the event would be unspeakably disturbing, forcing me to throw out that tiger-striped bedspread that, though I might loathe it, was the favorite of my wife, who, while not exactly my soul mate, could at least expect me to show her the respect of preserving her bedspread. The intruder must have known all this, and he must have calculated it with a malice only comparable with that of cabdrivers. An environmental malice, I'd say, that impregnates the skin of all the inhabitants of this capital city and imbues them with an unpleasant smell, the smell of stagnant water or dead bird; a malice that doesn't escape my notice even though my natural tendency toward optimism manages to take it for granted, overlooking its consequences and leading me to continue along the rigorous path of a life that, if not exactly based on the model my mother would have preferred, does satisfy me to some extent. At least it satisfies me to the extent that if it were not for that turd, found in ridiculous circumstances in the very center of my bed, I could today say–despite my marriage, my unemployed status, and my absolute lack of perspective in relation to the future–that I'm happy, to the precise and sufficient extent that happiness is the inertia of which I spoke earlier, the inertia that carries me gently from one Saturday to the next, showing me the most agreeable paths of existence, the ones that avoid danger and death, making incomprehensible but ultimately fortunate detours, or fortunate to the precise and sufficient extent that they don't land you in prison, because prisons are horrific in this country, or so I've been told.

Similar stories that I have heard: some burglars, after the robbery, shit at the scene of the crime. A signature, a personal mark, a *little detail.* The initials of two lovers carved into a tree trunk, crap to autograph a crime–it's the same thing; the desire for permanence, when you come down to it. But this burglar, if he was one, reversed the order: he didn't take anything. The turd wasn't a symbolic payment for any removal. Just crap, like a menhir on the tiger-striped bedspread. A semifluid totem. A fucking shitty insult. When I was capable of returning to the bedroom, I held my nose, screwed up my eyes, and folded the bedspread over the little gift. I disposed of it, not without worrying about how much it would pain Cecilia to lose her horrendous feline bedspread.

I told her I'd taken all the bedding to the self-service laundromat. That I'd sat down to read a celebrity gossip magazine, and when I got up to see how the wash was progressing, I'd found the machine empty: no tiger-striped bedspread, no sheets, no pillowcases. I was even careful to offer her precise details of what I'd been reading: breast implants, infidelities, probable u-turns in the sexual preferences of certain television stars, things like that. It was an absurd explanation, but no more absurd than the actual truth. Cecilia threatened to go to the laundromat to complain, to demand the return of her bedspread. I was sharp enough to dissuade her with the promise of new extravagances: I told her they were selling a bedspread exactly like hers, but violet, on the corner of Dr. Vértiz and Río de la Loza. Later, I'd think up another lie to cover the first one. The causal series of lies is no less rigid than its parallel version in the real world. At times the two series become entwined for a moment in a single causal sequence we term, for pure convenience, the first person singular.

The question of the authorship—intellectual, but also material—of the perfect turd kept me awake for many nights following the event. Now, due to my unemployment, the enigma has expanded into the daylight hours, and I can't shake off the grotesque, affectedly symmetrical image of the turd in the center of the bed. I think that if I had any money, I'd hire one of those detectives who advertise in the classified sections of newspapers and set him on the trail of the scatological felon. Given this, I regret having disposed of the evidence since no DNA test can now be carried out, nor can single hairs, mistakenly left between the bedsheets during the dastardly act, be extracted, nor a faithful reconstruction of the scene of the shameful deed made.

When I was dismissed from the museum, I had some meager savings. The greater part of my earlier reserve funds had disappeared with the costs arising from my recent marriage: outings to the movies, a leather handbag, board games, alcohol . . . anything to relieve the forced regime of living together. Given my penury, I decide to investigate the dark rationale behind the events myself, and given the lack of evidence, and my complete and insuperable ignorance in relation to my point of departure, I decide the investigation will be simply speculative, rational. The first question I have to answer is how the subject who shat on my bed entered and left. After discounting hypotheses in the general area of spontaneous generation and mystical manifestation, I tell myself he must have entered through the door of the apartment, like anyone else. Another option, which can't be completely discounted, is that he entered through the window overlooking the lot; the other window, the one that looks out on the interior courtyard, has bars. If he entered through the window, he must have used a ladder (coming from the vacant lot) or a rope (coming from the roof); either possibility involves a logistical deployment at odds with the speed of the events. He must, therefore, have entered through the door. But the lock didn't show any signs of having been forced, so the intruder (a) has a key to my apartment or (b) knows someone who has a key to my apartment. Or even (c) the intruder comes from a parallel reality, another time and space, and just crossed the threshold separating it from this world, appearing directly on the tiger-striped bedspread, squatting, with the crap at the point of exiting through his anus. But no, option (c) is unthinkable. It's an option that can only be conceived by theoretical physicists. Or mathematicians. Or science fiction writers. Or schizophrenics, which is to say, none of the above.

Naturally, even when all the loose ends of the break-in have been tied, the motive for the misdemeanor will still need to be clarified. Either the poo has a meaning or it doesn't. If it does, then it can be thought of as a sign and is waiting happily in its loathsome image for me to venture onto the course of its exegesis. If it has no meaning beyond that of perturbing me, it can feel satisfied with itself, can pull up its pestilential anchor and set sail for other, more fragile sensibilities.

I allow myself a rather unscientific deduction: if the intruder has keys or knows someone who does, he must also know me (I changed the locks as soon as I moved here), and if he knows me, he knows the shit on the bedspread would perturb me, but also that I could find in it a pretext for reflecting on other regions, perhaps less traveled, of human existence. The intruder is a sower of clues, a plotter of consequences, sufficiently wise to even anticipate these reflections of mine. Everything would seem to confirm that the intruder is the person who knows me best, the person most naturally close to me, my–until now–unknown brother.

2

Living with Cecilia is self-inflicted torture. Her scorn for me grows with the weeks, festering like a tenacious parasite in the inches of mattress that separate us each night. Sex, the last bastion of our reduced cohabitation, has, in this situation of overt antagonism, become watered down. In the mornings, Cecilia leaves for the museum, and I wander around the local streets in search of clues and evidence. (I think maybe some malevolent neighbor had been watching my movements for months before dealing the final blow. Now he amuses himself observing my increasing desperation, like a psychoanalyst who is entertained by the perversions of his patient, provoking them with decidedly indiscreet mother-related comments.)

My mother, unpredictably, interpreted my unemployment as a necessary pause in my existence, a moment for doubt and reflection that might, with a little luck, sooner or later return me to the paths of an enlightened life. She calls me more often now. Tells me a new stationery store has opened in Los Girasoles, and that the event, in its provincial magnitude, has generated a great deal of excitement among the natives. She says that not a few of her university colleagues have gone there to sport their most solemn apparel among the aisles of indelible-ink pens. I suspect she is lying, that my mother wants to seduce me with stupid stories so that I'll yield to the folksy nature of her anecdotes and move to Los Girasoles. Once there, she would undoubtedly do her utmost to convince me of the need to enroll in a degree program: there is no better way, in that

town, of killing time. She will attempt to convince me of the advantages of divorce. Or rather, the disadvantages of marriage. Of the
inherent machismo of the very idea of marriage, the senselessness of
stable relationships, the enormous number of marriages that fail or
end in murder. She will explain that, according to research, the only
type of marriage that avoids all these pitfalls is the marriage between
homosexuals, which is already legal in the capital. She'll attempt to
convince me to go bi. She'll give me flowers. Dresses. Plastic pricks
with more or less realistic veins and bulges. No. I can't go to Los
Girasoles on my own. If I do, it will be with Cecilia, who at least is a
woman, and my wife, and is conservative, and conservatism is a positive force in a world that is falling apart at the seams. Conservatism
is the keystone of a wall. The conservative person is an exception,
a landmark. A turd in the middle of a tiger-striped bedspread.

This idleness has brutally confronted me with the meanness of
my spirit. Not only do I spend a great deal of time thinking stupid
thoughts, but the curse of the ability to reflect obliges me to recognize that I spend a great deal of time thinking stupid thoughts.
An acute case of misanthropy is gestating somewhere deep within
me: I conceive my relationship with humans as a, to this point,
necessary evil, the reasons for which are increasingly less clear. At
this stage in the game, I consider full communion with a group of
delightful people to be completely unattainable. The loss of my job
and the resulting isolation have only confirmed my belief that the
inexorable path I follow leads to an unprecedented, unpredictable
level of misery. The only type of communion with people to which
I can aspire is through objects. For example, by observing the tea
bags I collected at one time, which simultaneously refer me to
the humans who produced them and the humans who saw me consume the product. Then I understand that society as a whole is
a machine, kept perfectly oiled by relationships of courtesy and
the stock and household appliance markets. And I understand that
humans are good.

Cecilia returns from the museum laden with supermarket bags.
From her grim expression, I suspect her patience is reaching its limits. As soon as she comes through the door, she starts making sarcas-
tic comments intended to wound my manly pride. Fortunately I've

never developed any such pride, and I find no satisfaction in defending a dignity I don't possess, so I observe Cecilia with a mixture of pity and indifference, accepting that, within her scale of values, the situation of having a useless husband is a deeply unhappy one.

All of a sudden I am invaded by empathy: I comprehend I've made this woman unhappier than she was before. As a form of compensation, I tell her that tomorrow, one way or another, I'll get together the money to take her to Acapulco for a few days. She quite rightly says Acapulco is a horrible city, full of garbage and death and vulgarity and ferocity and drug trafficking and places where they'll give you a blowjob for two pesos (she doesn't mention that last one, but it's true), and that she'd prefer to have a holiday someplace where there's not even the remotest chance of finding a corpse with its throat slit on the sand, a few yards from the filthy hotel. So I suggest we pay a surprise visit to my mother in Los Girasoles. Cecilia is concerned about the insuperable distance between my mother and me. It seems an idyllic opportunity to strengthen our family bonds; she is satisfied.

3

Cecilia had already expressed her wish to own a car. Now, with the December holiday season getting closer, and the trip to Los Girasoles an inalterable fact, her expression of that desire has taken on a more urgent tone. While she understands our economic situation is, to put it mildly, precarious, she continues to go on about the car, as if setting out to needlessly squander money were a means of evoking fortune. I share the underlying current of magical thinking on which this logic is based, and that's why I love Cecilia. She is, in her superficiality, everything I envy in flexible souls. So I borrow what seems an enormous sum from a cousin and buy Cecilia a small, red, secondhand car.

Moments of happiness. When it seems as if everything is exasperation and fear, as if the life I've been leading will fall apart around

me at any moment, that's when I finally enjoy minor, everyday pleasures. I've almost completely forgotten the grotesque episode of the
poo on the bedspread. At least I don't think about it so often, and I've
decided to temporarily abandon my investigation. Like a parting of
the waters, a sign of the need for change, the shit on the bedspread
is a positive, fortuitous event.

Cecilia is content in her job. She asked Ms. Watkins for a raise,
and the director, out of pity for our situation—for which she is, in
part, responsible—awarded her one, though lowering the requested
sum by a couple of percentage points. I don't know how she managed to square the books, because the museum budget depends on
the federal budget for culture, which wanes with each successive
day. And although this recession in the cultural industries is a direct
consequence of the government's contempt for anything intended to
make existence more bearable, I can't help but wish for, and tacitly
encourage, the collapse of state culture and the whole ridiculous
meritocracy it has installed, forcing people to spit on each other and
to make hatred and suspicion their only mode of survival. Because
the only people who rise up the pile are those who can fuck up everyone else, the ones who seek their neighbors' ruin and the ridicule
and disgrace of their colleagues, now their permanent adversaries.

But the fact is that Ms. Watkins gave Cecilia a raise, and Cecilia
is looking more kindly on the world.

The imminence of the holidays and the prospect of leaving the
city make the days more pleasant. My mom was happy to have us
stay with her, and I noticed in her mood a notable reconsideration
of my virtues, as if she thought that idleness had purified me. And
indeed it has: I now understand how wrong I was in trying to perse-
vere with office-ism. Only premature retirement, I'm beginning to
understand, justifies undertaking a college degree. (I even consider
doing one.) Mexico City seems to me like the oppressive monster
it in fact is, forcing a permanent regime of avarice on its inhabitants, from which they will only be released by a violent death or
a prolonged respiratory tract disease. The province of the spirit is
the only pleasure I defend. In light of this, I reevaluate my childhood in Cuernavaca, my father's house, the pieces of waste ground
that are not hemmed in by buildings but stretch out immeasurably

mysterious, gorged with life, across the poverty-stricken hillsides. The vacant lots so large they are called fields. Salvation is, ultimately, in the bucolic.

These reflections fully endorse my decision to seek out vegetal life, in the lowercase sense, in the adjoining lot. But I now understand that the lot is not wide enough to save me from the infinite idiocy, cruelty, and injustice of the city. And that is why someone shat on my bedspread. Civilization is a violent outrage, a clash of the most basic instincts of every citizen. There is no culture that offers redemption from this disguised barbarity, no poem or play that makes this extreme mendacity of the soul more bearable.

All there is in the city is pointless argument and swaggering, gratuitous animosity and the degradation of others. I now know that all jobs, with their eight office hours and their vertical structure and their system of rewards and punishments, are demeaning to the limits of what is humanly tolerable. And all wage earners–the culture bureaucrats who try to pass off the endless battle for the suppression of others as rational discussion of ideas–are themselves victims and perpetrators of the daily dose of filth, from which nothing, absolutely nothing except resignation and silence and ostracism and the margin, can save them. I, now, am going to conquer that margin, among the shrubs of the terrestrial sphere.

Of course there's a touch of the spasmodic in my sudden aspiration for the rural condition. Something of a last-minute remedy for the oppressive sensation of being in the process of dying. Because I am dying, that is certain: cooped up in a damp apartment, next to a lot inhabited by only a hen, married to a woman whose form oscillates in my spirit between the beloved (to be polite) and the incomprehensible.

In the past, the solidity of an imposed, semi-tyrannical routine allowed me to not worry about what I did with my idle hours. Now all my hours are idle hours, and ideas have time to grow inside me until they become monstrous; feelings have the space and silence to slowly soak into my nerves and reach the darkest regions of my spirit; the contradictions of which I'm made up have enough air to accelerate their combustion, making the collection of minutiae that sustain my existence inflammable and even perilously volatile.

4

Finally, the holiday season comes around. Cecilia's small, red, secondhand car will be good for traveling the highway, even though I don't drive and have no intention of ever doing so. She, then, will be responsible for getting us there. At heart Cecilia isn't bothered by that detail, as I had calculated would happen. Resigned to my uselessness, and having accepted it as one of my principal features, she's unsurprised that it should manifest itself once more in this new impossibility. She suspects–and she's right–that in the coming years I'll gradually renounce more and more activities, until I end up sprawled prostrate in a wing chair, observing a collection of tea bags on the coffee table, dribbling a little out of the corner of my mouth, and uttering, with ridiculous emphasis, the word *egg*.

In any case, Cecilia likes driving, so we set out for Los Girasoles, provisioned with a whole bag of ham-and-cheese sandwiches and several small rectangular cartons of grape juice. The highway, once we've left Mexico City, is packed with vacationers, station wagons with inflatable dinghies on the roof. As we travel farther from the city, and the gap between one house and the next widens, I feel I'm shrugging off an exaggerated weight, something irksome on my shoulders, sinking me ever deeper into myself, into the most wretched regions of myself.

The highway makes me think of all the things that happen. Of the madcap or impossible pace of the days that don't just pass but deny their existence, or turn back on themselves, or anticipate by whole weeks the actual date of their coming. So the accelerations and decelerations Cecilia inexpertly imposes on our family speedster tangentially express that frenetic leaping and prancing of the days, those moments of wonder and those emergency stops of individual perception before the passage of time.

The highway makes me think of all the things that happen. For example, of the waterways I used to construct when I was a child, on the slopes of the waste ground across from my father's house in Cuernavaca: they were PVC tubes, joined together with anything that came to hand, that formed circuits around which the water and my small Lego toys nimbly slid, although they would sometimes get stuck, or an unexpected leak would prematurely carry them off into the sand of the waste ground. (*Prematurely*: like the things that happen when you're in a hurry.)

The highway makes me think of all the things that happen. For example, of the way human relationships keep changing, in the same way as the Mexican landscape—there outside the car window—changes from conifer forests to vast expanses of maguey. Just like my relationship with Cecilia, which went from indifference to hatred, from there to the unmitigated discord of our opinions, and then, gently, approached tolerance, a discreet form of love, in neutral colors, routine.

"Doesn't the highway make you think of all the things that happen?" I ask her.

"Oh, Rodrigo, the things you say, you'd think you were a numbskull . . . Wouldn't you like a sandwich?"

5

Far from generating a more open world, as I suspect was their intention, my parents' generation became obsessed by, and eventually succeeded in, destroying the only frame of staked-out certainties in which it was still possible to enjoy something approaching happiness for a period of time longer than that of an orgasm.

This redundant lecture is just to say that, contrary to any notion of progress, I have, throughout the course of my brief adult life, insisted on behaving in what I imagine to be the same way as my grandparents. My ambitions are restricted to the absence of ups and downs. For that reason, unemployment and the mere thought of doing something radical, like leaving the city for good, of my own free will—this is just a working hypothesis—seem to me minor but significant concessions to the reckless worldview of my parents; as if I felt myself obliged to recognize, at least by intuition, that it's possible to lead a life that is different from the humdrum existence of an office worker. A sincere, I'd almost say shameful strand of hope, of renewed enthusiasm for the possibilities offered by the vast world, is inveigling itself into the general grayness of my spirit.

The highway is uniform and boring. I doze off every so often without being aware of it and am woken by Ceci's voice asking me to pass her the money for the tollbooth. At the toll station we're surrounded, like all the other cars, by vendors, appearing out of nowhere and offering local products: a bag of guavas for ten pesos, a little box of quince jellies, tabloid newspapers.

My mom was born in Ciudad Satélite at almost the same time as Ciudad Satélite itself was born. At the tender age of fifteen, she came to the wise conclusion that her environment was oppressive, and she continued to battle with it for a couple of years more, until she managed to establish herself as a language teacher in a primary school—her English was more or less respectable—and effective agitator among the mass of students just starting out at college. Her jet-black, curly hair, high boots, and determination were all the rage in the eighties, a decade marked by the notable ideological lag of its youth, who in Mexico behaved just as the rest of the world had fifteen years earlier: anarchic behavior that, in the end, changed nothing despite the very widespread belief to the contrary.

My dad studied agronomy because he believed that in this way he could gain a level of nutritional self-sufficiency with respect to a system he loudly decried, but after two years of analyzing the effects of fertilizers on the rubber tree, he decided to switch to law, and that was when he met my mother. (I sometimes like to say "my mother" because the very words impose a certain distance.)

They fused into a legendary couple who were observed mockingly by the most cynical kids and with flagrant envy by the most candid. My parents represented free love without the need to leave the family model: their freedom was based on nothing more than a certain high-sounding rhetoric and a slightly faster pace of walking than the rest. In every other way, they were like any couple of the day. But they themselves created their own conceited myth and set themselves up as the model of heroic marriage. When my mother got pregnant with me, the aura of ineffable transgression, of seditious activism, gave way to a portrait of middle-class life, and the specter of Ciudad Satélite hovered over them like an ominous fate. By the time I was born, my father had temporarily given up his academic ambitions and dedicated himself to manufacturing scented candles, which he then sold in boutiques of questionable luxury. My mother, on the other hand, enlisted in a less belligerent form of activism and studied for a master's in human rights, working as an assistant on a commission whose head used all his arts to conquer her and carry her off to live with him in his house in Colonia Portales, where she stayed for a little over a year. I lived for a time in Cuernavaca, beside a vacant lot that marked my stunted relationship with Madame Nature. Then came Coapa: my mother took on the role of the incorruptible, single woman, and while my dad, in Cuernavaca, was prospering in the paraffin business, she and I lived in the grubby neighborhood where I tasted–puberty, a divine treasure–the sweet delights of drugs and unrelieved ordinariness.

When my parents saw that I could walk unaided, though still unsteadily, they turned their backs: it was no longer necessary to pay attention to what I was up to. When I was able to make my own way financially with relative confidence, they moved far away. From that time, the relationship with my father waned to the bloodless point it has reached in recent years, while my mother, as I've said, calls from time to time, in an offhand manner, disillusioned by my characteristic lack of daring and run-of-the-mill dissatisfaction. So, to visit her now, with Cecilia, may be the nearest thing to an adventure I'm likely to experience in years. An adventure whose only plotline consists of emotional upheaval and reproach, uncomfortable silences and rain. The ordinary, gloomy rain of Los Girasoles.

The closer we get to the town, the more military roadblocks we encounter. Los Girasoles is still a peaceful place, but around it a multitude of shantytowns and shady settlements–the sort that are never mentioned in the national newspapers–are in the habit of adding to each of their components a prefix that is very fashionable in this country: narco. They are narcotowns, with narcoschools–both elementary and high–and narcobreakfasts for thirty-five pesos, by a narcosquare. And so on. And that's the reason for all the military roadblocks, which give Cecilia the idiotic and reprehensible sensation that something good is being done.

"Oh, thank goodness for the army. Even if we do have to stop every couple of miles."

"Why do you talk such garbage, my love?"

"It's not garbage, Rodrigo. It means they're putting ever so many people in prison."

6

My mom thinks I lead a largely dishonorable life. Perhaps she's right, but her way of saying this is so blunt, so passionately convinced, that it makes me distrust her recommendations.

"Before you lost your job, you were living a miserable life; now you're living a miserable life without any money. The only way you're going to do something useful is by studying for an undergraduate degree, so you can then do a master's and work fewer hours a day."

"Anyway, I wouldn't know what to do with the free time, Mom. And I don't mind working eight or nine hours a day, especially if it's in an old building like the museum."

She plays with her black mane and lets her eyelids droop, as if tired, silently discrediting my words. My reply is automatic because, deep down, I enjoy exasperating her: admitting, even for a minute, to the truth in her suggestions would represent a symbolic defeat equivalent to emasculation without anesthetic, and I've got no desire for that.

While this is going on, Cecilia is in the small cactus garden belonging to the house, which, luckily, is right in the center of Los Girasoles, where you can still see some dwellings with internal cactus gardens and high ceilings, and not just quick-build residential estates, as is the case on the outskirts.

My mom, Adela, takes us for a walk through the center. In the small main square is a man selling balloons, giving an absurd touch of color to the shade of the fig trees. It's the only part of the town that in any way resembles the central and southern cities of the republic: everything else is closer to the uncultivated north or the excruciatingly Catholic stillness of the El Bajío plateau.

Cecilia and my mom walk a few steps ahead of me, but not a word passes between them. Cecilia looks eager, as if she is trying to please her impossible mother-in-law, alert to any sign of good faith or a disposition for conversation that this might imply. But my mother walks on unconcernedly, as if indifferent to her visitors' attentions, thinking her own thoughts, inscrutable, giving me sideways glances, as though she were evaluating me with the corner of her eye, of her conscience, of her wasted or even regretful maternity.

Someone—in fact, Cecilia—suggests going to the movies, but my mother explains that the only movie theater where they show anything new is several miles away, in a ghost mall that probably belongs to the narcos since it stands there, ostentatiously, in the middle of nowhere, completely empty at any time of the day or night, except maybe Saturday afternoons, when some of the university professors drag themselves along to it, hopeful of finding something, anything, on which to spend their salaries and their discount vouchers.

Setting that plan aside as being complicated and too much trouble, we sit on a metal bench with the paint peeling off, next to an orange-juice stand on the edge of the square. The fruit on the stand looks wrinkled. My mother still seems absent, and Cecilia tries to catch my eye in a look of complicity that I suddenly don't want to share.

7

We sit down and switch on the TV. The fabric of the armchair is slightly faded at a certain level, from use. I point this out to my mom, but she doesn't deign to acknowledge my comment, waving it off with her hand. Outside, the heat of the afternoon is giving way to the cold of night, without measurable nuances between the two states.

I interrupt the rapt contemplation of Cecilia and my mother with a new comment, this time about how good it is that there are no mosquitoes in Los Girasoles. The comment is once again ignored, this time without even the gesture.

On the screen is one of those live, trashy talk shows. There are three couples, all around forty; a blonde, slightly vulgar presenter is opening and shutting her pound of lip silicon before them, admonishing them with amazing rudeness. As far as I can tell, the topic of the program is "I cheated on my wife with my own wife." The three husbands, apparently, all had sex with their respective wives. They even regularly had sex, just like any other couple, but for some reason that was impossible to communicate, during one of these encounters they were overcome by the certainty that they were committing adultery. And the feeling was shared: both the man and his wife were aware, for a moment, while they were high on pleasure, that they were being unfaithful; not with someone else, but right there during that sexual act, as if they knew their spouse simultaneously was and wasn't him or herself. And that led to a surge of jealousy. The woman was suspicious of every one of her partner's activities; the husband spied on his wife and treated her roughly or even violently (in one case, it seems, it even came to blows). For all their promises that it would never happen again, their trust in each other had been irrevocably undermined, and all for screwing each other, but deep down, in some strange way, committing adultery. Little by little, they say, monogamy was restored by means of stubbornly repeating an idiotic routine.

Disconcerted by the direction the program is taking, I get up from the armchair, ready to go to bed while thinking that, in the end, this is perhaps the only way to survive marriage with a degree of dignity. Forget the midlife crises and the sudden preference for youth and motorcycles. Forget the summer affairs and the red-velvet bars to which you go with the dentist's secretary. Forget the prostitution and the unexpected discovery of closet homosexuality. Endogamous adultery: that's what's missing, dammit.

I'm hardly on my feet when the doorbell rings. My mom, not moving from her chair, unsurprised, asks me to answer it, adding, "It must be Marcelo." I give her a questioning look, but she continues

watching the TV as if nothing had happened. I've never heard of
Marcelo. Cecilia, in the meantime, has fallen asleep in her armchair, and I know it's not humanly possible to wake her so that she
can be with me in this moment of deep uncertainty. Why does it
seem so natural to just open the door to him?

Between the house and the gate leading to the street is a minus-
cule garden with a gravel path. The bulb in the lamppost intended to
illuminate the sidewalk outside has blown so that I can only distinguish, beyond the high metal railing, a masculine figure, taller than
me, his right hand gripping one of the bars. The light from the other
street lamps shines behind him, eclipsing his face.

This, I imagine, is the Marcelo guy. He greets me with a suspicious degree of effusion, speaking my name as if we were old
friends. I open the gate wide to him, feeling perplexed, while running through the most obvious possibilities: a neighbor who has
only come out about his homosexuality to my mother, who is egg-
ing him on to start a civil liberties campaign in Los Girasoles; a psy-
chologist hired by my mom to convince me to return to education or
get divorced; and finally—always finally—the most sensible possibility: he's my mom's new boyfriend. His friendly, deferential manner
points to the last option, although I find one aspect of the situation
disconcerting: he's Spanish. The accent gives him away. And in my
mother's bellicose imagination, no one who's Spanish can—short of
renouncing his ancestry—attempt to display a benevolent attitude
toward a Mexican without it being understood as a disregard for
the dignity of that person (it's a relatively historical matter, very difficult to explain). So Marcelo makes an effort to be pleasant from
the outset, but the tension caused by his Spanish blood gets in the
way of this noble intent, and his amiability ends up being offensive,
grating, uncivilized.

Marcelo takes his place in the TV soirée with strange sponta-
neity. Cecilia has woken and, after greeting the stranger with obvious
coquetry, has started asking him questions, while on the now-silent
screen the programming continues autistically. My mother laughs at
Marcelo's ingenious replies, and Cecilia, without fully understanding them (they often include highbrow references), also laughs, but
with a hesitancy that gives her away.

Marcelo addresses me, trying to include me in the sudden intimacy of the scene.

"Rodrigo, your mother tells me that you're interested in belles lettres."

"Me, interested in letters? Really? You could say that I take an interest in some words, or parts of words. Lately I've been feeling a particular predilection for vowels," I reply, attempting to avoid my tone being interpreted as droll.

The conversation quickly veers toward politics, guided by the iron will of my mother's opinions. Marcelo is ambiguous: he concedes that the left in general has merits, but he despises the Manichaean sense of history. In the face of such an incredibly abstract affirmation, Cecilia takes her leave, alleging drowsiness, and goes to bed.

"Are you coming, Rodrigo?"

"No, my love, I'll catch you later." When she hears my reply, Cecilia shoots me a reproachful glance, giving me to understand that she was trying to leave Marcelo alone with my mother. The conversation about politics continues its sinuous course. Marcelo has taken a cold beer from the fridge, and I finally understand what all those bottles are doing there: he's a regular visitor to this house. It seems, in short, a fairly new but stable relationship.

Well, I think, maybe this Marcelo isn't as much of a cretin as he seems. He's said a couple of things that are not, to my mind, completely misguided: that talking across the table after dinner seems to him a revolting habit, that amusement parks have more revolutionary potential than rhyming jingles, that he had only been in Mexico City for a few hours but had been able to "perceive its close liaison with the Devil."

In the living room light–one of those so-called energy-saving bulbs–Marcelo appears less attractive than I'd first imagined. There are clear traces of acne beneath his straggly beard, pockmarks that extend down to his collar, and into which he sinks his thumbnail when absorbed in what he's saying. He's fair enough to appear European, but not that fair. My mother, who's never been able to completely rid herself of her Marxist discourse, and these days uses it only out of sentiment, must think he's a class enemy–his Italian shoes, his obvious preoccupation with style. Yes, she must think he's a real stiff-necked Spaniard, that he knows nothing about the real world, just a rose-tinted version of it. She must get a kick out of thinking, "He's a class enemy and I'm fucking him; class struggle is here, in my sweaty, proletariat bed."

My mother, of course, is not a member of the proletariat, although in her desire to be one, she took a course in indexable lathe tooling when she was young. She's never been able to explain what an indexable lathe is.

8

Four days and their associated nights have passed, and Marcelo is still here, as if it were the most natural thing in the world. One morning, he disappeared and came back half an hour later with a bundle of clothes and four orange juices that he shared among us. I asked him about his house. It seems that he was conned via the internet in relation to the price and space, the description and photos of the place. He can't bear the house he's rented; he says it's infernally hot and that the residential estate is full of dubious people. But he can't leave: he paid who knows how many months in advance, and there are various penalty clauses for early departure in the contract. To my mind, it had become for him a matter of principle. Marcelo seems to be the sort of person who invokes principles at the drop of a hat. He hopes to raise controversy every time he says–and he says it very frequently–that he's a vegetarian; he must be disappointed by my absolute indifference to such provocations. As far as I'm concerned, he could be a coprophage. It's all the same to me.

Marcelo is a couple of years younger than my mother. ("Just like Ceci and me," I think.) But at that age, as at the beginning of adolescence, the difference between a man and a woman is obvious. Or maybe it's just that Marcelo leads a healthy life, including gyms and visits to the homeopath and "a glass of wine in the evenings." No doubt, a lot of olive oil. And I'm certain he's never worked in an open-plan office. You notice these things immediately. When someone has worked in an office, a film of boredom spreads over his face and stays there for the rest of his life. His skin, for all that the sun and exercise might try hide it, loses its glow, becomes thin. His vertebral posture is never the same. There's a classic curvature around the lumbar vertebrae that no ex-office worker can correct, not even with yoga or Arab dancing. The clothing of an office worker is also an irreversible aspect of his demeanor. If he's lived in this nine-to-five routine, it's impossible to regain a dignified, presentable style. It makes no difference if he consults Italian men's formalwear magazines: the starched collar and the mediocrity of his shoes will be permanent shackles.

Marcelo seems like a stranger to this world of weighed-up sacrifices. He's the sort of person you'd expect to have a healthy hobby: five-a-side soccer on the weekends, energy drinks, massage parlors where they call the prostitutes "helpmates." He looks young, so young that instead of two, there are five years between him and my mother. And it's not that my mom is really showing her age. She makes superhuman efforts to keep herself in shape. Almost suicidal diets, expensive depilatory treatments for her hairy body, cowboy boots she buys in the most expensive store in Los Girasoles, and the discreet but ever-present foundation makeup.

Marcelo has a certain tendency toward good humor that I find suspicious. He's always asking me about my interests and even shows curiosity when he's with Cecilia. It's as if he believes that all human beings have something interesting to say, waiting there inside. He couldn't be more wrong.

Despite all this, he's a likeable guy, and even if his likeability can become almost intolerable after a few hours, his company is, in general, positive, or at least neutral. He shows himself to be obliging, but then he uses the opportunity of that conquered ground for a crushing display of theories. He proselytizes for the most innocuous causes ("a reevaluation of Epicurus," for example). His capacity for enjoyment, if not completely atrophied, is clearly dampened by his love of analysis. He's the sort of person who, when watching the most recent Disney movie, uses the word *multiculturalism*, or, when it's over, posits without the least visible trace of sarcasm, "It's a metaphor for almost everything."

Normally, I'd have thought my mother would have found those attitudes, those almost comical attempts to be intelligent, downright pathetic. Yet she seems fascinated by the man. Marcelo's most imbecilic comments receive an almost immediate echo of approval from her, and at times I feel afraid that he's simply testing her, trying to define the limits of her affection. I then discover an unprecedented impulse: to defend my mother against the possibility of disillusion. I've never before worried about anything like that: it was always she who was constantly trying to convert me to the hopeful club, with little success. She took me to events organized by her NGO, convinced that when I saw a little suffering my heart, embalmed in cynicism, would soften. She showed me documentaries about famine in Africa.

But with Marcelo, things are different: her personal enthusiasms lie in abeyance while she's laughing at the frigging Spaniard's jokes, as if twenty-five years of academia and social work were not enough to deal with the cover of *Hola!* magazine.

I learn about how they met, without really paying much attention. Something to do with a rough town somewhere in the vicinity, a crummy bar, something about my mom's car breaking down and Marcelo giving her a lift back to Los Girasoles . . . It all sounds as if it's come from a bad novel about drug trafficking. (The reader discovers, some pages in, that she's the head of a "fucking tough" cartel, and by then he, the professor of philosophy, has already become trapped in her web of corruption and deceit.) There's something about the rhetoric of other people's love stories that makes me feel sick, a tendency for bedroom hyperbole that, particularly when it's my mother speaking, gives me the urge to seek out once again that neutral office-worker tone, or death.

9

Cecilia has discovered literature: to my shame, she has bought a horrendous edition of *Jonathan Livingston Seagull*. The book appears to have been designed by a self-help professional: purple borders, title in italics, whimsical shading, and photos modified to look like drawings. In the evenings, she reads a couple of pages while my mom and Marcelo discuss minority rights. Then she gets all grandiloquent, says if you concentrate hard enough, you can dream that you're flying, and that benefits your everyday life. That's what she says to me before we go to sleep; then she has a lime tea (I save the bag) and curls up on one edge of the bed, smiling at the wall.

Inspired by her self-help book, she's also written some roughly heptasyllabic verses. She dedicated them to me, and they were about roses. I couldn't actually say it straight out, but instead formulated an unspoken warning: Love me any way you will, except in outmoded stylistic forms.

Cecilia now tells me things about her childhood. She hasn't said so, but everything indicates that an uncle or godparent tried to rape her when she was seven. At least I think that is what she's insinuating; she says, for example, that the bastard gave her photos of little girls like her. The story is dark and makes me shiver, but Cecilia relates it all calmly. I attribute the ease with which she addresses the subject of abuse to her economic background: there are atrocities that are never questioned in low-income families (nor in the ultra-high ones, of course; the middle class has a monopoly on scandal). She also tells me, for example, that two of her mother's children died. "One of them was still in her tummy," she says.

One night, I can't sleep. The silence in Los Girasoles is so up front that it wakes me. I look out the window and know I'll be lying there until dawn, listening carefully for some familiar noise: a car engine, a siren, bottles thrown against a wall. But there's no sound. Cecilia is sleeping on the other side of the bed. It irritates me to think that in the other room my mother is lying next to a stranger. That we are two couples, sleeping in two rooms of the same house. Like *acquaintances*. It really irritates me.

I go to the kitchen for a swig of milk. Here the milk comes in glass bottles with labels that are always falling off. And the vegetables have the misshapen, earthy look of healthy things. If I were in my apartment right now, I'd look out at the vacant lot, in search of the complicit hen. There's a street lamp on the opposite sidewalk that shines onto part of the lot below my window. The hen could be there, under the white light, waiting to be abducted or called to heaven.

The milk here is too thick to quench your thirst. All sorts of things here are too thick to quench your thirst. As if an invisible dust comes in from the plains and soaks up the moisture on your tongue, in your throat. When I urinate, it comes out darker than usual. In the city, my urine is almost transparent, unless I drink too much or ingest foodstuffs of an ochre hue or eat beetroot. But here my urine is dark. And so is the night.

I fill a glass with milk and drink it down in one gulp. I hate rustic furniture; to be exact, the pieces of rustic furniture that are always the decorative focus in Adela's houses. As I'm walking back to the bedroom, to try to fall asleep next to Cecilia, I hear a moan in the adjoining room, Adela's—my mother's—bedroom. I think Marcelo must be mounting her. That he'll be emptying into her a milk as thick as the brand they buy and that it's one of the worst conceivable drinks in terms of its thirst-quenching properties. I can't help it: I stop by the door of that room, even though I know anything I hear may perturb me. In a certain sense, I'm seeking out perturbation, as a strange confirmation that I'm human, the son of her, my mother.

Inside the room, the mattress is wheezing like a child on the verge of an asthma attack. They'll have to take it to hospital, I think. They'll have to give it an intravenous shot of Salbutamol. But the mattress suddenly becomes silent and then starts again, breathing slowly and monotonously now, like a swimmer doing the crawl. Every fourth stroke, the twisted mouth surfaces on the right-hand side, just under the armpit, and the swimmer inhales. Then the face goes under again. The hand cuts into the water like a knife and then turns to push the liquid down toward the feet. And then another inhalation. When the face comes out of the water, or rather when one side of the face comes out, the swimmer hears, for a moment, the surrounding hullabaloo: people cheering him, on-your-marks whistles, the splashing of his own legs, and the noise of his body in friction with the water and, above all, the noise of his own respiration, of his mouthful of air, which, when he puts his head down again, is immediately silenced. That's more or less what a swimmer doing the crawl sounds like. And that is also how the inside of my mother's room sounds, though perhaps with fewer competitive elements (there are no whistles, or people cheering Marcelo as he mounts her). I think they could go on like that all night. All week. Cecilia will wake up; she'll say she dreamed she was flying, and my mom and Marcelo will still be swimming.

I feel a strange pain in the pit of my stomach. I stop myself from hearing all this by going into the bathroom, which is right between the two bedrooms (between hers–my mother's–where they're swimming, and mine, which isn't mine, or only in a provisional sense until we–Cecilia and I–return to our apartment by the vacant lot). I turn on the light and sit on the toilet seat with my head between my knees and my arms pressed tightly into my abdomen. The pain is still there, and now it's throbbing. It throbs, and I feel as if my esophagus is filling with blood, feel the taste of metal rising up my gullet. I kneel down by the toilet, hug it like a pre-Columbian idol, and vomit into the bowl. After the couple of rather loud bouts of retching have worn off, I let a thread of spittle that seems endless fall from my mouth. I think I have an enormous coil of spittle in my belly that is unwinding very, very slowly. It's the milk from the glass bottle, the thick milk. It was the milk that caused me to vomit, and it's still there in my body in the form of an endless thread of spittle. Now I'll have to stay here the whole night, like a beast bleeding to death, facedown.

But no, someone is knocking on the bathroom door, and I have to cut the thread of spittle with my own fingers, leaving everything that has still to come out in my stomach. "Just a moment," I say. From outside, Marcelo's voice asks if I need any help. As if.

I open the door and sit on the toilet seat, doubled over, hands pressed to my belly. He says the noise woke him. I know that's not true, that he was swimming with my mother or rocking the child on the verge of an asthma attack–the aged mattress. I know he was coming in her, spilling his endless thread of thick, milky spunk while I was vomiting something similar. Anyway, I apologize for having woken him. "No problem," he says, "I was worried." Why was he worried? Has my mom told him I'm a worrier? That I'm weak and have a natural tendency to feel fucked up? That she *worries* about me? That everyone around me ends up entering into a relationship based on worry, their worries about me but also, to a lesser degree, the worry other people make me feel about myself?

"Nothing serious. I'm not used to farm milk. It's coming up." Marcelo's facial muscles tense almost imperceptibly at the sound of the word *coming*, which I pronounce with a particular emphasis. Now he knows I know he was swimming with her. He knows I heard him, or thinks I saw him, rocking the child on the verge of an asthma attack and then starting his race, which–from the sound–seemed less a speed race than a test of stamina, like swimming the English Channel, or with a rope tied around your waist so you have no possibility of advancing; the thing is that I heard him swimming–and he knows it–on Adela, she underneath him, raising his head to breathe on one side of my mother, of Adela.

From now on, he'll have to look at me the way you look at someone you've seen defecating–that obvious mixture of intimacy and denial.

---------------------------------- **10** ----------------------------------

Cecilia did indeed dream that she was flying, or that's what she says. So I say that I dreamed I was swimming in a pool filled with milk; the image inspires me, and I amuse myself by telling her the particulars of my fictional dream. Around the pool, I say, there was a forest littered with trash, and while I was swimming–with my eyes closed–I *knew* a lot of people were watching me from the side. Eventually, I got out of the pool, shivering, and saw Isabel Watkins, Marcelo, my mom, and her, Cecilia, standing there. Endless threads of milk were streaming from my torso and head, and everyone else was smiling, as if approving my performance. Then I looked behind me, and on the other side of the pool of milk, an asthmatic child was wheezing, making a horrible noise. The child was very dark-skinned, in strong contrast to the pool, which looked more like it was filled with almond milk than the bovine variety, now that I come to think of it. No one seemed to notice the dark, disturbing presence of the asthmatic child, and they continued to applaud my prowess as a milk swimmer. Angst was taking hold of me, and I dived into the pool, swam across it, and got out on the other side, ready to assist the asthmatic child. But the child wasn't there, and there was no one back on the other side either: not Cecilia, my mom, Marcelo, or anyone else. I was alone, without a towel, next to the milk pool. I got back into the white liquid. Then the milk began to thicken, and it was increasingly difficult to do the arm and leg strokes. The milk got thicker, and the pool was somehow involving me in an abduction phenomenon—I put it that way, "abduction phenomenon," because Cecilia knows the term and always uses it when she wants to express actions that are beyond human understanding, though it's not particularly appropriate—until I gave up swimming and let myself be pulled to the bottom.

Cecilia is powerfully impressed by my fictional dream. She anxiously tells me I have to concentrate every night and think of positive things ("Like your pets when you were small," she explains), and that once inside the dream, I have to try to look at my hands. She also says she'll get a book on oneiromancy—she doesn't use that word—to see what the swimming pool filled with milk means.

There's something satisfying about lying to Cecilia, even when it's just innocuous lies like that. She never doubts what anyone says or compares the information she receives with the facts. I could swear to her that I'd walked on water and she would end up accepting it. I believe that, in part, I like lying to her because I envy that capacity of hers for taking things on board as if they were true. I, in contrast, harbor an innate distrust of almost everything, and although until lately I thought that made me a more intelligent person, I'm beginning to suspect it only makes me a more nervous one.

Anyway, I have to take full advantage of this ordinary pleasure, I tell myself, the pleasure of lying to Cecilia. There are few things that make my day: devising arbitrary collections, righting wrongs related to turds on bedspreads, pampering hens. The few ritornellos in my character that make me different from other men while simultaneously destroying me, in the way a drop of water repeatedly hitting a stone gives it a unique shape, while also producing or accelerating its ultimate eradication.

Marcelo has been distant the whole day, ever since I heard him swimming with–or on–my mother last night. He hasn't tried to convince me of the virtues of vegetarianism nor the need to reevaluate Epicurus. He made no effort to display his exaggerated friendliness while we were eating. He's been sitting in the living room, scarcely moving, turning the pages of a book with a boxer on the front cover. I discover that I actually find his silence and distance less tolerable than his love for being friendly, though this is probably because the reasons for his silence and the reasons for his distance–which are the same reasons–have to do with the fact that I heard him swimming on–or with–my mother. All things considered, it's my fault, and being guilty is like having vanilla ice cream in your pants pocket: you can pretend it doesn't exist, but sooner or later it will melt and make you feel uncomfortable, and the stain will be there for all to see.

Out of politeness, but also out of guilt, I go up to Marcelo, who is, as I said, sitting quietly in the living room, and ask him about the person on the front cover of the book, who seems to me to be French due to the simple fact that the book itself, its title, is in that language, which doesn't really mean anything. (There are books about Pancho Villa in French, for example.) Marcelo stops reading for a moment and looks at the cover of the book, the stony or deranged–it seems to me–expression of the Frenchman who might well not be French. "It's Richard Foret," he says, "taken in 1916, two years before his death. He was mad," and Marcelo's tone when saying this is also, in some way, the tone of a madman, of a person whose contact with the rest of the human race has been destroyed by a terrible event or idea. But then Marcelo suddenly changes his tone and goes back to being the sane (perhaps too sane) person who tries to convince me of the advantages of vegetarianism and the need to reevaluate Epicurus and says, "My research is on him; it was because of him that I came to Mexico, in the beginning," and on stressing the "in the beginning," he is alluding, it seems to me, to the less obvious reasons for his Mexican expedition, maybe reasons like meeting Adela–though he couldn't have known about that in advance–or generally meeting someone who would make him feel alive and swimming again.

"And what have you researched so far? Have you discovered anything yet?" I ask him with a touch of spite, as I know that the sort of research a professor of aesthetics does rarely translates to "discoveries"; they only interpret and offer opinions based on a greater or lesser knowledge of the topic, always taking the opportunity to discredit the interpretations and opinions of others. Marcelo then tells me that he's hardly done anything yet, that he'll have to spend some time in Mexico City, or even Monterrey, or the port of Veracruz, all places Foret passed through, he says, before disappearing without a trace from the face of the Earth–that's how he puts it, as if we were in a bad movie. I'll have to find some unpublished letters, says Marcelo (to my surprise, since it contradicts my prejudices about his kind of research), letters written by Foret from Mexico City and never sent to his wife, Bea Langley, who was waiting for him in Buenos Aires, or replies from Bea; she must surely have written to him from Buenos Aires to plan the details of their life together, to say "I'm pregnant, Richard. You're going to be a father"; to say that Duchamp–as she had discovered in a letter from Picabia–was also planning to come to Buenos Aires for a while. Marcelo insists that he'll have to find all those undiscovered documents to work out the reasons for Foret's madness and disappearance, though it seems increasingly clear, he adds, that there are no reasons for madness, but possibly accomplices: silences or landscapes or people who accompany it, who create a favorable environment for it to blossom and regularly water its monstrous flower. I tell him I've heard of Richard Foret–what I really want to say is, "I'm not illiterate"–but have never read him, or don't remember reading him, which is true. And Marcelo, for the first time since I met him, with a degree of sincerity that damages his image, tells me that he hasn't read him either, or has read very little and, what's more, has hardly understood anything of what he's read, but that for some reason, independent of his–Marcelo's–inability to read him or his–Richard Foret's–inability to be read, he is obsessed with him, or was obsessed with him when it came to choosing a topic and location for his research during his sabbatical year; now he's not so sure that he's still obsessed. There's a tinge of sadness in his voice, as if losing obsessions or interests also involved becoming detached from an important part of oneself (not from an arm but maybe a little finger), an irretrievable part. And all of a sudden I feel empathy with Marcelo, and sympathy, and a willingness to live for a while with that Spanish professor who swims the crawl with my mother, and also with that boxer on the cover of the book, who was an obsession of his (Marcelo's) and then stopped being one. My obsessions, though more enduring than Marcelo's, have something unknowable about them; they rest on a foundation of impossibility that, when it becomes apparent, leaves me prostrate and exhausted, as if things tire me more when they don't come to fruition, when they abandon me before their due time.

I wonder if I should tell him, tell Marcelo, something about the vacant lot, or about the tea bags, or the hen, or the perfect turd that appeared one day (that seems long ago) on Ceci's bedspread. Tell him I'm also undertaking aesthetic research, or not aesthetic but simply related to life, research that concerns the warp and weft of existence. And I'm also abandoning it (or it's abandoning me; I'm not sure), and I feel tired and betrayed, with no inducement to continue living. But it's probably too much, telling him all that; we probably haven't reached that point. We don't know each other well enough, and Marcelo prefers to go on being the guy who does the crawl on my mother and just wants me to be the on-loan son he has to worry about, the son he has to accompany in the early hours while he vomits or expels an endless thread of thick milk, hugging the toilet bowl, the sacrificial stone that has never, in fact, been anything but a toilet bowl. Most probably Marcelo couldn't care less that I became obsessed and then stopped being obsessed by a hen, a vacant lot and a turd. And he certainly couldn't care less that I have a pornographic photo from the eighties in my wallet, and particularly that, before my marriage, it was my custom—not completely voluntary—to masturbate twice on Saturdays. Who would be interested in all that? And how, above all, could it interest someone who has such a high opinion of himself? And Marcelo has a high opinion of himself.

Most probably I won't reveal my secrets to him. And he'll take up his book by Foret—or is it *about* Foret?—even though he's not obsessed with him, and will finish his research—without going to

Mexico City or Monterrey or the port of Veracruz–in this lost town of Los Girasoles, living with Adela and mounting her, swimming with her every night, until the end of his existence.

— 11 —

The holidays are almost over. We celebrated Christmas without too much fuss: a turkey and salads that we bought from a small restaurant in Los Girasoles; a good provision of wines, chosen by Marcelo, who thinks himself a connoisseur (in the supermarket checkout line, he told us the story of a wine grape the Chileans had stolen from the French–or vice versa, I can't remember which–in addition, naturally, to having previously paused to consider the good qualities of each bottle before putting it in the trolley); and a rather unenthusiastic exchange of presents. Cecilia gave me the book on oneiromancy she had promised to buy. We, Cecilia and I, gave Marcelo a fountain pen like the ones Ms. Watkins uses (though surely less expensive) and my mother an elegantly indigenous shawl.

The day after tomorrow will be New Year's Eve, and after that we'll have to return to DF. I'll have to return to my–aesthetic?–research on the origin of the turd on the bedspread, and Cecilia will return to her full-time job at the museum, where perhaps some colleague will leave a scrap of paper on her desk and propose matrimony, and quickly take her from me. Return to DF, and its cruelty.

An alternative occurs to me: to stay here for at least a week longer, without the yoke of marital companionship and with my mother and Marcelo working all day at the university. Then I could spend my time walking around the four bearable streets of the town and striking up rural friendships with some of the locals (friendships, for example, based on whistling from one side of the square to the other, and the ambiguous gesture of raising a hand to the crown of a straw hat).

Returning to the city right now seems to me a rather unattractive option. If I at least had a tyrannical routine to go back to, everything would take on meaning, but what I'll be returning to is the uncertainty of having no job and the uneventful days steeped in idleness; days that are empty, like a Chinese fortune cookie they've forgotten to put a message in, leaving you with the twofold sensation that you have no future and that you've just eaten a capsule of air, of nothing, of antimatter.

No, I have to stay here, in Los Girasoles, or even venture to some other place. Cross to the United States undocumented and send remittances to Cecilia while I break my back picking strawberries, or move to a neighboring town and join one of the local cartels, or set up an innovative business right here and squeeze out the salaries and bonuses from the professors at the University of Los Girasoles (squeeze out, for example, the bonuses Marcelo and Adela, my mother and Marcelo, receive). But any one of those alternatives would require an exhausting deployment of ingenuity, and for the moment I'd prefer to sleep in late and walk in my underwear to the kitchen to drink—straight from the bottle—a swig of thick, repulsive milk. So, I'll stay here alone in Los Girasoles, if I can manage to convince Cecilia that this is best for us both (I'll have to invent something, which will give me an extra satisfaction; I like telling her lies), and that it doesn't mean I'm going to leave her for good. (In the family setting she comes from, if the husband sleeps away from the marriage bed for more that two nights, the most likely explanation is that he already has another life—wife included—at the opposite end of the very same street.)

So I talk to her. I ask her to sit down when Marcelo and my mom have gone over to Marcelo's horrible apartment to see how it all is and, one imagines, to play at swimming together on another mattress filled with asthmatic children. I tell her—Cecilia—to sit down, and she goes slightly pale since never before, I believe, have I threatened to talk seriously with her about something, about anything; all our previous conversations have been uninspiring, or at least have not required such a sensationalist gesture as asking her to sit down. In fact, I don't think I've ever asked anyone to sit down before, I've only seen it done in movies, where they always ask a person to sit down when they're about to give him a piece of news that could throw him. (If you fall from a sitting position, it hurts less or

does less harm than if you fall from a completely upright position,
which is why people prefer to sit down before hearing something
that could precipitate a fall; I suppose, I imagine, I guess.)

Cecilia sits down next to me in the living room and asks, with a
twinkle in her eye, if I've succeeded in flying in my dreams.

"No," I say, "I want to talk to you about something else. I'm
going to stay here in Los Girasoles for a few days longer. Marcelo
tells me a friend of his at the university needs someone to copyedit a
book he's written so that it sounds less academic and he can send it
to a publisher in the real world. I could do it from home, but I need
to talk to him first, when the new term starts." I know I'm touching a
sensitive spot: she might have read *Jonathan Livingston Seagull* and
now professes a blind, arbitrary faith in the power of dreams and
other shit like that, but what really concerns Cecilia is the issue of
my unemployment, and only a promise of work would convince her
it's necessary for me to stay, even if doing so feeds her most deep-
rooted fears. The story about Marcelo's friend comes to me on the
spur of the moment, and I don't stop to consider before opening
my mouth that I'll probably have to ask him–Marcelo–to back me
up in public, which clearly implies that my mother will find out
about it, and I'll have to decide whether or not we should make her
party to the lie or keep her out of it. The best thing, I think, will be
to keep her–my mother–out of it and convince Marcelo to maintain
the pretense in front of the two of them, Cecilia and Adela, my wife
and my mother.

I also tell myself that while the lie only justifies a brief delay in
my return to DF, a delay of at most one or maybe two weeks, I can
always invent, on the hoof, lies that function as extensions, lies that
get tangled together and follow each other like the stories in the
Thousand and One Nights and put off–as in the *Ibidem*–the fatal
moment, the moment of my return to a gray life, to the unbearable
loneliness of marriage, which is more lonely than all other forms
of loneliness, than sane, effective lonelinesses: the loneliness of the
desert, of the widower, the loneliness of men who live surrounded
by cats; marital loneliness is, I insist, more lonely than all the above
because it imposes the necessity of being other, even in the sacred
space of the shower, where you have to go on pretending that

you are like this or like that, are interested in this or that detail of shared life, pretend that progress and the feasibility of a savings plan, the eradication of the damp in the living room walls, the advisability–or otherwise–of getting cable television, really matter. And in contrast, in this modality of simulations, what is impossible, or at least not to be recommended, is the public acceptance of our fallibility, of our devotion to collecting, of our miniature versions of the eternal return of the same that make up the course of the weeks: the contemplation of a vacant lot; the speculation about the way of life of a feathered animal that can't, however, fly; the particular abnormality of the gland of eroticism that makes us masturbate twice, thinking monstrous things, every Saturday.

So I talk to her, to Cecilia. I ask her to sit down, and she does, and I tell her what I've outlined above: the lie about the possible job and the promise of a financial recompense not to be disdained. I round off the story with an homage to us, to us as a couple, appealing to her recently discovered interest in self-help–about how good it is that we can communicate our needs and understand that temporary separation, that state of being alone, doesn't mean we aren't together on a deeper plane. Finally, and maybe going slightly over the top, I tell her we can try hard to dream of each other every night, and that in the dreams we have together, we'll be closer than anywhere else since we'll fly hand in hand over the tops of scented pine trees, and won't have to worry about anything except meeting with voracious dragons or other predators of the oneiric skies.

A little confused, Cecilia agrees to my proposal. At the beginning of my soliloquy, when I was talking about practical matters, she seemed slightly distrustful or sad, and then, as I insisted on the importance of finding a job, even if it wasn't permanent, a smile appeared on her face, and I understood (or intuited, or invented for myself) the idea that she was thinking of her dad, my father-in-law, and in the restored pride of being able to say to him that I'm a good man, and that I'm saving again for that property, the promise of which gained me her hand and her sham virginity. Finally, when the story goes off on a transcendental tack, and I talk about abstractions and the subterranean feelings that unite us, Cecilia looks serious (about the abstractions and subterranean feelings, not the rest), gently frowning and not looking me in the eyes–like when you're making small talk with another human being–but an inch or so, or maybe less, to the right, as if she can't focus or is contemplating, beyond my face, the landscape of scented pine trees and the tremendous battles we'll fight against oneiric, aerial dragons on the symbolic plane.

And Cecilia says yes, I should stay to see what happens with Marcelo's friend, and she will drive the red car back by the same route and return, as is her duty, to the apartment next to the vacant lot, and the museum, to complete her tasks as an efficient secretary, no longer the frustrated pain in the ass she was with me when we were colleagues, but finally kind and docile and married and relatively happy with her life, even if her husband tells lies–she knows, deep down, that he does–and now has neither a job nor the least scrap of enthusiasm, and doesn't even join her in the marital bed to consider their future options. Well, she doesn't say that, but Cecilia does say yes, I should stay to see what happens with Marcelo's friend, and she'll drive the car back, and I can catch up with her again, as soon possible, in Mexico City. And that's it; we don't say another word, just switch on the television (my mom does have cable) and watch an entertaining documentary on the secret life of snakes, and I think that the secret life of snakes is their whole life, not just some aspect or moment of the night or a recurrent dark thought–as is so often the case for human beings–but all their life: from the moment they wake up until they succeed in swallowing a field rat whole, and also when they shed their skin, slithering out of themselves. I don't say anything to Cecilia about all this, not, of course, because I'm in an uncommunicative mood–I am–but because I think she has already had enough with all the stuff about flying together and dream dragons chasing us. You could say I believe Cecilia has, for today, heard enough of my thoughts on reptiles–even if they are oneiric–and now, on the screen, snakes are secretly slithering out of themselves and secretly watching their prey and finally, secretly, snaking between the plants, so there's no need to harp on the topic. Sometimes, even when you're in a communicative mood, you have to leave things unsaid, keep the words–secretly–to yourself and trust that the people around you are thinking the same things, or something similar, and trust in the possibility of a silent empathy, an empathy related most specifically to space, to the possibility of sharing a space and inhabiting it at a given moment in history, which, in the case of Cecilia and I, is this one: this given moment in history.

------------------------------ **12** ------------------------------

I thought talking to Marcelo would be more difficult. I had, perhaps, too blind or too naïve a faith in his moral integrity. I thought that lying, the very idea of lying, would be not only alien to him but also reprehensible. That he would feel a sort of congenital disgust at lying in the abstract and, therefore, an acquired disgust at my concrete lie. My lie demanded a degree of complicity on his part that I now regret, because the complicity hatched in lying is always more powerful than the complicity hatched in the bright light of truth, in the same way that wicker woven underwater is hardier than wicker worked beneath an unforgiving sun. It's the same for everything; it's said, for example, that there is no friendship more enduring than that formed in prison, or at least when turning a blind eye to legality and consensus. And neither is there a more solid love than the one that is persecuted, or rather that would be hunted down and punished if its existence were known, so forcing the parties in question to lie habitually. Secrets and lies unite one man with another, and one man with himself, and perhaps they also unite snakes, whose secret lives are intensely secret and so must be more united than any other being under the light of the moon.

That's the way it was with Marcelo. Almost immediately we passed from a cordial, if tense, relationship to becoming conspirators as soon as he'd agreed to participate in the game of my duplicity. He was fascinated by the idea. I didn't have to go into details as he said he would take care of everything. That the professor implicated in the story, Velásquez, was in fact a friend of his for whom my mother felt a hyperbolic aversion. She would never ask him any questions since she couldn't bear his presence or to hear news that involved him, even in a secondary role. Marcelo also arranged the matter of the possible extension of my visit: if I wanted to stay for a while longer, I only had to say I was going through certain aspects of the document I felt unsure about with Professor Velásquez. That instead of merely correcting copy, I'd become an authentic, fully fledged, personal editor, and that word had spread like dust in the aesthetics department, and there were already other researchers ready to put their books, their theses, their articles into my blessed hands.

I told Marcelo we should think it over, that it all sounded too complicated, and that for the time being I only needed the first excuse, the one I'd broadly outlined and he'd refined with a skill that revealed—against all expectations—a habit of lying, and even a perverse delight in doing so. As a coda to our conversation, Marcelo said that if I got fed up with living at my mom's house, I could spend a few days at his place in the residential estate of Puerta del Aire. It wasn't particularly pleasant, he said, or close to the center of town, but if what I needed was to be alone and think my own thoughts, it was a good spot with no distractions. I didn't know if he was proposing this because he'd realized that our shared lie would oblige him to live with me for a longer period and, hence, be a little discreet about his sexual relations, or because he genuinely wanted me to attain spiritual maturity through living ascetically; my guess is that it had more to do with the former. In any case, I decided to take him at his word later on, not because I thought any good would come from staying in Puerta del Aire, but because I took pity on him and imagined that neither he nor my mother would want me vomiting up her thick milk every night for much longer.

The whole conversation took place in the street while Marcelo and I were walking to the store, at Adela's request, to buy some things we needed for the New Year's Eve dinner. I explained to him that I'd already told Cecilia the lie, so all that was needed to put the plan into action was to tell it to my mother when we got back. On January 2, Cecilia would get into the red car and travel, in the reverse direction, the highway that had drawn so many reflections from me on the outbound journey.

13

And so it went: on New Year's Eve we had a meager, vegetarian dinner—Marcelo had complained about the Christmas turkey and suggested cooking something without meat. And Cecilia got into the red car and set off back to routine, and my vacation changed from being a temporary, reversible rest to a limbo of idleness, promising great satisfaction, or great disillusion, or simply hours and hours of looking at the wall. And my mom returned to her university work, which didn't take up too much of her time, and Marcelo went back to his small office at the university and spoke to Velásquez and told him about our lie, hatched from his supposed book. And I woke up alone in the morning in Adela's house without having heard anything too upsetting in the night—no swimming contest, no asthmatic child—and sat by the cactus garden and felt myself to be a little freer, a little lonelier, and a little older, in the venerable sense of old age, which can, I imagine, be positive, to the extent that it allows you—will allow me, if I get there—to think only about the things each morning offers. In my case, the morning offered me the difficult choice between either staying in my mom's house or moving into Puerta del Aire. But instead of weighing these options, as I would when making a decision during office hours, when one considers the pros and cons and makes a rational decision based on a quantitative calculation—more pros and fewer cons beats fewer pros and more cons—I endeavored to sit silently for a few hours and then suddenly decide one way or the other, basing this decision on, for example, climatic conditions—things related to the moment, which is always unfathomable and irrational. And I wanted it to be the moment, and perhaps the climate—not the climate as a matter of clouds, but something else: the climate defined as the totality of objects that surrounded me, the material climate that is derived or emanates from the harmony and secret communication between inorganic things; objects are traitorous—that would make me suddenly decide to go to Puerta del Aire, to Marcelo's tasteless little house, where, what's more (now come the pros and cons), away from any watchful eye, it would be easier for me to pretend I was copyediting Velásquez's book. And where it would be easier for me, I supposed, to quench my thirst without having recourse to my mother's thick milk, the thick, maternal milk that comes in bottles with the labels falling off. And where, moreover, it would be easier for me to avoid the reasons for my sleeplessness–swimmers doing the crawl, children with asthma–and give free rein to my collector's impulse, which is neither a destructive impulse nor a creative impulse, but simply this: an impulse to accumulate without any great degree of coherence, an impulse to conserve and find a space for the things that already exist, that apparently have always existed.

14

Marcelo rings the doorbell of his own house, in which I've installed myself. The bell emits a shrill, piercing screech that continues going round and round the spiral of my ear long after the external sound has faded, like the way the sea continues to be heard in the spirals of seashells, or so they say. I know it's Marcelo because no one else has rung the doorbell; no one else would, or at least I can't think of anyone who would. I've been here for two days, and no one has rung the doorbell. Just Marcelo, yesterday, who rang and came in to see how things were, to see, I suppose, if I'd destroyed the horrendous furniture or had a problem with the security guard, to whom Marcelo has, apparently, taken a certain dislike. Or it could be that Marcelo came yesterday and, as seems likely from the sound of the doorbell, has come again today because he's genuinely interested in what's happening to me; in what's happening to me inside my head, I mean. This is an option that seems–against the grain of my habitual skepticism in relation to the human species in general–probable, and I say this because yesterday Marcelo sat in the armchair opposite me, in the afternoon, at this hour, after leaving the university, where he'd probably done nothing, or at least nothing of any note, nothing worth mentioning: he didn't mention anything he might have done, or even thought. He sat, as I said, opposite me, in the armchair opposite the armchair where I myself am now sitting, and asked, in a tone of voice new to me—more serious or more sincere, perhaps, if sincerity can be identified in a tone of voice—what I'd been thinking. "What have you been thinking?" he asked, as if he was really interested in what I think, as if I myself was interested in what I think and was capable of retaining and then transmitting it and letting my thought fall into the other person's mind and then germinate, timidly, and grow into a tree, or at least a small plant of thought, of ideas, of communication. Something of that kind, so they say, though using less hackneyed similes, is possible between people, though it's never happened to me.

Marcelo rings the doorbell of his own house, a dwelling that was never, strictly speaking, completely his own since just as soon as he came to Los Girasoles, he says, he realized that renting this glorified apartment (it would be an exaggeration to call it a house) had been a mistake, and it was perhaps for that reason he had sought, or at least opened himself to the possibility of, a love affair, of being infatuated by a local, or reasonably local woman like my mother, who wasn't born in this town but has lived here for some years—I've forgotten how many—and, in any case, is more local than Marcelo since she is at least from this country. Marcelo rings the doorbell of his glorified apartment and, hearing the bell, I realize his glorified apartment is, in fact, after only a few days, my glorified apartment. And I say that it is, in fact, mine because I have a proverbial ability for setting up home, for occupying a space in a human, cultural way, for impregnating the space with the smell of my actions, which don't need too much repetition to become everyday actions—it's enough for me to do the same thing twice, on two successive days, for it to become a ritual, identifiable activity, my way of inhabiting that portion of air in this house in Puerta del Aire, which is the not unpoetic name with which they christened this awful, soulless residential estate. But the glorified apartment is not only mine in the, let's say, *intangible* sense of my having actively appropriated its space but also in the, let's call it *tangible* sense of having placed in that space a series of objects (not many) that indicate an organizing mind different from Marcelo's—objects are traitorous. There are, for example, some pieces of volcanic, or at least porous—I know nothing about geology—rock that I found in the sun-scorched streets of Puerta del Aire. Pieces of rock that I liked, I'm not quite sure why, and brought here and distributed around the apartment in an order that could be described as random, though is, in some way, comforting: I am comforted by the visual continuity the pieces of rock confer on the whole house–they are, you could say, its decorative focus.

Marcelo rings the doorbell of his own–my own–glorified apartment, and I get up from the armchair and open the door, which he himself could have opened since he has keys, but which, I guess, he prefers not to open out of respect for my privacy. I open the door, and he comes in and sits in the armchair opposite the one in which I was sitting–I think he must have noticed a sign, the depression left by my weight on one of the armchairs, and for that reason sat in the other one: objects are traitorous–after, naturally, greeting me in a slightly chilly way, the way Europeans do. (But, I ask myself, have I ever in my life greeted any other European person?) And having installed himself in the opposite armchair, he asks what I've been thinking, as he did yesterday, as I suspect he will do tomorrow, as I hope he will continue to do for some time (the time I'm here, in his glorified apartment, for example, or the time our relationship lasts, which can't be forever, I tell myself: nothing is), because I like the idea of someone asking me fairly regularly what I've been thinking–it's never happened before–although I'm not sure if I have today, in contrast to yesterday, anything to tell him.

Marcelo sits in the opposite armchair and asks me what I've been thinking–"What have you been thinking?" he asks–and in his tone I once again note a tinge of sincerity, or at least a consideration for his fellow man I hadn't thought him capable of. A sincerity or consideration I hadn't, in fact, thought any of my fellow men capable of, since not one of them had ever before made the effort to ask me what I was thinking, unless my thoughts had immediate–real and verifiable–repercussions in his own life: people are, in the end, a bit egoistical. Marcelo is also a bit egoistical, like other people, but apparently he is, in addition, a fellow man, in the sense explained above: he's interested in my thoughts. (Oh, fellow men, sailing around under the flag of egoism so they won't be noticed in the busy crowds; fellow men walking hurriedly out of the metro station, or serving coffee in a greasy café in the downtown of an enormous city, or working in offices and bothering you with all kinds of stupid stuff so you don't know they are fellow men, so you think they are *people,* or even *frigging people:* the frigging people who bother you and plague you and aren't interested in what you're thinking; but they don't fool me, I've got it straight now: everything is full of fellow men; you drop your guard or get distracted, and fellow men come out from under a stone; even a piece of volcanic, or at least porous, rock–I know nothing about geology–can have fellow men under it.)

"I've been thinking of my fellow men," I tell Marcelo, and he gives me a strange look, as if saying–thinking, I mean–"This guy's as crazy as a coot" or rather–he's not a local–"This guy's lost his marbles." But I haven't lost my marbles, quite the reverse: I feel sane. Although, of course, you can't trust your own sensations: in their way, lunatics also feel sane; only our fellow men can give us a hint about our own mental health, and if the fellow men are themselves crazy, there's no way of knowing who's the lunatic. It's the same with societies: when the frigging people, all the people, are crazy, the one sane person seems crazy–I think, for example, of the Nazis and those who opposed them.

Marcelo says, "You mean you've been thinking about your fellow *man,* don't you? It's really an abstract category: there are *people* in the plural, but your fellow man is uncountable . . ."

How to tell Marcelo he is fundamentally wrong, and with him all of Christendom?

15

Cecilia calls me on my cell phone in the evenings, just around sundown. My cell phone only has reception at the front door of the glorified apartment (it's an exaggeration to call it a house), as if on crossing the threshold you were entering hallowed ground, a sort of temple with horrible armchairs, in which it is no longer necessary to communicate, or in which any possible form of communication

depends on the telepathic abilities of the tenant, which is me. I don't
have telepathic abilities, or I haven't developed them or been shown
how to, so in the evenings, when I see nightfall coming on–the air
cools, the dust settles–I sit on the front steps with the door open and
put the cell phone down beside me, waiting for Cecilia to call and
entertain me with the tangled narrative of her day. She is, in some
sense I can't quite put my finger on, let's say a postmodern narrator.
She tells me about the museum, about Ms. Watkins's latest uncalled-
for remarks, about Ms. Watkins's latest lovers, and about the latest
arguments she's had with Ms. Watkins. (Offices are like monarchies;
that's why if anyone starts to go mad–even subtly–in an office, their
whole conversation becomes centered on the words and actions of
the monarch. His, or in this case, her, presence then threatens to
overwhelm everything else: the monarch is behind every conversation, like an internal enemy, and his, or in this case, her, recurrence
in the sphere of ideas harms the enraptured person and his family.
He, or in this case, she, is included in every topic, if only remotely.
The possibility of being fired writhes like an overexcited boa con-
strictor in the subconscious of each and every subject, and when one
of them breaks–when one of them, due to personal circumstances,
collapses–that possibility seems to announce itself in innumerable
ways, and its asphyxiating form begins to tighten its hold on the body
of the hireling. When this person finally senses the inescapable grip
of the snake, the boa stops; the possibility of dismissal is dimmed
and retracts or lies still, as if tamed; then and only then can it be
said that the office has matured inside the hireling. Then and only
then can the monarch feel satisfied, and go out for breakfasts that
last the whole day without fear of a possible riot or an act of irrever-
ence in his, or in this case, her, realm. Cecilia, unfortunately, is that
unhinged element in the office toward whom Ms. Watkins seems to
have directed her entire constrictive potential.)

   So here I am sitting on the front steps, waiting for Cecilia to call
and tell me more details of the life of Ms. Watkins, the sovereign
of that office in which, until not long ago, I acted as a tame knowledge administrator. And in a certain sense, although I hate those
conversations, I'm also grateful for them, because hearing about
Ms. Watkins reminds me of my office days, and when I remember

them, I can perceive the at times elusive continuity of my existence: I see myself as a person to whom things happen, and not as two or more unconnected guys who only share a name and a certain speculative propensity.

But Cecilia doesn't call this evening. And night falls slowly as I watch the paving stones soften, or so it seems to me. When I'm at the point of giving up, of going inside and assuming Cecilia isn't going to call today, the security guard of the Puerta del Aire residential estate appears at the end of the street, walking with a confident, strangely rhythmic step. He has the military air that in this country forms a halo around anyone in uniform, making him a potential son of a bitch. The pistol at his waist gleams for an instant when he passes through the milky light of a buzzing street lamp surrounded by moths. The guard walks toward me, and although the light is now behind him, making it impossible to see his face, I suspect he's looking at me, assessing my expression and posture in case it's necessary to eradicate me. (*Eradicate* is a word the uniforms use to try to professionalize their most audacious thoughts.) But he doesn't eradicate me. He walks up, and I raise my eyes, slightly intimidated.

"Everything all right, young man?" he asks. I know it's a rhetorical question, that he couldn't, in fact, give a fuck whether or not everything is all right; he just wants to chat for a while or show me he's doing his job properly. The double standards of security guards: they want you to know they have power, but they can't suppress that sense of inferiority, that inevitably servile attitude against which their spirits struggle, with high-handedness being the outcome of that struggle.

He introduces himself as Jacinto Nogales Pedrosa ("at your service," he adds). I introduce myself as Rodrigo Saldívar, honoring my elusive dad and the–also elusive–truth. He tells me there have been "incidents" in the area during the last few nights and that I should be careful. He's a good sort, I think. Though I understand why Marcelo might warn me about him: his personality is ambiguous, maybe too ambiguous for an outsider to understand. Even for me, his ambiguity is disturbing. Only provincial people can tolerate such a high dose of ambiguity without feeling themselves in the presence of the unspeakable.

We chat for a while. His speech alternates with pauses so long that at times I believe our conversation is definitively over. But he goes on. And he goes on saying things that don't necessarily have anything to do with what we're talking about, or don't have anything to do with it at first, though later it seems they do, but only in a tangential, elusive, unexpected way. He asks me, for example, about the phone I'm holding, about the brand, its quality, and so on. I briefly explain it's a simple cell phone with good reception. We say nothing for quite a while, and when he speaks again it is to describe his wife. He tells me she's good-looking, with a beauty spot on her face. He tells me she's a mute, a deaf-mute. Then he talks about his children, who are not deaf-mutes, and finally he returns to the topic of the phone, of how he lost his–the reason: he never used it because his wife is a deaf-mute. Stories that bite their tails, or at least chase their own shadows. Bite their own shadows.

Jacinto continues on his rounds, and I go back inside the house. Why don't I call Cecilia? Maybe she fell asleep before the time we had tacitly agreed on. Or had gone to see her parents and would return later. Or she had to stay a couple of hours late in the museum due to some sudden whim of Ms. Watkins. I'll call her tomorrow, I think. And I think that I like talking to her, even if we have little to say to each other. Even if we only talk about Ms. Watkins, and the damp, and how I'm doing with my nonexistent task. At least she's not a deaf-mute.

--- **16** ---

Discovering conversation, the possibility of a real exchange, is a rare event. In general, we proceed without bothering about what those around us understand or fail to understand, and have recourse to language for simply practical matters, to come to an agreement. Conversation, in contrast, forms the basis of a dialect as it unfolds. Conversationalists weave a language of their own, constructed from winks and inferences and keywords, in which words don't mean what they mean, or always mean a little more than they mean, in a warped, unpredictable way. In the context of complicity, conversations proliferate like climbing plants covering the castle of language, reinvigorating it, negating the aridity of the brutal stone. The layers of conversation are multiple. It often happens that a word stops meaning the thing enunciated and begins to mean another word that in turn can indicate another, and in this way, ad infinitum, the words in the conversation refer to themselves and multiply like a hen in a hall of mirrors.

Marcelo sits down in the opposite armchair and tells me my mother is worried about me. Not only because I haven't submissively become a member of the academic community, a topic she is completely incapable of dropping, but also because she suspects I'm going mad. Marcelo says my mother says that I said something very strange to her about poo when she called the other day at seven in the morning and woke me from a deep sleep. I laugh.

"I might have," I say, "but at that hour, we're all mental cases. What's odd is that I never said anything about shit on any one of the thousands of days she woke me up for school."

Marcelo laughs. He tells me that when he was a child, he was sent to a camp in Extremadura every summer, a camp run by nuns on a high yellowish plain, with temperatures reaching 140 degrees Fahrenheit, where they supposedly taught the children to speak English. One year, he had to share a bunk with a boy around fourteen years old, from Galicia, who walked and talked in his sleep. Marcelo had the top bunk and the boy was in the bottom one, so the Galician's soliloquies ascended during the night and filtered through Marcelo's mattress, keeping him awake. Unable to sleep, Marcelo decided to note down the things his bunkmate said. He tells me he still has those childhood scribblings. He has them in a very handsome notebook with a black cover, a brand you can no longer get in Madrid. (Marcelo digresses here; I force him to return to the anecdote.) Mostly the Galician boy sleep-talked about shit (that's why he recalled the event). In an anguished voice, he said things like, "No, that shit's not mine, honest!" And then he also talked a lot about cars: he recited the makes and models of the cars of the day, listed their characteristics, criticized their weak points. Marcelo's anecdote once again faded into unedifying details, and I stopped paying attention. I was left with the first part: a sleepwalker who talks about shit. A sleepwalker who dissociates himself from his shit. He must have been someone like that person who came into my bedroom in DF and shat on the tiger-striped bedspread.

Marcelo suggests that I come back with him for dinner. He says that my mom—Adela—has arranged to go to a party teeming with resentful female academics, and he's decided to do his own thing. He invites me to this thing. I accept.

IV

THE FUTURE OF ART

Marcelo Valente walked to his car under the unforgiving sun, wading through the cloud of scalding hot, yellow dust raised by the vehicles leaving the university in single file. The professor squinted to prevent being blinded by the dry earth. This being the case, he had difficulty finding the right key for the car. He coughed. In a low voice, employing Castilian idiomatic expressions, he cursed the arid environment and that fine desert dust that floated in the air throughout the University of Los Girasoles, covering the papers on his desk and drying his skin. He finally managed to locate the lock and speedily got into the car, slamming the door behind him before the cloud of dust could enter.

He had arranged to meet Velásquez in a restaurant in the center. It was Friday and no one had to go back to the university in the afternoon, so it would be a long lunch, washed down, no doubt, by plenty of tequila. Velásquez wanted to introduce him to a friend of his, a gringo practitioner of the plastic arts who had set up his ceramic sculpture workshop in an old, half-ruined house in the center of Los Girasoles, and had, in Velásquez's words, "an absolutely visionary artistic project."

That description naturally inspired a justifiable degree of mistrust in Marcelo. In general, Velásquez's recommendations were difficult to take on board. He had once lent him a movie, "an indisputable classic of the Mexican counterculture," that turned out to be one of the worst Marcelo had ever seen: women undressing in trucks with slogans like "Fucking Fast"; pallid vampires sweating out-of-focus; overweight heroes. The visionary gringo artist didn't sound much better, but you never could tell.

They were to meet at the Barraca de Pedro, a restaurant with a simple name but pretensions to haute cuisine, where local dishes were reinvented with a sophistication that, in Marcelo's opinion, removed all their charm. He had been there a couple of times before, first with Adela and then with Velásquez, and on both occasions he had ended up drunk. The array of tequilas, mezcales, aguardientes, and local wines on offer was almost suicidal. The prices were absurdly low.

Marcelo arrived slightly early, at five to three, and was surprised to see Velásquez already installed at a table, laughing uproariously. It was unusual for him to be on time. The gringo was tall, tanned, and too wrinkled for the age that his bearing and presence suggested; he looked as if he had been weathered by small-town life, and his rough-hewn hands did not in the least suggest the delicacy of the pottery he supposedly worked on. He had long, graying hair tied in a ponytail and was wearing a white shirt of some coarse material, with the sleeves rolled up to just below the elbows, faded denim jeans, and snakeskin cowboy boots. He was also laughing, sitting opposite Velásquez and absentmindedly stroking the leg of an adolescent who couldn't be more than eighteen (and that was, in fact, exactly how old she was, as Marcelo would discover a couple of hours later, by then infected with the collective jubilation, taking advantage of the girl's removal to the bathroom to discreetly ask Velásquez her age).

Marcelo introduced himself and shook the rough hand of the gringo, who said his name was Jimmie. He kissed the cold cheek of the adolescent, who didn't say a single word and whom Jimmie introduced as Micaela. When he sat in the only free chair–facing Micaela, on the right of the gringo–he noticed that already waiting for him were a shot of tequila and a cold beer, still misted from the change of temperature after its removal from the fridge, as if they had calculated his arrival to the exact second.

They talked about anything that came to mind as the waiter brought their dishes and placed them in the center of the table, delicacies Velásquez and the gringo ate with their fingers, Marcelo sampled rather ineptly (they were not designed for his strict use of a knife and fork), and Micaela observed with calculated disdain.

Jimmie was from California, from a town an hour from San Francisco that used to be full of manual workers and was now inhabited by Vietnamese immigrants. He had spent his childhood and teenage years in the Bay Area, surrounded by hippies, and told the story of an elder brother who died in the waves after going swimming while high on drugs. Jimmie was ten years older than Marcelo and had done everything: from cycling across the continent to working as a cleaner in the Apple offices in Silicon Valley. He had been living in Los Girasoles for a couple of years, after an argument in San Miguel de Allende with a landlady from New York who had thrown his things out into the street. "Goddamn son-of-a-fucking-bitch gringos," said Jimmie, resentful of his compatriots, like any good Californian.

Marcelo talked about Madrid, about the Movida years, about women. He gave Jimmie a summary of his Mexican trip: the relationship with Adela, the house he had unsuccessfully rented and that was now occupied by Adela's son, his project for a book on Foret's passage through the country. Velásquez intervened with witty, usually misogynist comments while Micaela sat with a rigid smile on her face and occasionally rested her head on Jimmie's shoulder. Marcelo attempted to include the girl in the conversation; he asked her what she did. "I study," she said in a voice that was almost a sigh, and smiled timidly, more for Jimmie than Marcelo.

The afternoon passed quickly, and the lamps of the interior patio of the restaurant illuminated a fountain when darkness finally fell. By this time, Marcelo had developed a tolerance for tequila much greater than he had had on his arrival in Mexico, and he was now able to recognize the moment when the next round would be accompanied by catastrophe. He was far from that point. But not so the gringo, who seemed more affected by the drink, or by life in general. It was he who proposed they move on to his studio, where he kept—he said at the top of his voice—much better tequila than the dog piss they served there. Micaela looked smilingly at him, imperturbable. Marcelo calculated that if the gringo passed out in the restaurant, it would be more complicated to transport him to his bed than if he lost consciousness near that bed, so he seconded the idea of moving on to the studio. He hesitatingly asked Micaela if she needed a ride somewhere else first, but the child shook her head very slowly, swinging her straight black shoulder-length hair, and told Marcelo she lived with Jimmie.

Marcelo offered to drive the five or six blocks that separated the restaurant from Jimmie's house, and they walked unsteadily over to his car. The gringo had begun to lose his fluidity in Spanish and compensated by inserting words in English; Marcelo noticed, by the change in her expression, that Micaela didn't understand that language. It was perhaps for that reason, or simply because of his state of intoxication, that Jimmie passed completely into English and told Velásquez and Marcelo, in an awkward confidence, that he had met Micaela near Nueva Francia; the girl's family was very poor, and she, according to Jimmie, was a brilliant woman, like a Martian, completely unexpected in the familial and social context in which she had been reared. He spoke about her in the way a naturalist would when describing some indigenous flower. Jimmie gave the father five thousand pesos and took the teenager, promising the family they would come back from time to time to visit. "She fucks like an angel," he added, this time in perfectly clear Spanish, to which Micaela reacted by distancing herself slightly.

The studio was an old building, from the same period and in the same style as Adela's house but in much worse condition and a great deal smaller. The paint was peeling from the walls, or they had only been painted in patches, and in the kitchen the original roof had been replaced by a sheet of rusty metal that allowed a view of the night sky in places. Luckily, it didn't rain much in Los Girasoles. All the interior walls, except for the one delimiting the back bedroom, had been knocked through. A number of load-bearing columns divided the elongated space, along which were scattered pots, shards of pottery, and ceramic plates painted with horrendous designs (horses with auras, blue suns, women drawn in profile whose hair metamorphosed into flocks of birds).

Jimmie rinsed out some glasses and carried them, still wet, to what could be considered the living room: three Acapulco chairs set around a low, rectangular table. Each of the men took one of the chairs; Micaela disappeared into the bedroom and came back with some pillows, which she put on the floor to make herself more comfortable.

Indoors, Jimmie seemed more sober, as if only the air-conditioning or the desire to insult the waiters had aroused him for a short time. Now he poured tequila for the other two men (Micaela had taken a can of beer from a small icebox but scarcely touched it) and talked about his projects with relative fluency. He was thinking of organizing an exhibition right there in the studio so that the wealthy residents of Los Girasoles would buy his ceramics. He knew the designs were horrible but defended his right to sell them, alleging that people liked having ugly things in their homes. In fact, added Jimmie to Marcelo (much to the satisfaction of Velásquez, who had been waiting for this moment the whole evening), his real passion was not ceramics but contemporary art; the problem was that in this bleak wasteland it was impossible to explain to the natives ("or even worse, to the academics," he added scathingly, with a wink to Marcelo) what contemporary art really was. Though he knew, he said, that Marcelo was a man of the world, and in Barcelona ("Madrid, Madrid," Marcelo interrupted), right, in Madrid then, he must have seen contemporary art projects much closer to his own area of interest. In fact, that was why he had told Velásquez that he wanted to meet him: to invite him to join this new project—the word was repeated like a mantra in his discourse—he was putting together. It was going to be a magnificent *exposition*, he said, a performance unlike anything that had ever been done before. He had been in training for this for years, although he had only discovered it a short time ago, and only now, said Jimmie, did he understand that all that training was destined for this moment and this place. By "all that training" he was of course referring to a bunch of unconnected anecdotes spiced up with sex and prog rock.

Jimmie went on talking, and Velásquez seemed to have fallen asleep, although it turned out he was listening carefully with his eyes closed. Micaela was looking at her owner (no other word occurred to Marcelo to describe the relationship between the girl and the gringo) with an unsettling mixture of submission and disdain. Marcelo listened to Jimmie and gradually understood that it was he, and not Velásquez, who had wanted them meet, and that Jimmie in some way subjugated the people around him, crushed them with his conversation and anecdotes, reducing them to mere spectators, to supporting actors in the movie of his life. He talked about his artistic project with the conviction of a real estate agent. It was, he said, the future of art. By that he didn't mean that art would advance by following his model, but that his project thematized the future of art, or rather a vision, a foretaste of that future. To explain this he had to go back to his youth in San Francisco, after the demise of the hippie dream.

In 1975, when Jimmie was twenty, there had been a lot of talk about certain CIA programs related to mind control. Everyone knew all about it: these days, Hollywood most likely lives on stories like that, added the gringo. What happened was that the radicalized hippies who had been arrested for supposed communist affiliations, and then later released, talked about interrogation sessions using hypnosis and experiments with LSD. At first, naturally, no one had believed them; one more invention of anticapitalist paranoia. But then the affair had reached Congress, and Senator Ted Kennedy had demanded clarification. The declassified documents spoke of a group of psychiatrists recruited by the CIA to develop the program, utilizing hypnosis as an interrogation tool. One of these psychiatrists, maybe the most notable since his name was mentioned many times in Senator Kennedy's reports, was Dr. Francis Cameron. When the scandal broke and the guilt was, more or less randomly, apportioned, Dr. Cameron disappeared for a few years, then, in the mid-eighties, became famous for founding a private counterespionage business based on techniques related to hypnosis: E-Sight Enterprises. They offered services—pharmaceutical, technological, nutritional—to companies—Coca-Cola was even mentioned—anxious to discover if an employee had leaked information to the competition, in infringement of the confidentiality clauses in his contract. E-Sight Enterprises was a failure in financial terms, despite the free publicity given by the tabloid press, who published whole articles on the sinister Dr. Mind, as they nicknamed Cameron, in which they speculated on his pacts with secret societies. But the company had gone bankrupt, and Cameron was out of a job, so he recycled himself as a champion of alternative medicine and other emergent concepts of the New Age in San Francisco at the end of the eighties.

It was there that Jimmie came across him: just another hippie doctor—one of the old guys, burnt out on acid, who preached against the use of vaccines and examined the color of your aura for five bucks. Jimmie was in the herbal business and sold those delirious doctors piles of cacti stolen from the indigenous reservation in the south of the country. It was illegal, but his was the least of illegalities in a universe that changed paradigms every couple of weeks, with the Berlin Wall coming down and various mafias staking out generous areas of the u.s. criminal underworld for themselves before the government decided who their next archenemy was going to be, now that the Soviets had gone out of fashion.

Jimmie brought Dr. Mind some rare cacti and climbing plants that no other medicine man had ever ordered, and talking the matter over one afternoon in his consulting rooms in the Mission District, they had ended by exchanging confidences. Cameron took a liking to him (there was an insinuation of a homosexual relationship in the story told by Jimmie, who spoke of the man with great tenderness) and told him about E-Sight Enterprises and the years before, when he was working for the CIA. In the beginning, Jimmie didn't believe a word of it, although he thought he had read similar stories years before. But Cameron had kept documents from the company that explained the method used in the hypnosis (patented) and set out guidelines for the training of hypnotists specializing in counterespionage and other pleasantries.

Jimmie saw in all that a possibility for getting rich, so one night, while the parascientist was asleep, he broke into his house (or was already inside; the anecdote didn't make this clear), stole the papers, plus three thousand dollars in bills, and spent six erratic weeks driving to Guatemala (he stopped off here and there), never again to return to San Francisco.

The narrative flow of his flight was uneven; he amused himself for several minutes telling, with a wealth of detail, what he had eaten in a certain wayside restaurant in Chiapas, then dispatched a couple of years of his life in a single blow with a vague explanation of the profession ("attack-dog trainer") he had taken up during this interval. Marcelo thought, in the end, it was the story of an obsession that, like a hurricane, returned periodically and departed as violently as it had arrived. Jimmie had come across hypnotism in a moment of desperation, just when he thought his life might consist of stealing cacti from the Indians for five more years and then dying of a heart attack brought on by the abuse of toxic substances. The friendship with Dr. Mind and the promise of salvation that underlaid his conspiratorial nonsense poured down on the gringo like the bucket of meaning he needed to become fully awake.

Maybe, thought Marcelo, there were some E-Sight documents, stolen by Jimmie, that described, in broad outline, the process of hypnosis. Although it was more likely, from his viewpoint, that the gringo had fled his country for a more common reason: pursued by the law or the ghost of a love affair drugs had snatched from him. The point was not the truth of the story, but the pell-mell way Jimmie told it and the delirious look in his eyes. A deeper truth could be perceived in these outward expressions. And finally, wasn't he himself, Marcelo, very similar in this sense? A man intermittently gnawed by trivial recurrences, a researcher of lives constructed on the knife edge of lies, an imposter convinced of his false story. If he were, for a moment, to strip Jimmie of his most superficial layer, to draw back the curtains of his eccentricity and his adaptation to the stereotype of a Californian in love with drugs and the Third World, what was left was not so different from what Marcelo himself hid under the dermis of sophistication and behind the shield of arrogance. Of course, looking at the matter clearly, all men, stripped of a precise number of superficial attributes, are essentially the same, in the way that the centers of all onions look alike, and what one has deep inside is essentially boring: superimposed layers of tissue bathed in blood, a few entrenched fears, urine, shit, desperation in the face of death. Only in the way these elements articulate with the external conditions—material, political, economic, climatic—do men acquire true interest as objects of study. There is nothing in the noumenon that allows us to concern ourselves with the next guy.

Marcelo strayed off into these vain considerations of a philosophical nature, but in the meanwhile, out there, in the world of material determinants, Jimmie continued talking like a street vendor with echolalia. His story had reached the vicinity of the present, and he was having a fine time discoursing on his artistic vocation and the need to use hypnosis for the good of the cultural world, now barren due to a handful of hypocrites who had betrayed the romantic spirit of art through their cold, financial calculation. In short, Jimmie was spitting out the traditional megalomaniacal rant of all those who propose to do something radically new (that idea gave Marcelo a warm feeling).

Some months before, at the kiosk in the center of Los Girasoles, Jimmie had bought the tabloid he read religiously every Sunday. In a poorly written article, he had discovered that Dr. Mind was dead, and for that reason, he finally, after years of waiting, felt free to apply the CIA and E-Sight techniques of hypnosis for his own benefit. He had already made a few experiments, hypnotizing Central American prostitutes and queers garnered from the streets during his years of bumming about. Any mistake in the technique and the patient would wake up in the middle of the session, screaming and attempting to scratch his eyes out, but Jimmie had persevered until he had polished every detail and could now put even the most reluctant subjects into a trance. Once, he said, he had hypnotized a dog in Ciudad Juárez.

At some point in this hazardous form of amusement, Jimmie had, however, realized that Dr. Cameron's method had certain applications unforeseen by its creator: doors that opened in the middle of the hypnosis that only an experienced therapist could enter without leaving his patient an idiot. Tunnels to unknown regions of the mind that Dr. Cameron had overlooked, concerned as he was with dragging a clumsy confession from a poor student or, later, from an employee who had attempted to take early retirement by selling a couple of formulae to the highest bidder. Jimmie's ambitions were more expansive. He didn't give a shit about the superficial layers of the consciousness, he said. What he was interested in was diving deeper, immersing himself in the gloomy depths of the frontal lobe.

At this point in the story, Jimmie's voice became more serious. Even Micaela, usually so impassive, looked on edge, like a child waiting for the moment of opening the presents at a party. Velásquez had emerged from his profound meditation and, although he already knew the story, was staring spellbound at Jimmie. Marcelo Valente, trained in the toughest schools of philosophical reason, resisted the effects of the story, but didn't deny the charm of the narrative, to which the gringo's accent added an organic contribution.

The dramatic pause gave Jimmie the opportunity to serve another round of tequilas. Micaela continued to take timid sips from her can of beer, sitting on the floor on her pillows. Marcelo Valente glanced at her and for the first time understood her beauty. She wasn't a child of eighteen; she was a very old woman, with the eyes of one who has seen things go up in flames too many times; she had regressed to her physiological age, thought Marcelo, from some unlikely place.

After downing his tequila in two swigs, Jimmie took up his narrative. Memory, he said, didn't have a linear structure, as we used to imagine. Within it, all the images from our past were superimposed in a chaotic, random manner. The scenes shuffled together there were not the sediment of time but instantaneous constructions that could take in elements from any lived moment. Sometimes, said Jimmie, during a session of hypnosis, the patient's images of a memory didn't correspond to any previous lived experience. Among the family photos of a trip to the beach, a strange element would timidly sneak in, one that didn't correspond to that or any other memory. They generally appeared in the form of an object–objects are traitorous: a piece of plastic, the function of which is hard to explain, or a gleaming white machine surrounded by rust. Jimmie termed those strange elements that appeared during hypnosis, falsifying the memories, "hypnotic fetishes." And he had discovered, as he went on to add, that hypnotic fetishes were not imaginary constructions but anticipated future scenes that we would perhaps never see: kitchen appliances, toys our children or grandchildren would use quite naturally some Thursday morning, or multisensory sculptures that would make the visitors to future art galleries shudder. If, during the hypnosis, you managed to concentrate on those fetishes, you could learn about those future art forms and carry them into the present. That was, to cut a long story short, the project.

Marcelo, whose pragmatism had waned during his stay in Mexico and, in particular, during his recent conversations with Rodrigo, had listened with respect to the anecdotal part of Jimmie's monologue: the intrigues with the CIA, the eighties, the counterespionage business, the financial disaster, the birth of the New Age, the illegal deals, the homosexual relationship between the budding fugitive from justice and the discredited psychiatrist, the betrayal and the flight south, the experiments with hypnosis. He adored the story. He had even thought, during a moment of distraction while Jimmie was rattling on, that he had to find a way to put some of it into his book, to relate it somehow with Foret's months in Mexico and his disappearance. They'd lap this up in Madrid, he thought. They'd no longer see him as an academic with a talent for taking full advantage of the perks of the office, but as an authentic researcher of the passions of the soul, an explorer of the depths of consciousness who had, in the New World, discovered a parallel logic capable of renewing the stagnant thought of Western philosophy through the unlikely terrain of the aesthetics of madness. These were the delusions of grandeur he childishly gave himself up to from time to time on discovering, for example, an author no one had read. The idea of being a pioneer in some subject, of finding a bundle of yellowing papers in some provincial library that would position him as the man who was capable of rescuing some forgotten aspect of philosophical thought, stirred him to the core of his being. Shining in the pedestrian grayness of academia was such a complicated enterprise that he had dreams of himself as the Christ who would open the gates of a new conception of the world, and then all those miserable wretches would recognize his true worth.

Obviously, there was one aspect of Jimmie's narrative that he was uneasy about: it was absolute nonsense. The belief that one could secretly look into a future art gallery to anticipate its content by a hundred years was enough to have the poor gringo locked away for life. He decided, nevertheless, to humor him and then later, when he got Velásquez alone, sound out the extent of Jimmie's derangement.

Micaela stood up and went to fetch a glass from the dilapidated kitchen. Jimmie had his eyes fixed on Marcelo Valente, who was attempting to avoid the question that would inevitably follow.

"What do you think?" Jimmie eventually asked. "Do you want to join the project?"

Marcelo stammered feigned admiration and praised the gringo's narrative talents. "But I'm not sure," he then said, "what all this has to do with me."

Jimmie hit his brow with the palm of his hand, like someone who has remembered that he's left the stove on three blocks from home. He took a deep breath and began a new monologue at the very moment Micaela returned to the room and sat cross-legged in her place, putting her empty glass down in front of her without having served another round of tequila to the others, as Marcelo imagined she would.

The thing was that the objectivity of the method, its ability to effectively predict or anticipate the future, depended not only on the hypnotist's training and the willingness of the hypnotized subject, but also on confirmation by others of the content observed during hypnosis. That is to say: a fetish could be a fetish or it could be the fruit of the individual's imagination, and only during a collective session of hypnosis, with everyone involved simultaneously diving into the future, or into the subconscious, or wherever the hell they were supposed to be diving, could the form of an unmistakably anticipatory object be defined. Everyone would search for the same fetish during the session and, given that they were intimately connected, thanks to the group exercises undertaken beforehand, the anticipatory potential of one member of the group would empower the other hypnotized subjects. On their return from the voyage, they would describe the object to each other, then they would proceed to construct a replica in clay or latex or whatever.

Jimmie paused for as long as it takes to smile. His eyes opened enormously wide and seemed bluer than ever. Marcelo glanced at Velásquez, his ally in reason in the midst of barbarity, but Velásquez was looking fixedly at the gringo and appeared to have jumped the gun on the hypnosis session. Marcelo saw his friend had, some time ago, become ensnared in Jimmie's web, and that his predilection for all things magical, perhaps due to his American origins, was much greater than his (Marcelo's origins were, when you came down to it, European and rationalist).

Marcelo had to make some response, and he knew what it should be: this was all madness and too much like the Mexican B movie Velásquez had recommended to him. He had no intention of getting involved in any such game, and if it hadn't been for the tequila, it would all have been a waste of time. But he didn't say any of that.

His desire to please at any cost was stronger that his convictions, and he didn't want to generate disaccord between the gringo and Velásquez, since the fat professor must already have said something about his willingness for the gringo to risk inviting him. So, Marcelo agreed with feigned enthusiasm. He said he was ready to participate in the collective hypnosis session, that they should get out the pocket watch or whatever was needed.

Jimmie gave a triumphal smile, and Velásquez's previously stern face appeared to relax into an expression of relief. Micaela stood up and, after lifting her skirt to her waist, slid her white panties down to the floor, where they lay like a dead animal. She took Marcelo's glass, which by then contained not a drop of tequila, and placed it under her skirt. After a moment of general expectation, the tinkle of urine was heard and Micaela took the glass, with a little piss in the bottom, from beneath her skirt. She repeated the ritual with the three other glasses and finally arranged them all in the center of the table; then she poured a shot of tequila into each glass of piss. Jimmie drew the girl to him, sat her on his knees, and kissed her on the mouth. Velásquez was the first to raise his glass, and he then clinked it with those of the gringo and the girl. The three looked simultaneously at Marcelo, and he wondered if they had rehearsed this gesture beforehand. His head hurt, and he thought, "I'm drunk; I'm so sloshed I'm seeing things, and this is not happening." He raised his glass and enthusiastically clinked it against the others.

He had never tasted anything so delicious.

2

There was just one last thing to be done before the preparatory sessions of hypnosis could begin. Each time Jimmie mentioned it, he lost his cool. According to him, it was dangerous to initiate a session of collective hypnosis with an even number of participants. Once, in Trinidad and Tobago (When had he been in Trinidad and Tobago?

thought Marcelo, without believing a word of what the gringo was saying, or only half believing it, as if departing from the promise that it was necessary to compensate for his exaggerations with a veil of incredulity, even though, at heart, one might feel darkly attracted by his exaggerations, by the prospect that they might not be exaggerations), he had tried it with a group of four, and the results had been disastrous. Marcelo interrupted: "Aren't there supposed to be three of us? Micaela, Velásquez, and me, with you directing us?" No, Jimmie also intended to enter the hypnosis, to guide them from the inside, or something like that. Marcelo thought about Foret, about the photos from his final years, where he still looked like an elegant gladiator, a type of dark superhero, living his double life as a poor poet and fifth-rate boxer, his life as a beggar and the prince of brawling, his multiple lives dedicated to love, and that other life, the only redeeming one, the life he shared with Bea until the summer of 1918. Marcelo thought about Foret because there was nothing in his own predictable life story with a high enough level of mysticism or madness with which to compare and measure the madness of what was taking place. He turned to the great ones. That, thought Professor Valente, is what tradition is: a series of parameters for measuring the madness of the things that happen to us. He believed, with Protagoras, that man was the measure of all things. And Richard Foret, in this case, was man.

Micaela already had a lot of experience in individual hypnotism since Jimmie had been inducing deep states in her for months (Before fucking her? Marcelo wondered), but it was possible that, in a group session, the girl would be unable to control the course of the hypnosis.

The reasoning seemed to him, at best, muddled, but after many failed hints from Jimmie, and Velásquez telling him bluntly, Marcelo understood they wanted him to persuade his "stepson"–as they called Rodrigo–to join the project. Marcelo had never thought of Rodrigo as his stepson, but he now realized he could justifiably be considered as such since Adela and he had been living together for a good while, and were talking about the possibility of prolonging this situation, even after Marcelo's time in Los Girasoles came to an end.

To Marcelo, the warning–foolishly repeated by Velásquez and the gringo since the day they had drunk Micaela's urine–not to tell Adela anything seemed curious. Only Rodrigo was to be told, and then he would accept the warm invitation to lose his wits and keep the secret from his mother.

3

Jimmie had seen Rodrigo one day walking through the streets of the town. He had said hello, thinking he was an acquaintance, and the young man had replied with a nod that, to Jimmie, at that moment, seemed touched with some antique grace. He had done his research: Rodrigo was Adela's son, he had been chucked out of his job in DF, left his ugly, vulgar wife, and had been staying in a small house on the Puerta del Aire estate since the beginning of the year.

The relationship between Jimmie and Adela was, to put it mildly, dire. In Los Girasoles, everyone knew everyone else, and both Adela and Jimmie frequented those circles surrounding the world of academia, where the professors gave mutual demonstrations of their aesthetic sensibility and theoretical versatility: jazz–or even trova; many of them didn't know the difference–gigs in some café in the center of town, yoga classes given by a professor of economics in the front room of her house, group exhibitions of the photographs taken by the teenage offspring of those same professors.

They had met at one of those events, two years before, neither of them now remembered exactly how, and had flirted listlessly, more to shake off the tedium of provincial life than to get laid or have a real relationship. The fact is that they had exchanged phone numbers–in fact, Adela had given her number to Jimmie, who didn't have a phone at that time–and arranged to meet for a drink during the week. The date had been a complete failure. Jimmie turned up smelling of marijuana and had forgotten what Adela looked like, so he sat down at a table near Adela's where another woman, much younger, was drinking a beer alone. Adela watched from her table, filled simultaneously with compassion and rage. The young woman, in contrast to what might be expected of someone who has been suddenly accosted by a dirty gringo smelling of marijuana, had taken it well and let the stranger buy her a drink. Jimmie, convinced he was with Adela, the professor he had met a few days before, didn't understand what sort of game she was playing. He followed her lead and acted as if it were the first time they had spoken, convinced that her use of a pseudonym–the Adela who wasn't Adela had told him her name was Natalia–signaled a degree of perversion that would be useful when it came to sex.

Natalia and Jimmie drank and laughed for two hours, closely observed by Adela without anyone noticing her presence. At the end of those two hours, Adela had drunk, all alone, as many beers as Jimmie and Natalia together and, she realized, was in an almost perilous state of inebriation. Eventually, plucking up her courage, she stood and walked to the table where the gringo was charming the young woman with his anecdotes. Initially Jimmie thought she was a waiter and held out an empty bottle without looking up, muttering thanks. Noting that Adela didn't take the bottle, Jimmie turned his head and found himself looking at her face, bathed in tears of humiliation. "I'm Adela, you moronic gringo. You stood me up for her at the next table." Jimmie made a wry face when he understood his mistake. Adela walked unsteadily to the door.

Many things could have happened at that point. Jimmie could have caught up with her and spent hours begging her to forgive him. They might never have got as far as anything approaching a stable relationship, but at least they could have remained friends, which, in a small town like Los Girasoles, was something worthy of consideration. But Jimmie opted for the worst possible reaction. Charmed as he was by the low neckline of his impromptu companion, he said, in a voice loud enough for Adela to hear, "There are some weird, disturbed people in this town, aren't there?" The girl's laugh wounded Adela even more deeply than Jimmie's question, which condemned her to ridicule.

4

Rodrigo listened to Marcelo's confused, long-winded story, sitting in what was now his armchair, while the Spaniard sat rigid, apparently uncomfortable, facing him. Velásquez had wanted to be there when he explained the plan to the "stepson," in case he stumbled over some point or forgot some fundamental fact that needed to be addressed, but Marcelo felt Rodrigo would dismiss the proposal immediately if he suspected from the start just how divorced from reality Velásquez now was. So they were alone again, as they had been during their earlier conversations.

He told Rodrigo about the gringo and lingered over a very extended description of Micaela, emphasizing her disturbing beauty and the fact that, despite all odds, her piss tasted divine. He told him there was a lot of alcohol splashing around, and that although there was certainly something ridiculous about the whole affair, what mattered was meeting up with these people every so often—a couple of times a week maybe, or three nearer the time for the actual hypnosis session—sharing something of the disquiet of Los Girasoles.

Rodrigo listened with a poker face. It was impossible to guess what was going through his mind, Marcelo thought, and all the better, because he could be thinking about the possibility of making a sudden return to DF—back to his wife—putting a distance between himself and that bleak, dusty plain, where sensible people ended up giving in to the darkest whims of the soul, to the most grotesque claims of an unknown gringo, to simple, unadorned madness, clearly pronouncing each of that word's syllables, few though they might be, because madness only has two audible syllables, but is followed by a long series of sounds that seem to seep toward the interior of the word; syllables that are never pronounced, but throb within the word and are, in a certain sense, alluded to when someone says "madness," especially if they say it consciously, thinking of the multiple, not necessarily pleasant forms of madness, that word of infinite syllables.

Rodrigo listened with a poker face but inside was not really listening, or he was listening and responding and carrying on an angry, inaudible dialogue in which he posed counterarguments and swept aside excuses related to what Marcelo was telling him. That dialogue went more or less like this:

"Frigging Marcelo. He's got an amazing proclivity for weird situations. Where can he have found those people, those stories of piss drunk at midnight in dark hovels full of ceramic plates? Is he telling me lies? Inventing an absurd story to see how credulous I am, to report straight back to my mother about my reaction to all this? No, that can't be it. Not after the conversations we've had; after we've jointly revitalized the dry, dusty house of language with a couple of good conversations. But if he's serious, what the hell does he expect from me? On the other hand, drinking the piss of a beautiful young girl sounds pretty tempting. Disgusting, but tempting. What's more, drinking piss is an infallible indication you're in the presence of the sacred, or something like it. It's easy to imagine this is the sort of thing that ends in a whole pile of people committing suicide, here in this remote town full of academics. The way I see it, it would be pretty sad to die with a capsule of poison between your teeth and a message tattooed on your skull, next to three or four other guys who drank piss, here in a town full of people dedicated to higher education. But I've got nothing else to do. I've been cooped up here for weeks. Cecilia is desperate for me to return to DF, and this is just the sort of stupid plan I could use as a triumphal end to my stay in Los Girasoles. So, I'll drink piss with them a couple of times, let them hypnotize me, then I'll go back to DF and look for a job as a knowledge administrator someplace. As a bulletin writer somewhere. As a waiter, if I have to. And I'll be a worthy man. The poor but honorable man my wife deserves: poor, honorable, and unhappy because of my flagrant uselessness."

5

And so Rodrigo had in the end, if rather vaguely, agreed to join the hypnotists at least once, just to hear Jimmie's explanation of the project firsthand. That was the most Marcelo could get from him, and he was satisfied.

A few days after that conversation with Marcelo, Rodrigo decided to make a foray beyond the walls of Puerta del Aire and go out for a drink one evening, on his own, in the center of Los Girasoles. Marcelo had lent him a little money to cover his expenses, and so that he could pretend he was receiving payment from Velásquez for the phantom proofreading he was phantasmagorically undertaking.

He asked Jacinto Nogales Pedrosa, the security guard, for the number of a cab service, and was set down in a street flanking the main square. He walked around the colonial part of town without much idea of what he was looking for, and even went a little farther on to the market, where, despite the fact that the stalls had closed, things were quite lively.

The cantina he entered didn't look too much like the typical local joint: it was, rather, a touristy spot serving regional brews. Only a couple of tables were occupied, and a jukebox was pumping out deafening boleros.

At one of the tables, the darkest and farthest from the bar, Rodrigo made out two foreign girls, looking half-lost and too naive for a country like Mexico. After a couple of shots of tequila at the bar, he plucked up his courage and went over to their table. They, the foreign girls, were very young, and Rodrigo was surprised to see them alone in a bar, without a man or responsible adult to chaperone them. One was good-looking, in a gamin kind of way, with a pretty nose and outlandishly long black eyelashes. Her hair was short, and she seemed, from her smile, more willing than the other to strike up a conversation.

Rodrigo asked if he could sit down, and the girl with the long lashes answered with a smile while taking a cigarette from a packet and rummaging in her bag for a lighter. Rodrigo decided that what could have been indifference was assent and took the seat beside her. The other girl seemed more concerned with the ambiance of the cantina and only gave him a distracted, aloof glance, the way you look at someone who comes up to offer goods for sale at an inopportune moment.

The girl with the lashes was called Domitile and was French. She spoke faltering Spanish but incorporated into it Norteño expressions, as if she had learned to speak by deciphering narco-corridos. They were both nineteen and had been living in Mexicali for eight

months on a cultural exchange–as they explained–which allowed
them to spend a year in Mexico learning the language before returning to begin their university studies in their respective countries–
the more standoffish one was from Poland. Rodrigo was surprised
by the unlikely fate that had befallen them, and jokingly apologized,
in the name of all Mexicans, for the ugliness of Mexicali. Domitile
agreed, smiling widely again, and explained that they were now on
a group trip around the whole country, with the aim of experiencing something besides the unbearable heat of their adoptive city. In
comparison with Mexicali, Los Girasoles seemed–according to the
French girl–like paradise. The rest of the group was in a hotel on
the outskirts of town, and they were the only ones who had dared to
leave the comfort of their accommodations to seek a little local color
and sample something of the way of life in the town. They had ended
up in this cantina thanks to a guidebook–a particularly bad one–that
only suggested anodyne places that were, therefore, characteristic of
every town and settlement mentioned.

The Polish girl, with obvious annoyance, moved her seat away
from her companion's cigarette smoke, and Rodrigo took advantage of this distance to strike up a more intimate conversation
with Domitile. She was from Nantes, had never before been outside France, and had chosen Mexico in the hope of finding a more
humid climate and the constant sound of danceable music, only to
be confronted with the fact that neither of these things existed in
Mexicali. The Norteña music was, for her, little less than dodeca-
phonic, and she invariably suffered a nosebleed every afternoon
due to the exquisite sun of the city and the desert dust. Her journey around Mexico, though brief and organized by people unac-
quainted with the local terrain, was in some way redeeming the
previous months of suffering. She even thought Los Girasoles was
pretty, compared with the neighborhood in which she had lived
in Mexicali, in the house of a middle-class couple who had given
the two girls room and board in exchange for sending their son to
France the following year.

Domitile didn't know much about Mexico, and what she did
know was information that Rodrigo, a resident of the capital and
more used to the southern cities, didn't share. She told stories about

quinceañeras where the people fired into the air after a quarter of an hour spent swigging from a bottle with no label.

Rodrigo learned that the other girl was called Daga, or rather that she had an unpronounceable name that she had exchanged for this simpler nickname while in Mexico. Daga muttered a beautifully enunciated "Mucho gusto" when she felt herself being referred to, and then asked, in a Spanish her companion must have envied, if he liked the music in the cantina. At that moment, a deeply emotional song was playing that Rodrigo had heard one too many times the year before, at the exit of every metro station and in the streets crammed with ambulant vendors around the museum. He said no, he didn't like Mexican music, or at least not this kind, and that the only Mexican music he did like was the *son jarocho* and some rock 'n' roll numbers from the sixties that were extremely free translations of songs from the States: "Angélica María, for instance, or the incunable Rockin Devil's," added Rodrigo, making erroneous use of an adjective that, to him, always sounded like it meant famous. Daga looked as if she had no idea what he was talking about, and Domitile explained that Mexicali only had rancheras and narco-corridos, and that they still hadn't worked out the difference between these two genres despite having spent various months being forced to listen to them, in the same way that prisoners in Guantánamo had to listen to Barney the dinosaur. To Rodrigo, this political allusion sounded, quite rightly, frivolous, and he thought his relationship with these outsiders was, from that moment, condemned to unmitigated failure.

Rodrigo ordered a round of beers and two tequilas (Daga didn't want one), and they clinked glasses in a not especially cordial toast while he returned to his private conversation with Domitile. She had not yet been to DF but would be going there in five or six days, she couldn't remember exactly when, and Rodrigo recommended a couple of neighborhoods not to be missed during her nocturnal excursions, when she again left her boring group of students in the boring hotel restaurant to go out and sample the local nightlife of that monstrous city. Domitile wrote down the names in a notebook she carried in her bag and thanked him for the information with disarming innocence. She said DF was what she was most looking forward to because she'd read the French translation of Bolaño's *The Savage Detectives* as soon as she'd learned that she had been awarded the annual exchange grant (in fact, what she said was "anal exchange grant," but Rodrigo turned a deaf ear to the imbecilic pun and inwardly pardoned Domitile's poor command of the language). Rodrigo told her he hadn't read *The Savage Detectives*, even though he had in fact done so and hadn't liked it, and preferred to sound ignorant rather than question the adolescent's tastes. Domitile attempted, without much luck, to summarize the plot of the novel but stopped short to include Daga in the conversation, referring to one of their traveling companions whom they had secretly nicknamed Ulises Lima (Daga had also read Bolaño, apparently).

They continued drinking and tried to agree on which one of them would go to the jukebox to choose the next record. Rodrigo gave way under pressure from the others, alleging his knowledge of the field, and walked to the jukebox, taking a five-peso coin from the pocket of his pants. As he began to flick through the sheets of the cantina's musical menu, a drunk who was sinking into sentimentality in a nearby chair shouted, "Don't put on anything stupid, you fucking sod," and Rodrigo felt too intimidated to choose a song based on his very personal criteria, so he returned to the table and said, "We'd better be going." Domitile understood the situation and looked serious. Daga was already serious and simply took her bag from the back of her chair and sprang up, as if she had been wanting to do so for several hours.

They left the cantina, and Rodrigo realized that Domitile was having difficulty walking, as if she were very drunk or some bug had bitten the sole of her left foot. He inquired and discovered that the girl's unsteady gait was a mixture of drunkenness and accident: she'd twisted her ankle a few days earlier, at a waterfall they had visited in another state; besides which, she was sloshed, and when she was sloshed she always walked a bit oddly. From her explanation, Rodrigo understood that Domitile had only ever been sloshed in Mexico, and he thought of her parents' concern when they learned that Mexicali was Mexicali and that laws in Mexico were mere suggestions.

Domitile started saying her elder sister was still calculating the price of things in francs, but that she, born seven years later, didn't remember ever having seen a franc and that euros seemed to have been there forever. She laughed inappropriately, unconcerned whether either of her companions shared the joke, if that's what it was. They walked around the market in search of another open bar and during that search passed along a street lined with prostitutes.

The only open cantina they came across had a more dubious air than the one they had left, although to an inexperienced eye, it might have been the very same cantina, which is exactly what Daga said when they looked inside: "It's the same cantina." In any case, they decided to try their luck and went in. It was much more crowded than the other and was so noisy that all three of them, without saying so, felt sheltered in some form of anonymity. They found an empty table, and when they sat down, after borrowing another chair, Rodrigo thought he had no clue what he was doing there. This cantina also had a jukebox, and the music it was pumping out seemed like an exact copy of the other: boleros about the stoical endurance of the nostalgia for a lost joy. It was obvious he wasn't going to get either of these girls into bed, much less the two of them together, nor did it seem probable that their conversation would be particularly enlightening. He considered beating a retreat but was beset by a vague sense of guilt and decided to stay with them for at least a while longer, so as not to leave them at the mercy of the drunks.

But his guess that the drunks would keep their distance on seeing him sitting with the foreign girls was completely mistaken. They hadn't finished their first beer before a short guy, his head almost shaven, wafted beery breath in his face, shouting into his ear a request to be introduced to his friends. Rodrigo didn't know how to react and chose what was, perhaps, the worst possible option: he said they weren't his friends, that he'd only just met them, and didn't think they were interested in doing anything or getting to know anyone. Seeking complicity with the drunk, he said he'd already tried it on one of them and been told to fuck off, and they'd also told him they had big gringo boyfriends who were coming to pick them up a little later in another bar.

The drunk with the almost shaven head and the obstinacy of someone used to getting his way continued to insist, even though he

appeared to have swallowed Rodrigo's explanation and taken the
bait of the sham friendship. Forgetting about his prey for a moment,
he pulled up his chair until he was practically on Rodrigo's lap and
began telling him about isolated episodes from his life. He had a fat
wife, and a daughter he was proud of, whose picture he had as the
background image on his malfunctioning cell phone. He was a
state policeman, and if Rodrigo had any problems during his stay in
Los Girasoles, he just had to mention his name, Oliver Rodríguez,
to free himself from the injustice his colleagues shamelessly doled
out. "You gotta grease the wheels if you wanna move," the policeman pronounced, making it clear he also took advantage of outsiders to make it comfortably through to payday.

It needed a few more wiles to convince Oliver Rodríguez that
the two gringas didn't want to fuck him, and that he should leave
the table of the impromptu trio and return to his solitary corner,
where he knocked back a couple more drinks before departing–all
the while talking to himself–through the wooden swinging doors
leading to the street.

And it was while Rodrigo was watching, with relief, the departure of Oliver Rodríguez, the drunken policeman, that he saw Micaela
cross the threshold in the opposite direction. The girl's solitary presence in the doorway only lasted a second before Jimmie came in
behind her and swept the room with the expert gaze of a person prepared for any eventuality. A second or two that, for Rodrigo, seemed
to extend in time like a wet shirt thrown up by its extremities, two
elastic seconds, or maybe three that seemed to last five or six of
the seconds we normally experience, sometimes with greater shame
than glory but always without the power to stop the passage of time,
as he would have liked to have stopped it at that instant, because
Rodrigo had forgotten about Domitile and Daga and thought the alcohol must have been adulterated, since there was no other way to
explain the intense heat rising from his stomach and manifesting
itself at the back of his throat as an extreme dryness, as if all the dust
of Los Girasoles had been summoned to appear in his throat, as if
someone had ordered a cemetery to be constructed in his mouth
and people were throwing handfuls of earth onto the simple coffins
of their most recent dead.

There are coincidences in real life that appear to be dictated by the cliché that rules songs of love and vengeance with an iron fist, and there are coincidences that appear to be neither forced nor gratuitous but essentially necessary, inevitable, and evident, and that no one, having experienced them, would dare say were the creations of an affectedly falsetto voice or an eccentric personality, but are, rather, events with undeniable religious echoes, even if these coincidences involve, as in this case, a song of love and vengeance issuing from a jukebox. Because as soon as the door of the cantina allowed the policeman to leave and set up the arrival of Micaela, suddenly, in the middle of a line, the song playing was interrupted and another began, as equally new to Rodrigo as its predecessor, but in some way related or foreseen, like those songs we hear one single time in our childhood and never again until the day they are played on the most unlikely radio program, and then we remember we have already lived that moment. The words of the song were clear, and the voice was not nasal, unlike all the others that had pulsed through the cantina. It was a female voice and a sad song, like the sad, female figure who entered at that moment through the wooden door and let her eyes wander in the semidarkness until they met with, at the darkest, most distant table, Rodrigo's, in an elastic, unreal moment of more or less two seconds that both of them would remember as the clearest they had ever experienced. Because there are clear moments when the air really does seem to be a docile material that allows us to understand the world, and there are dirty, noisy moments when any degree of lucidity will be immediately held in check by the insipid material of things that impose themselves like symptoms of a very serious disease we all agree to call "world," or "cruel world" if we are tragedians.

Micaela walked in and the gringo, Jimmie, appeared behind her, and when Jimmie appeared, Rodrigo understood just who those two people were—Micaela and Jimmie—since they couldn't be anyone else and perfectly matched the description Marcelo Valente had offered a few days before when suggesting the possibility that Rodrigo join the hypnotism project, the project related to the future of art.

Rodrigo stared fixedly at Micaela's crotch and joyfully told himself he would soon be drinking piss from that font of eternal youth, although he then thought he wouldn't like to be young forever; youth was a nebulous, larval stage in which everything seemed more important, and nothing annoyed Rodrigo more than importance, as if he only aspired to a Nirvana of household appliances in which the greatest danger was buying a dishwasher on credit.

As soon as he saw Micaela, he became convinced it wouldn't be such a bad idea to take part in the hypnotism project Marcelo had invited him to join a few evenings before. Jimmie and the girl sat at a nearby table, and he listened distractedly to Domitile, who was speaking a few inches away, her breath agreeably seasoned with alcohol.

6

A stabbing pain in his temple suggested the night had gone on much longer than necessary. Blurred images of things he regretted floated around in his head. He made an effort to impose a chronological order on that inferno that, by nature, responded to a different logic. Inebriation sets up shortcuts in time, and it might not be such a good idea to try to mold it into a sober form. But despite it all, Rodrigo attempted to do just that.

He remembered having stared insistently at Micaela sitting next to Jimmie a few yards away. He knew, since the loose change in his pocket clearly reminded him, that he had sent a couple of tequilas to their table by way of the waiter, something he had only ever seen done in movies. To round off the cliché, he had lifted his glass and serenely nodded in a toast to them, and Jimmie had looked at him with an expression of surprise that didn't seem possible in someone so knocked around by life. Later, Jimmie came up to the table at which Rodrigo sat with the foreign girls–who interpreted it all as a series of steps in a local custom–and thanked him for the drinks, squinting his eyes to study him better. Eventually the gringo asked, unnecessarily, if he was Adela's son, to which Rodrigo responded with a drunken smile, a pause perhaps too long to be pregnant and a few words that might have been pleasant, but sounded, after that pause, odd: "Among other things." But they understood each other, and Jimmie was immediately hugging him with manly enthusiasm and beckoning Micaela to come over, bringing with her his tequila, and meet "our new group member" as he put it, in an obvious allusion to the collective hypnotism plan.

Domitile and Daga seemed startled by the presence of the gringo, with his fugitive-from-justice air, but they relaxed on seeing the shy innocence of Micaela, who was the same age as them and showed no fear of that other person. Jimmie set himself up at the head of table and took charge of keeping them well supplied with liquor, even Daga, who had previously declined anything but beer. Maybe due to her clearly low alcohol tolerance, she and Domitile soon exchanged roles, as happens with friends who spend a lot of time together. Daga laughed raucously, continually changed seats, applauded the spineless boleros on the jukebox, and touched Rodrigo with increasing confidence, while the French girl became cautious and monitored the state of inebriety of the others with the superior air that only adolescence can confer.

Jimmie attributed the meeting with Rodrigo to some secret force of destiny that was winking an eye and encouraging them to embark on the hypnotism project with even greater verve. He was wary of talking about the project in front of the European girls, wary of their knowledge of occult matters, but took advantage of every lapse of attention on their part to tell Rodrigo, shouting in his ear, some of the details of the affair. He talked about Marcelo's initial reluctance and his later conversion to the creed of hypnosis, and the interest he now showed in discovering the future form of art by means of that technique. He also spoke of Velásquez and his propensity for slipping into states of altered consciousness. "Prof Velásquez only needs five minutes to get into the asshole of a trance," explained Jimmie, resorting to technical language. "And once he's there, his visions are as clear and detailed as if he were right here, now, with his eyes open." The allusion was inaccurate because the cantina was full of smoke, and the noise of the boleros mingled with the crude comments the waiter directed at the drunks, thickening the atmosphere and fogging everything.

The gringo was a professional snake oil salesman. There was no doubt that he had a certain sensitivity when dealing with people that went beyond the mere power to convince. Jimmie was able to see a person's inner vulnerabilities and attack them mercilessly; he knew how to overcome resistance and which strings to pluck for each individual. In Rodrigo's case, the strategy was obvious: on stressing the joint nature of the hypnosis project, he was not only appealing to one of his most longstanding, secret aspirations but also tangentially hinting that it was Micaela who held the group together with the strange Indian-princess magnetism she exuded.

They poured their own drinks, or their glasses were freshened by Jimmie with the skill of a Turkish con man. Rodrigo downed one shot after another, and it became increasingly difficult for him to pretend his attention was on the gringo's words and not the lock of black hair that had escaped from behind Micaela's ear, a lock she gracefully replaced, time after time, very slowly, always with the same movement, as if it were a tai chi position taught to her by a Chinese grandmother, the purpose of which was to tame wild animals. Rodrigo began to see double, and two Micaelas were more than his nerves could bear. He felt stabs of guilt for staring so fixedly at a woman who was not his wife, but then he remembered his wife, and the evoked sound of her voice seemed to him so unworthy of brushing Micaela's ears that he resolved never to introduce them. He had also, naturally, forgotten about the teenagers whose names began with the letter *D*.

At a given moment, Domitile asked Rodrigo to go with them to find a cab since her friend was drunk, and their absence had probably been noted in the hotel, causing alarm among the other members of the group. Rodrigo briefly explained the situation to Jimmie and promised to return shortly, not because he found the gringo's conversation particularly entertaining, but because he couldn't take his eyes off Micaela. Faced with the girl's extravagant beauty, both Daga and Domitile had seemed suddenly anodyne, Europeans more insipid than celery sticks who didn't deserve a place in his desire for longer than half a jerk-off. Despite the fact that she was almost the same age as them—as has already been mentioned—Micaela seemed older because her silence was not the mute expectation of someone

who is learning, but the grace with which the magnanimous allow
chaos to proliferate around them for a time.

Rodrigo left the cantina with a girl on either arm—an achieve-
ment that earned him the respect of a number of the most stupid
drunks in Los Girasoles—and the three of them headed for the main
square, where he remembered having seen cabs waiting for customers when he was walking alone. On the way, Daga threw up
noisily into some bushes, and Rodrigo held her forehead like a
patient father. Domitile seemed worried but, nevertheless, thanked
Rodrigo for having been their escort for the night. They exchanged
telephone numbers, and the girls promised to call soon, even though
they would be leaving for another city—they couldn't remember
which—the following afternoon, so the possibility of meeting them
again seemed fairly low.

When he returned to the cantina, having put the girls into a cab
with instructions to take them straight to their hotel, Micaela had
disappeared.

It was this fortuitous disappearance that had contributed to fix-
ing in his mind the image of Micaela with the bewitching aura of a
blueprint. If he had met her again on his return, still accompanied
by her irritating partner, Micaela would have seemed a more terrestrial creature; if not just an ordinary girl, at least one of flesh
and blood. But her disappearance placed a wax seal on the meeting
and allowed it to rarefy in his memory. To satisfy that feeling of
imperfection the evening had produced, Rodrigo was obliged to see
Micaela again soon, alone if possible, without the annoying presence of Jimmie, for whom he felt contempt mingled with envy.

7

He had to wait a week for the second meeting to occur. A long week,
cooped up in the house, during which Rodrigo experienced a sense
of loneliness more profound than the one that, until then, had lulled
him to sleep each night. If his life, including his married life, were

indeed that of a loner, it suddenly seemed the fact of having met Micaela, of having glimpsed or sketched out in his warped imagination the possibility of an old age at her side, was essentially modifying the density of the loneliness that had never even come close to disturbing him.

Loneliness is always the same, but not the lonely. The discourse we hold back in front of others has a different weight to that which we speak aloud when no one is listening. In a certain sense, one offers inner comfort since it is a form of intimacy. The other, in contrast, makes a hollow in the world, in whose furthest corners the words ricochet to remind us that they have no taste.

Rodrigo called Cecilia one cloudy afternoon. She sounded unusually cheerful, and there was no indication in her voice of the well-known reproach that normally underlay her tremulous vowels, sometimes prolonged into a loving complaint ("They'll seeee. You'll be back sooon," she would say to him). But this time, nothing: a precise description of the atmosphere in the office, a detailed account of her father's most recent attempts to eliminate the damp in the living room—the old man had taken up the task again, with modest results and an irrational sense of victory . . . in fact, a trivial, if not completely comfortable conversation, without the mild, balsamic triviality of couples who tie each other down with the chains of their inexhaustible affection. Or perhaps Rodrigo's mood—equivalent to the one that invades a sensitive soul when he considers the possibility of having contracted an incurable disease—was tingeing his perception of the world and other people with a violet hue, the violet of his sporadic migraines and his frequent periods of melancholy. Micaela—like a tumor, the nature of which is still unclear—glowed in his memory, threatening to either spread through his hypothalamus or discreetly dwindle under the benign, chemotherapeutic effects of distance. Rodrigo couldn't decide which was more worrying: that love existed and had, a few days before, wormed its way into him, or that the adulterated tequila in the cantina had played a dirty trick on him. In the former case, he would be obliged to renounce, out of simple coherence, the greater part of his cynicism, something he found worrying since his cynicism was, as far as he knew, his only recourse for externalizing a sharp intelligence; in the latter, the unbearable confirmation of the mediocrity of the world would weigh on him for several decades, until a merciful case of Alzheimer's would turn his stern, pensive expression into one of drooling innocence. The dice of his life, as someone given to cliché would say, had been cast.

Marcelo came to visit him on Wednesday afternoon. He had heard from Velásquez of Rodrigo's meeting with Jimmie and the charming Micaela in the cantina in the center. (The gringo had told Velásquez.) He asked about his impressions of the pair, and Rodrigo looked upward and turned his eyes significantly to the left, a zone he reserved for dark thoughts or the most serious considerations, considerations that left him, after some hours of deep conjecture, with a trochaic murmur in his chest.

Marcelo Valente was less talkative than on previous occasions. However, he embarked on a topic that he rarely touched: his relationship with Adela. He told Rodrigo he had "cultivated" a growing affection for his mother, and that verb immediately reminded Rodrigo of his wild, vacant lot in Mexico City. "*Il faut cultiver notre jardin*," he recited to himself, with a nod to Voltaire, while Marcelo continued his speech. The Spaniard had moved on to his future plans. He wasn't sure what to do with his essay on Richard Foret and Bea Langley. Gradually, during the months of study and the rereading of love letters, whirlwind poems and unfinished, romantic manifestos, Marcelo's interest had moved from Foret to Langley. He was no longer so much interested in the mysterious disappearance of the boxer-poet as in Bea's life in the aftermath of that event.

"I'd like, I think, to focus on what happens after the letters of 'The End' fade from the screen. Sure, Richard Foret disappears in the Gulf of Mexico, or is killed in the revolutionary turmoil, or simply vanishes without a trace, as people skilled in the art of bad writing say. But Bea continues in the world afterwards. She's pregnant with, and then gives birth to Foret's posthumous daughter; she returns to her native London only to discover it is a city that has nothing to say to her; she travels to Buenos Aires and then, again, to Mexico in search of clues to Richard's whereabouts, even though she knows very well there is no hope; she writes poems that don't attain global fame or change the face of literary modernism but that give her moderate pleasure and arouse the admiration of a few friends; she lives something like forty or forty-five years after Foret's disappearance; she sets up house in Paris because it is the only city where she feels like a stranger, and to have seen everything before is a more than institutionalized way of life; she raises a daughter with whom she hopes to remedy, karmically, the neglect of her first two kids (both of whom, in time, turn out well, although they retain an indelible core of resentment). Beatrice Langley incarnates a drama more private—less spectacular, if you will—than that of her dead husband, but no less intense for it. Foret's life is the stuff films are made of; Langley's is the stuff of a novel that, rather than ending with a bang, extends over hundreds of pages until the ink begins to fade and the words become illegible."

Rodrigo listens in silence to the monologue of his—the word comes into his mind—friend and thinks that in reality Marcelo is obliquely talking about his own life, and Adela's. It's clear that in a short time they have become an authentic couple. His mother absent-mindedly strokes Marcelo's neck at breakfast; Rodrigo does not remember her doing anything like that before. What Marcelo is saying, by means of the story of Richard Foret and Beatrice Langley, is that he wants to stay in Los Girasoles; he is not willing just to remember it all as a more or less happy sabbatical trip, the only product of which will be a monograph on a dead poet and an arsenal of memories in which Adela's thighs have a starring role. He wants to stay, to renounce his lifelong, vain ambition to gain modest fame through his books; he wants to *"cultiver son jardin,"* the garden of bluish cacti and perennial weeds in Adela's backyard in Los Girasoles.

Rodrigo also wants to cultivate his garden but has yet to find it, unless it is that lot filled with thorn bushes where a hen scratches around night and day in search of worms. Which is his garden? he wonders. A placid life in that small town, like the one Marcelo wants, going to spiritualism sessions with a crazy gringo and a girl he silently desires? Imbibing urine every couple of weeks as a member of an exclusive pro-contemporary art sect? Conjugal life with Cecilia in DF and resigning himself to feeling constantly out of place in relation to everything that exists in his grimy routine? Or is his garden death, a patch of dry earth to which his bones are added;

the grief, initially, of his loved ones and then an oblivion that slowly falls like a golden mantle on the heads of Adela, Marcelo, his father, Cecilia, and that at times, being fallible, falls back for a moment–during what would have been his birthday, let's say–to allow them to dream of an Eden that doesn't exist and from which Rodrigo contemplates, with peace in his soul, the actions of those who are still alive? Or is his garden nomadic, the negation of that fixed custom of being oneself, a custom you have so diligently cultivated until this moment? Which is his cultivable garden? Which is the piece of the world given to him on loan, even if it is only to set fire to it? Which is the corner crammed with supermarket bags full of cadavers where he will erect the temple of his indifference?

8

A couple of days after Marcelo's visit, Rodrigo walked through the empty streets of the Puerta del Aire residential estate, looking at the drawn curtains and the pickup trucks as if they were desert mirages, until he reached the security booth, where the guardian, the Cerberus of all this abandon, the tough, immutable Jacinto Nogales Pedrosa, called a cab that would take him along a route stretching farther than his wallet to Jimmie's studio, the provisional temple of that religion invented in the clamor of a few tequilas, of which he was at the point of becoming an acolyte.

The devastation reserved for us by the confirmation of an ominous truth is more subtle than that offered by our first glimpse of that truth. A man can wake every morning and look out his window to check that, there outside, the end of the world–in the biblical and material sense of the topic, setting aside metaphor–is still unraveling in five-hundred-foot flames, and the shock of that everyday confirmation operates inside him in a way that is less visible but more heartrending than the first vision of that same apocalypse. Repetition is a bitch with an arched spine that peacefully and conscientiously gnaws at the bones that keep us upright until it brings us down.

Some such words, to cut a long story short, were passing through Rodrigo's mind as he entered the dusty house and found Micaela sitting cross-legged on a straw mat. It was no foggy alcoholic delirium that had made him see her, in that cantina, cloaked (in the Catholic usage) by a virginal mantle of gold thread and with a halo of grace around her fawn-like head. All that was still present and even, perhaps, accentuated by the gloomy space in which he now found her and the sweaty, incense-laden greeting Jimmie offered him. There are women who are specialists in benefiting from the contrast with their environment.

Rodrigo tepidly extended a hand to Jimmie, who didn't hesitate to trap him in a lateral embrace while destroying the metacarpals of his right hand in an irritating impersonation of camaraderie. Frigging grimy gringo. The aroma of dark tobacco exuded by the rags for which he served as a bony clotheshorse made him wretch. Men who use olfactory resources as statement should be hunted down by the forces of law and order, he thought as he detached himself from the unctuous foreigner in the way one detaches a piece of chewing gum from the sole of one's shoe.

The atmosphere in Jimmie's studio was so insalubrious that Professor Velásquez dissolved into a *trompe-l'oeil* worthy of David Copperfield. Only when he spoke–"How are things going with the editing of that phantom book?"–and rounded off his witticism with a wheezing laugh, did Rodrigo become aware of his presence, forgotten in one of the three Acapulco chairs delimiting the borders of the living room.

Although Marcelo had not yet arrived, Professor Velásquez was undiplomatic enough to tell Rodrigo that his place was on the floor, as there were only three chairs, and in that house, decisions were made by the "council of wise old men." The allusion to this fictitious authority could only be irritating. Rodrigo was obviously younger than the other three men–the gringo, Velásquez, and Marcelo–and was closer in age to Micaela, even though she was a decade younger than him. The fact that these gentlemen were involved in so eccentric an undertaking as deciphering the future form of art by means of hypnosis seemed to be aggravated by their show of insensitivity to two youths–though of very different caliber–like Rodrigo and

Micaela. There was, in Velásquez's reference to the "council of wise old men," not only a touch of rancor directed at their youth, obliging them to sit on the floor, but also a thinly disguised sense of inferiority. Velásquez, fatty Velásquez, whose cranial terrain was divided between areas of baldness and dandruff; Velásquez, the survivor of three divorces, the anonymous professor who years before had lost the ability to win over his students by any other means than blackmail; Velásquez, the brute, the man who had early on become fascinated by aesthetics–the aesthetics of the avant-garde–and had clung to it, disguising his interest as intellectual research, as if it were the last trace of his youth; that Velásquez had found, in the hypnosis project, the enthusiasm he needed to channel his eighth adult crisis into the sense of power he longed for.

Marcelo Valente's reasons for embarking on such an unlikely enterprise couldn't be very different. They were both men who, after a couple of decades given up to teaching, needed a new relationship with the world, a mirage of youth and delirium that would quash their dissatisfactions while erectile dysfunction was gaining ground and stripping them once and for all of their thirst for History–it is well known that History is a phallic aspiration denied to eunuchs, one that women access in a completely different, much more intellectual and tempered way, while men beat totemic drums around it.

For his part, Rodrigo's motivation was clearer. He couldn't give a damn about the future of art, the sense of power that hypnotizing others might bring him; he didn't need any other emotion than that provided by his long conversations with Marcelo in the house in Puerta del Aire, with the addition of an occasional altercation with his mother and the customary coitus with Cecilia on his return to Mexico City. He didn't particularly need to feel more alive or to gain a timely victory in an idiotic battle that is always lost before it begins. No. What Rodrigo wanted, for the moment, was to go on smelling Micaela for a little longer. And to gather sufficient sensual material to allow him to dream about her later. What Rodrigo needed were reasons to have regrets when he reached a half century and, looking back, say in a tone of moral sententiousness, "I should have . . ." He needed to be wrong; in short, to stumble and doubt, and to be moved in some unique way by the sense that the communion he had searched so hard for was there, with its legs crossed on the straw mat beside him. Rodrigo didn't need to feel alive, like other people: he needed to *be* alive.

He and Micaela made themselves as comfortable as possible on the matting, and a slight touching of hands as she maneuvered to make space for him revealed a skin whose softness was only eclipsed by the warmth it radiated. Rodrigo even thought the woman–it was an exaggeration to so describe her–might have a fever, so scorching was his perception of the contact.

Jimmie, as usual, immediately monopolized the conversation. Just as soon as he had handed out the cans of beer–he gave Micaela a glass of water–he sat in one of the three chairs–the other, like an invitation or an offence remained empty–and once again embarked on the tale of his discovery of hypnosis and his later work. Rodrigo had heard the story secondhand, by way of Marcelo's measured narrative, and had not imagined it could be as complicated as it actually was. Jimmie changed the details with each new version, and now he made it sound as if he had always, from the first moment, despised Dr. Mind and planned his stealthy betrayal. The digressions were also different from those he had embarked on when telling the story to Marcelo. On this occasion, he said almost nothing about the CIA experiments and instead spoke at length, without respite, about his time as an illegal herbalist in the late eighties.

Rodrigo listened patiently, considering whether he should say he had already heard the story from Marcelo. He felt sorry for Micaela, who must have listened to all those innocuous details of the gringo's drifting pilgrimage three hundred times. Velásquez, who in Jimmie's presence became, if possible, a little more opaque, vegetated in his chair as if that string of nonsense were a cradlesong lulling a child. Rodrigo's legs went to sleep. He wasn't used to sitting on the floor–a level that, in his view, was more appropriate for animals–but accepted the sacrifice because Micaela's scent, a mixture of incense and vanilla with something more unsettling, came to him like a perfect symphony.

Jimmie rattled out his anecdote for a while longer. As he was moving toward the finale, there was a knock, and Velásquez made the superhuman effort of detaching himself from his chair to open the door to Marcelo, who delayed his greetings and stood by his chair so as not to interrupt the gringo's monologue. Finally, Jimmie came to the end his story. Marcelo greeted, in this order, Rodrigo, Micaela, and the gringo—he had already absentmindedly clasped hands with Velásquez—and Micaela stood up—an eddy of more potent smells around Rodrigo, who followed her with his eyes—to attend to the visitors and fetch drinks, as was dictated by the rigorous patriarchy in which they lived.

It's unimportant to mention how much they drank. Suffice it to say that tequila, once again, was the liquor selected to prepare for the coming ritual. Rather than hypnosis, they spoke of everyday matters for a few hours until a chance silence fell on the room, and Jimmie took advantage of it to ask, in a commanding tone, if they should begin. Velásquez was the only one to give a clear answer, in the affirmative, while Marcelo and Rodrigo nodded rather unconvincingly, and Micaela remained, as ever, silent.

9

It's hard to say if the following morning's hangover was the result of the hypnosis, the tequila, the imbibing of adolescent urine, or all of the above. To tell the truth, he had, up until the last minute, been fairly skeptical about the real possibilities of the project. He didn't believe hypnosis was substantially different from, for example, the sleep that followed a bad migraine. He imagined it as a certain misting of consciousness and, at best, an exacerbated imaginary state directed by the words of an invisible guru. But the technique stolen from E-Sight Enterprises was much more complex; in this version, the process for attaining a hypnotic state seemed more like a satanic ritual than guided meditation.

First, as a warm-up, they drank Micaela's urine. Rodrigo observed with a fascination bordering on psychosis how the beautiful girl pulled up her dress in front of them and moved a wide-lipped glass to her vagina, the humid, rosy lips of which he thought he glimpsed for a brief moment. Desire then installed itself throughout his whole body. He wanted to believe that sooner or later he would manage to eat that cunt, slowly, for hours, but there was no element of reason he could cling to in order to imagine this would happen. Luckily, the taste of the urine dissipated those turbid thoughts. It was, without a doubt, an unexpected sensorial experience; the initial disgust at the smell rapidly gave way to an eagerness to down the drink in one gulp and, afterwards, a sensation of heat down the length of his throat. It tasted like an exotic cocktail, a kind of dirty martini with some top-secret ingredient that made the drink burn.

After that, Jimmie ordered them to perform a strange series of vaguely military exercises. With exaggerated effort, Marcelo and Velásquez copied the movements the gringo carried out more flexibly, as if he were already used to them. Rodrigo and Micaela, in contrast, had little difficulty replicating the gringo's extremely strange routine. Once that stage was over, Jimmie handed each of them a different object. Objects dragged from the dusty corners of his studio but that, in the hands of those involved, seemed so special it was odd they had not been noticed earlier. Rodrigo, for example, received a small toy truck, made of plastic, with an impressive level of detail. In the driver's seat a man in a cap could be made out, brutally killed, his shirt stained with blood, his mouth covered with electrical tape. The cargo space could be opened by operating a tiny plastic lever, revealing its disturbing contents: a shipment of doll heads.

Rodrigo accepted his toy and the instruction to examine it carefully. He wondered about the origin of that strange but realistic national souvenir. It was like a narco version of a Playmobil; probably, thought Rodrigo, some artist had constructed the piece for counterpropaganda purposes. He noted that Micaela had also received an object alluding to violence: a tequila shot glass in the interior of which stood the translucent shape of an AK-47 rather than the obligatory cactus of the glasses normally found in airport stores.

The objects allotted to Velásquez, Marcelo, and Jimmie himself had no such reference. They were, respectively, a large marble of the variety known as "cloverleaf," with twisted abstract figures in its interior, a carved stone scepter, and a pair of women's panties with a floral print that Jimmie sniffed in an unpleasant way, and which Rodrigo thought might belong to Micaela.

Rodrigo's was, by far, the most complex and detailed object. It immediately made him think, by free association, of the supermarket bag he had discovered in the waste ground, what was now a long time ago. He remembered his repulsion, his gloomy suspicions about the origins of those viscera, his fear of seeing them again on his second, and last, incursion into the lot.

Those images, in turn, transported him to the early days of his marriage and that disturbing episode, still unresolved, of the turd found exactly in the center of his bed, on the tiger-striped bedspread Cecilia had been so fond of. And as he was making a detailed reconstruction of the events, searching for some clue he might have overlooked, he gradually sank into the memory, like someone who finds himself trapped in quicksand–if quicksands still exist in spite of the zeal for explaining everything humanity has adopted without reservation.

The small toy truck was melting in his hands, or so it seemed to Rodrigo, and taking different forms: a hen, a handful of tea bags, a newspaper open at the classified pages. When Rodrigo attempted to halt the metamorphosis by looking around him, he discovered that it was, in fact, nothing other than hypnosis. Everything appeared to have been literally rubbed out, as if it were possible to pass an eraser over the things we see, leaving only blurred vestiges, colors, and lights in their place, but swathed in a myopia that veiled the limits of all things.

He was reluctant to believe that by drinking urine and doing a little exercise he had entered into such a deep state of hypnosis. Rodrigo suspected he had been drugged. Maybe Micaela's urine was psychotropic, and the only function of the frigging sinister truck was to distract him while the drug took effect. He had already, during his lysergic adolescence, experienced similar states of consciousness. Although what he knew about taking acid had prepared him for anything, what was disturbing here was the sudden, unforeseen nature of the thing.

The session, luckily, was short. It hardly gave him time to be frightened, and before he could be assailed by the desire to get out of that trance at any cost, he heard the distant voice of the gringo, deeper than usual, giving very precise instructions on how to terminate the exercise. Once he had "woken," had recovered the clarity of his senses, he was incapable of reproducing in his memory the instructions he had followed. He feared the possibility of being "trapped in the trip" if he repeated the experience, but Jimmie convinced him that this was unlikely.

His head was now throbbing, and his eyes felt sunken. He had been tossing in his bed in Puerta del Aire for over an hour, attempting to reconstruct the events of the previous night. When he thought of Micaela, a surge of lust took complete hold of him, and he had to masturbate quite aggressively, as if guided by the desire to rid his imagination of those images. He had always found it surprising how the world changed before and after ejaculation. Everything he believed, longed for, expected from life was transformed between one state and the other. Preorgasmic anxiety dissolved into a placid drowsiness; his desire to excel in some area faded into a discreet background shot. This time, when he had finished, he thought of Cecilia. He was still a married man, after all, and it now seemed like he had been away from his spouse for an eternity, although in reality it was little more than a month and a half. Marriage was, however you looked at it, an indelible stain: its reality couldn't be avoided by the fact of being far away. He felt more isolated than usual, as if the simple truth of being married, even when it might not involve a particularly intense relationship with his wife, was enough to raise a wall between Rodrigo and the rest of mankind. A wall that seemed to get thicker by the day.

Maybe that separation, that distancing from others, didn't correspond, or only partially corresponded, to his marital state. Perhaps it was just a mean trick of adult life. But Rodrigo related everything to his marriage, conscious that it was the most outstanding mistake of his troubled collection of mistakes, the mistake precipitated by a bad joke that had made him feel even further on the margin of everything. Was there any way back after that?

He dressed in the clothes he had worn the night before, made himself a cup of coffee with cream, and sipped it noisily as he walked around the room. His reflections on the nature of marriage had left him in a melancholy mood, and he felt the need to call Cecilia. It was Saturday, and she would probably still be in bed, either sleeping in or watching television with idiotic interest. He went out of the house in search of a better signal for his phone and keyed in her number while walking in circles on the deserted road. But Cecilia didn't answer.

Maybe due to his hangover, maybe as a secondary effect of the hypnosis, Rodrigo had, that morning, a mania for signs. He believed he saw a symbol in everything, indicating something else, as if the world were a tautological series of winks. The fact that Cecilia wasn't answering made him think of a more profound, perhaps even definitive absence. In some way he knew—spurred on by the paranormal phenomena he had recently been involved in—that Cecilia had left for good, that she would never again answer the telephone, that she had disappeared from his life with the same exasperating candor with which she had appeared in it. He imagined a diversity of possible reasons for that sudden distance: the original sender of that initiatory message left on Cecilia's desk had finally revealed his identity, demanding that the course of events be corrected to restore the proper story, aborted by an error in the plan; he also imagined Cecilia had been raped by the same delinquent who had broken into the apartment to shit on the tiger-striped bedspread; he imagined she had died of asphyxia because of an allergic reaction to the damp, or had just run off with some frigging neighbor.

These possibilities, however, didn't alarm him. Rodrigo's hopes lay elsewhere. The arrival of Micaela in his life had helped him put everything in perspective. It might be impossible to possess her, but the idea of a genuine relationship—unlike the one he had with Cecilia—had made an impression on him. In addition, his conversations with Marcelo had revealed the existence of a different style of involvement. All of a sudden, Rodrigo had an intuition of a certain meaning, a certain intention or at least a teleological murmur that gave order to the uneventful sequence of the days. He thought that Cecilia's arrival in his life had been necessary, that it had contributed to, and even set off, a series of events that had led to a key discovery: communion with others was possible. Perhaps by means of hypnosis, but nonetheless possible. That simple truth completely altered his perception of the world. Now, with that theoretical enlightenment, he suspected he would have to act coherently: abandon his cynicism and give himself up completely to the search for a comrade–the word inevitably chosen by his mother to refer to his girlfriends when he was a teenager, as if in addition to having sex, they were conspiring to "take to the hills to join the guerillas" and "bring down the oppressive government."

But Rodrigo didn't have to wait long for this enlightenment, as he liked to call it, to be eclipsed by another, more decisive one.

10

The second session of collective hypnosis, after that brief warm-up, had as its objective the consideration of the future of art. In the multiple, mutable forms they were offered during the trance, the participants had to discover a possibility for art, a concrete suggestion for a possible piece. Rodrigo wasn't very clear on how he was meant to direct his hallucinations toward a predetermined end, but he supposed that before the session, there would be a more detailed explanation of the process. There wasn't. Everything proceeded as in the last meeting, but this time they did it early in the morning, which made the ritual even more outlandish: tequila, disinterested conversation, more tequila. Jimmie, Velásquez, and Marcelo laughed loudly and almost shouted each other down in an attempt to seem manlier in the eyes of the ingenuous Micaela, who looked on in silence. Meanwhile, Rodrigo was distracted, distant, since he considered that–faced with such competition–it was wisest to adopt an alternative strategy. It worked: Micaela, against all expectations, asked him about his life–in general–in a neutral tone.

Here Rodrigo came up against what could have been an insurmountable obstacle. He felt an electromagnetic attraction for Micaela, but he knew that everything was against him: his life, hers, the totality of accidents that made up the world. He was, when you came down to it, a married man, and she was, practically, a possession of the grimy gringo. Micaela's simple question put him in a predicament. That is to say, she most certainly knew Rodrigo's story through having heard it from Marcelo in one of his conversations with Jimmie, but it is never the same thing to hear the whole story as to have it confirmed by the words of the principal person involved. At the exact moment Rodrigo pronounced the magic words ("I'm married"), a beautiful bridge, like the one in Brooklyn, would shatter and fall into the waters separating him from Micaela, accompanied by the explosion of fireworks.

Rodrigo, given his limited possibilities, chose a sincere but abstract response. The watchful presence of the three other men made him nervous. Even Marcelo, with whom he already had a more than healthy complicity, was completely transformed in the presence of the other alpha males and was displaying the weapons of his arrogance, a heraldry of idiocies. He noticed the three had clearly heard Micaela's question and had reduced the decibel level to fix their left ears on the development of Rodrigo's reply. He feared they would intervene, boycotting his prudence, openly pronouncing the word, *marriage*, which he had planned to avoid by means of philosophical tricks. Luckily none of this occurred, maybe because Rodrigo's response put a rapid end to it.

"My life has the disadvantage of not being completely my own," was Rodrigo's valiant beginning, alluding tangentially to marriage, but also preparing the way for a piece of high flying. He was, however, unable to continue, at least not aloud. The continuation of his reply was a gaze pregnant with implicit meaning that Micaela might or might not have understood. If he had managed to speak, had been capable of saying things openly once and for all, Rodrigo's reply would have continued, more or less, along these lines:

"The greater part of my time is spent in inertia, and that includes the most crucial decisions, which I take like someone picking a card from a deck held out to him. The result is never magic; I can't even perceive the adrenaline of objective chance or observe a conspiracy of symbols behind what happens. I just go on living. I tie myself up with nonsense, like someone traveling on top of a train who, to avoid a fall, uses elastic straps attached to a metal projection instead of a leather belt, which would be more sensible. I know that simile is exaggerated. But it's kind of like that: I feel I'm being pushed and pulled around the whole time. Chronological order seems like a crime to me. And the supposed need to know oneself irritates me. I can only imagine an introspective journey as a rocky descent in a toboggan made of bloody viscera. That's about as deep as my normal conceptions go. At the same time, I know I don't have what it takes to be decisively superfluous. I'd like nothing better than to give myself up to frivolity and spend Sundays enjoying the healthy amusement offered by enormous supermarkets, but I get bored very quickly. My relationships with people are always based on mistakes [here Rodrigo thought of his marriage again, but also of his friendship with Marcelo, which had only arisen after he had heard him and Adela fucking], and those fundamental mistakes linger like a shadow of doubt that distances me, emotionally, from everyone. Not even during sex can I completely forget that insuperable distance, even though that's when I'm closest to doing it. My level of empathy with human beings is near zero, though I once had a pet [Rodrigo is thinking of his hen] whom I loved in a, perhaps you could say, purer way."

He paused in his unspoken mental monologue. Micaela was breathing more quickly, or perhaps he was excited by her closeness and was projecting an image of desire onto her. He was afraid the hypnosis session would start too soon—though at the same time, he longed for the strange taste of Micaela's urine and the fleeting glimpse, too short to fix itself in his memory, of her Mount of Venus, her panties lying around her diminutive feet.

Micaela was looking at him strangely, as if she had intuited or even heard, by telepathic means, Rodrigo's reply. The three older men, sitting, as on the previous occasion, in their respective Acapulco chairs, continued bragging while Micaela and Rodrigo lay, perhaps too close, on the matting at their feet. Suddenly, Jimmie interrupted the conversation to announce it was time to commence the ritual: they had drunk enough.

Mechanically, they did the preparatory exercises, the calisthenics, following Jimmie's lead. After that, in betrayal of the men's hopes, Micaela shut herself in the bathroom with a jar and, out of the sight, if not the attentive hearing of the other four, took a long, uninterrupted piss. She came out, triumphal, with the brew ready and handed it to Jimmie, who ceremoniously poured it into the four shot glasses with their two fingers of tequila. They drank.

The objects given to them on this occasion were different, less significant, more neutral. Jimmie briefly explained that he didn't want to direct the course of the hypnosis in too specific a direction. Rodrigo received a lump of some sort of malleable clay or Play-Doh that made him think of the famous piece of Cartesian wax. He remembered the story of the philosopher, learned in his school days and returned to later with, by then, adult curiosity.

In his search for a truth on which to erect the solid edifice of his science, Descartes systematically discarded (the wordplay is intentional) less reliable sources of knowledge. And among those less reliable sources of knowledge, it is always said, are the senses. But the reliability of the senses can only be questioned by means of examples, that is to say stories, inventions, narrative. The zero degree, or almost, of narrative, but narrative nonetheless. The character of Descartes takes a piece of wax and describes it. He enumerates its physical attributes, its shape, its weight, its color. He cannot doubt what he perceives: he knows the piece of wax with apodictic certainty, or so he believes. A second character (little more than a hand, a neutral voice, a blurred face, a shadow acting as the agent of destiny) takes the piece of wax from the first character and, hiding it from sight, puts it close to the stove. Under the effect of the heat, the wax softens, and the second character molds it and evenly divides it into new fragments. Finally, he gives the first character the result of his operations: the same piece of wax having undergone a change. With it, he also offers a rhetorical question, directed not to the first character (who at this point in the work vanishes, or switches off like an exhausted automaton and ceases to attract our attention) but to the spectator, to the History of Understanding, perhaps: "Can the first character know if this is the same piece of wax? If not, how can the senses be unaware of such a fundamental relationship as the principle of identity, which is not contained in the material attributes of a piece of wax?"

That was, more or less, how Rodrigo remembered it. That was how he recreated it as the clay transformed into a worm in his hands.

Following the channel of his thoughts, while he fell deeper and deeper into a hypnotic trance and the world around him faded away, he recalled or began to recall the theory, or rather the example of the evil genius. Descartes let his imagination range too freely with that example, that inkling of a plot. There are some truths, like mathematics, that seem to us impossible to doubt. In order to doubt them and stand alone, triumphant, before the void, Descartes proposes the most delicious theory in the history of philosophy: we have been created by a god who obliges us to be mistaken. An evil genius who is amused by our blunders and laughs at the certainty we assign to the simplest sums. An astute god with the worst of intentions, who made us in the form of his boredom to see us fall into error as Thales of Miletus falls into a well. A god who sows signs in things and sends us out into the world with our faces covered in eyes to search for those signs and be dazzled by our stupid discovery. A bastard of a god, like those in myths that have a better sense of humor than the religious ones.

Rodrigo raised his eyes, forcing himself to defer his reflections, and the shock was so complete that he thought he had lost his wits. He was no longer in Jimmie's workshop, sitting on the floor next to Micaela, but in his bedroom in the apartment in Mexico City. The bed was made, but the creases in the bedspread—Cecilia's tiger-striped bedspread—showed evidence of a recent presence. As it seemed impossible to attribute to hypnosis this perfect, detailed recreation of his room, Rodrigo assumed he had fallen asleep and even allowed himself to quietly deride Jimmie, Velásquez, and Marcelo for believing in such an absurd project as the future of art. He didn't deride Micaela because it wasn't her conviction that had brought her there, but an irreversible series of events, circumstances somewhere between cruel and ridiculous that made up her distant, melancholy personality.

He decided, since he was there, to enjoy his dream and inhabit that lost moment from the past while he could. He didn't usually struggle against subconscious promptings, and this would be no exception: he was going to live this dream as if he had gone back in time to those days of unemployment and idleness next to the waste ground.

When he remembered the vacant lot, he naturally decided to look for the hen, his feathered accomplice, who would cluck in the dream as in reality, happily feeding on bugs and seeds. He went to the window and leaned out to get a better view. He saw the hen, walking in her characteristic way among the bushes, and he congratulated himself on the veracity and level of detail of his dream, which was representing the undergrowth and the chiaroscuro of the lot like a photograph. But behind the hen he saw something else: a movement of leaves, a cracking of branches, a glimpse of clothing moving a few yards away. Rodrigo leaned back slightly to avoid being seen, but it was unnecessary: the man who was walking around the lot in search of his feathered friend was himself. He saw him moving thorny branches aside and steadying himself by pushing his foot into the earth to get to the bird. He saw, in a flash of sunlight, his face in profile, in the way mirrors never show it and we are surprised to recognize in photographs. He felt dizzy.

He moved farther away from the window and, letting himself fall backwards onto the tiger-striped bedspread, felt a drop of sweat trickling down from his armpit toward his elbow, and a kind of nausea that made him press his hands to his stomach. As if in a revelation of a mystical nature, he suddenly understood what was happening. He didn't even struggle against it. He opened his eyes in a gesture of fright in the face of the incomprehensible, but each of his following actions seemed self-evident, without the least need for explanation or exegesis. He stood on the bed, lowered his pants and briefs, the elastic of which stretched over his ankles, then he squatted down and produced a perfect turd in the exact center of the tiger-striped bedspread. He didn't bother to wipe himself: he raised his pants, jumped off the bed, and contemplated his work. It was, without a shadow of a doubt, the same turd. That turd.

He contemplated it in ecstasy during what could have been a long moment: his perception of time was suddenly as malleable as the piece of Cartesian wax. He thought of—or rather imagined in fast-forward—all the events that had occurred since that day, since he came back from the lot with a pain in the back of his head and was disgusted to find that surprise. In some way, he said to himself, his journey toward abandonment, his perdition, his voyage around the void had begun right there. Or before, perhaps: the first time he decided to walk home from work instead of taking the metro. Or even earlier, when he first entered his childhood Thicket, the one this other vacant lot replicated. Or never, and the milestone didn't exist, just constancy, atoms falling in the void in perfect verticals and monotony.

When his thoughts had reached this point of irreversible abstraction, Rodrigo heard the key turning in the front door of the apartment. It was him, the first person, coming back from his expedition, injured and upset, to discover a piece of shit on the bed. He didn't give it a second thought: he raised himself up onto the windowsill and dropped down into the lot.

EPILOGUE

He opened his eyes, or they were already open and beginning to see again, he wasn't completely sure which. The world returned to normal: Micaela sitting a foot or so away on the matting; Marcelo, Jimmie, and Velásquez in their Acapulco chairs. They all looked to be asleep, their eyes closed and muscles relaxed. Velásquez was even snoring.

Rodrigo once more thought, for an instant, that the hypnotism didn't exist, and Micaela had slipped some strange drug into her urine to sedate them. But he had no time for explanations: he was awake and back in his five senses—fallible though they might be, according to the French philosopher—and after what he had witnessed, what he had done, what he had intuited during that dream, or whatever it might have been, he was in no mood for details. He slowly stretched, loosening the muscles of his legs, and moved toward Micaela. He woke her by touching her shoulder. The girl was, undoubtedly, sleeping less deeply than the other three. Rodrigo wondered what he had looked like from the outside while he was sleeping.

Micaela woke with little effort and smiled on seeing Rodrigo so close. She didn't appear to be nervous, but rather relieved by the solitude she was unexpectedly sharing with him. Rodrigo indicated, with a gentle squeeze of her arm and a meaningful look, that they should leave. And that is what they did. They stood up, careful not to make any noise, held hands, and walked toward the door of the studio.

Outside, the sun shone down on all things, leaving no shadow.

Coffee House Press began as a small letterpress operation in 1972 and has grown into an internationally renowned nonprofit publisher of literary fiction, essay, poetry, and other work that doesn't fit neatly into genre categories.

Coffee House is both a publisher and an arts organization. Through our *Books in Action* program and publications, we've become interdisciplinary collaborators and incubators for new work and audience experiences. Our vision for the future is one where a publisher is a catalyst and connector.

LITERATURE
is not the same thing as
PUBLISHING

FUNDER ACKNOWLEDGMENTS

Coffee House Press is an internationally renowned independent book publisher and arts nonprofit based in Minneapolis, MN; through its literary publications and *Books in Action* program, Coffee House acts as a catalyst and connector–between authors and readers, ideas and resources, creativity and community, inspiration and action.

Coffee House Press books are made possible through the generous support of grants and donations from corporate giving programs, state and federal support, family foundations, and the many individuals who believe in the transformational power of literature. This activity is made possible by the voters of Minnesota through a Minnesota State Arts Board Operating Support grant, thanks to the legislative appropriation from the arts and cultural heritage fund and a grant from the Wells Fargo Foundation Minnesota. Coffee House also receives major operating support from the Amazon Literary Partnership, the Bush Foundation, the Jerome Foundation, the McKnight Foundation, Target, and the National Endowment for the Arts (NEA). To find out more about how NEA grants impact individuals and communities, visit www.arts.gov.

Coffee House Press receives additional support from many anonymous donors; the Alexander Family Foundation; the Archer Bondarenko Munificence Fund; the Elmer L. & Eleanor J. Andersen Foundation; the David & Mary Anderson Family Foundation; the Buuck Family Foundation; the Carolyn Foundation; the Dorsey & Whitney Foundation; Dorsey & Whitney LLP; the Knight Foundation; the Matching Grant Program Fund of the Minneapolis Foundation; the Rehael Fund of the Minneapolis Foundation; the Schwab Charitable Fund; Schwegman, Lundberg & Woessner, P.A.; the Scott Family Foundation; the US Bank Foundation; VSA Minnesota for the Metropolitan Regional Arts Council; the Archie D. & Bertha H. Walker Foundation; and the Woessner Freeman Family Foundation.

THE PUBLISHER'S CIRCLE OF COFFEE HOUSE PRESS

Publisher's Circle members make significant contributions to Coffee House Press's annual giving campaign. Understanding that a strong financial base is necessary for the press to meet the challenges and opportunities that arise each year, this group plays a crucial part in the success of Coffee House's mission.

Recent Publisher's Circle members include many anonymous donors, Mr. & Mrs. Rand L. Alexander, Suzanne Allen, Patricia A. Beithon, Bill Berkson & Connie Lewallen, the E. Thomas Binger & Rebecca Rand Fund of the Minneapolis Foundation, Robert & Gail Buuck, Claire Casey, Louise Copeland, Jane Dalrymple-Hollo, Jennifer Kwon Dobbs & Stefan Liess, Mary Ebert & Paul Stembler, Chris Fischbach & Katie Dublinski, Kaywin Feldman & Jim Lutz, Katharine Freeman, Sally French, Jocelyn Hale & Glenn Miller, Roger Hale & Nor Hall, Randy Hartten & Ron Lotz, Jeffrey Hom, Carl & Heidi Horsch, Kenneth Kahn & Susan Dicker, Stephen & Isabel Keating, Kenneth Koch Literary Estate, Jennifer Komar & Enrique Olivarez, Allan & Cinda Kornblum, Leslie Larson Maheras, Jim & Susan Lenfestey, Sarah Lutman & Rob Rudolph, the Carol & Aaron Mack Charitable Fund of the Minneapolis Foundation, George & Olga Mack, Joshua Mack, Gillian McCain, Mary & Malcolm McDermid, Sjur Midness & Briar Andresen, Peter Nelson & Jennifer Swenson, Marc Porter & James Hennessy, Jeffrey Scherer, Jeffrey Sugerman & Sarah Schultz, Nan G. & Stephen C. Swid, Patricia Tilton, Stu Wilson & Melissa Barker, Warren D. Woessner & Iris C. Freeman, Margaret Wurtele, and Joanne Von Blon.

For more information about the Publisher's Circle and other ways to support Coffee House Press books, authors, and activities, please visit www.coffeehousepress.org/support or contact us at info@coffeehousepress.org.

LATIN AMERICAN TRANSLATION
FROM COFFEE HOUSE PRESS

Faces in the Crowd
by Valeria Luiselli
Translated by Christina MacSweeney

Sidewalks
by Valeria Luiselli
Translated by Christina MacSweeney

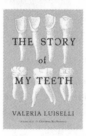

The Story of My Teeth
by Valeria Luiselli
Translated by Christina MacSweeney

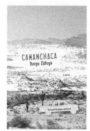

Camanchaca
by Diego Zúñiga
Translated by Megan McDowell